ON THE EDGE OF REALITY

AN ANTHOLOGY OF SPECULATIVE FICTION

Kevin Baker

Editor: Christy Lynn

Cover & Formatting: Joe Dugdale

This is a work of fiction. While some places and institutions are real, they are used solely to add structure and background to the stories and do not reflect actual circumstances.

Some characters may be a conglomeration of persons the author has met; still, they do not exist in reality.

ACKNOWLEDGMENT

A list of persons who helped me bring this anthology to the light of day would fill a volume in and of itself. There are a few, however, who pushed me over the proverbial hump. These include my wife, Tracee. Her kind words and belief in me were invaluable. The same may be said for Christy Lynn, author par excellence. Frankly, this book would not be before your eyes without her support and direction. I owe a big thanks to my sons, Gabe and Ben, whose encouragement means the world to me. I also want to give thanks to the author's group for their suggestions.

CONTENTS

The Expecting and the Hun

Jeremiah repeatedly tried to check the time but to no avail. The mortars had rained down nonstop for hours. Each time he opened the watch cover, dirt would fly on it, causing him to close it. It was a gift from his wife, Deborah. She had given it to him as a good luck charm, as much as a timepiece. She had their minister bless it; then, she presented it to a spiritualist to place a protection spell on it. Deborah told her husband that the seer said the watch was also a physical piece of a psychic bond. The timepiece attached him to her

He thanked his wife, yet he thought the whole idea of the charm was hogwash. Still, he was deathly afraid of losing it. He held it firmly, rubbing it between his fingers. It was something real, something that reminded him there was a world beyond trenches, mud, barbed wire, and corpses. He wasn't dreaming when he thought of home.

It was there, as real as the object in his hand.

Jeremiah felt a worm of fear crawling in his belly. He knew as bad as the artillery barrage was, it was when the bombing stopped, the authentic horror would begin. That was when the Huns would send their men over the trench and into no man's land - seventy-five yards of hell.

In that horrible, thin expanse of land between the two opposing armies was the scene of countless, ineffectual battles. There, the bodies lay like cords of wood. The stench of rotting corpses was so putrid that he repeatedly vomited for the first three days at the front. Now, two months later, he had become used to the fragrance. He could eat, sleep, joke, all with the dead, mere feet from his trench. The veterans said that is when you become a trench rat or long-timer. Part of Jeremiah hated himself for his nonchalance in the face of senseless, human butchery.

The bombardment suddenly stopped, and Jeremiah instinctually placed the watch in his left breast pocket – over his heart. A couple of men down the line started retching as the expectation of close-quarters battle became imminent. An eerie silence prevailed for almost a minute, then came the sound each side had come to dread - whistles. The shrill sound meant someone was sending men to take a trench. This time it was the Germans.

Jeremiah heard his officers barking orders. They were always the same, "man a position," and "be ready to fire." He had listened to the dribble pouring from his commanders' mouths countless times before. "We must hold the line." He, like all the other enlisted men, knew this to be true. However, they were uninterested in fighting for God and country, nor strategic purposes. It was survival. If routed from the trench, they would be cut down in the open field.

Across the wasteland, he saw the Huns climbing out of their trench. He had never seen so many. There was a sea of Germans advancing toward the Yankees. Even at a distance, he could see the fear on their faces. They came within fifty yards, and the Americans unleashed hell on them. Machine guns and rifles made the remaining stretch of no man's land a suicide march.

Jeremiah was shooting Germans at a pace of ten a minute. He was a good aim with the bolt action rifle and wasted no time between shots. They were falling by the hundreds, yet, they kept coming by the thousands. To Jeremiah's mind, they seemed like a wave that would inevitably swamp their pitiful defenses. He made the sudden, terrible decision to save the last round in his pistol for himself.

Suddenly, British infantry came down the line to support the Americans. The increased firepower made the enemy's advance tenuous. The Germans arrived within twenty yards of the trench when Jeremiah heard the order to fix bayonets.

With screams for more ammunition going unanswered, hand-to-hand combat became inevitable and imminent. The enemy was now within ten yards. With his rifle out of cartridges, Jeremiah fired five of the six rounds in his Smith and Wesson. Not two seconds passed from firing his pistol, just time to holster his sidearm, when he heard the ungodly order, screamed more in madness than a thoughtful command - "Charge!"

Along with hundreds of his comrades, Jeremiah came out of the trench like a long snake, piece after piece of the body, sliding out of the mud and into the breach. What ensued was savage, close-quarters fighting. The men of each side, having no need, or for that matter, the desire for sanity, left it in their respective trenches. Bayonets and knives were gutting men with all the brutal efficiency the Roman legions had practiced with their short swords.

Jeremiah's ears did not hear the screams, both primal and pitiful; he focused on only one thing, killing the next man in front of him. A grenade blast, while not hurting him, blew his rifle from his hands. He and a German charged each other with their knives.

The two men rolled in the mud, blood, and decay. Jeremiah drove his knife deeply into the German's leg. It was just when Jeremiah was about to pounce on his enemy that he slipped in the mud. His arm became tangled in barbed wire. He fought desperately to free himself, but it was evident he did not have the time.

The Hun jumped on him, trying to drive the American's own bloody knife into his chest. Jeremiah was losing the battle; the German was straddling him and had all the leverage. He felt the blade slice through his jacket. It hit his can of snuff and veered to the side, cutting deeply into his arm. He screamed in pain and rage. The German quickly grabbed his knife and raised it above his head. Glaring at Jeremiah, he let out a roar of triumph, then a side of his head disappeared. He fell on top of Jeremiah.

The two lay there, weakly panting. The shot man produced gurgling noises in his throat, unmistakably dying. The pistol fell from Jeremiah's hand. He had lost a good deal of blood from the knife wound. His world went fuzzy; then consciousness left him. The two men, deaf to the world around them, lay in the muck and gore, the watch Jeremiah's wife gave him resting between their chests.

***

Half a planet, and a universe away from the war, Deborah Weston lay sleeping. She slumbered on her side, as she had done for a few months. The young woman was eight months pregnant, the result of the last interlude between herself and her husband, Jeremiah. Like everyone else, he had just completed basic training and was given a ten-day leave before more specialized training. In this case, a mere two weeks of infantry instruction before waiting his turn to leave for *Over There*.

They had decided to wait until he returned to try for children. What gripped her bowels in fear was the real purpose of delay. It was the change of just one word for another: *If* he returned, instead of *when*. Daily, the thought of switching those two, one-syllable words brought her to tears.

Their last opportunity for lovemaking had been sudden and unexpected. They had driven to Central Union Station in Toledo for Jeremiah to catch his train to Camp Zachary Taylor in Kentucky. At the depot, they discovered, to their delight, the train was running three hours behind due to a delay in Chicago.

Deborah looked at the time as a gift, one she was not going to waste. They had the same idea as sparks flew between them. They hustled to the nearby 224-Knapp Royal Hotel and rented a room. Their coupling was desperate, passionate, and bonding. Afterward, they held each other until the clock cruelly signaled their time together, possibly forever, had come to an end. Little did either know; they had created life.

Even in sleep, her brain acknowledged a sudden light

and a presence near her. She dreamily examined the room, her mind still more asleep than awake. What she saw caused her eyes to widen in horror as she looked upon the form before her. She tried to scream but couldn't expel the sound from her throat. It was a German soldier, the left side of his face hideously torn away. Dried blood and dirt covered the specter's head and uniform.

His gruesome smile exposed bloody, stained, yellow teeth. He was holding a large knife in one hand and some form of beautiful light in the other. His smirk remained as he maliciously spoke. "Frau Weston, your husband did this to me."

Deborah tried to talk, but before the words could leave her throat, she felt something wet and grimy on her lips. She wiped it away with her fingers and looked at them. To her horror, she saw it was blood and dirt. That awful, disfigured thing had kissed her! Was she going mad? She thought this must be some horrible vision.

She regained her senses and her tongue and asked, "what manner of phantom are you, and why have you invaded my bedchamber?"

"Why, Frau Weston, I am a spirit removed from my corporeal body by your husband's pistol." His mouth turned downward in an angry frown. "When I died, the watch was between my chest and that of your wretched husband. Your charmed gift brought me here instead of to my family. Now, I may very well never say goodbye to my wife and children."

Deborah further studied her unwanted guest, this time considering his words, as well as his body. He possessed some fashion of physical form, but for what purpose, she didn't know. The German waited patiently for the pleas of mercy that would inevitably come. When she spoke, her words caught him off guard.

"I am sorry for your condition; war is a horror no one should have to live with, let alone die in. What is your name?"

"My name, Frau Weston, was Martin Swanger. I was a corporal in the Kaiser's army. I had a wife, Helga, and two precious children. Herman is four, and Ingrid will be three next month. I lived in a small town outside of Munich. I worked in a steel plant. Given my employment, the armaments department informed me there was no possibility of being pressed into active duty. That is why Helga and I felt secure in having Ingrid."

Martin stopped talking and appeared reflective, his eyes becoming distant. Deborah could see the sadness. He heaved a deep sigh and turned his attention back toward the woman sitting on the bed. "I hope Helga finds a good man. A wise and kind man. I hope he treats her well and raises our children as his own."

Deborah, despite her horror, felt her heart well up in

pity for this man. "Martin, I'm sorry for you and your family. This savage conflict placed a ruthless pain in your life and home. It has also caused heartache in mine."

"What do you mean, both our homes?!" he shouted. "Your husband has a chance to return to you and his child *if*." He stopped at that. And that word, which had haunted her since Jeremy's call to duty, hung in the air like a foul stench…*if*.

"Martin," she nearly sobbed, "what do you mean? What do you mean by *if*?"

"Frau Weston, the fortunes of war will determine your husband's fate. Your child is in our hands."

"My name is Deborah!" she screamed. Martin sat on the edge of the bed, and his hands pressed against her chest, over her heart. She rocked back and forth, tears rolling down her face. The young woman felt herself falling into some deep, black abyss. She laid back on the bed, welcoming the thought of her mind wiped clean, a blank slate.

Just as she was to give herself over to nothingness, Deborah felt a pain in her stomach; her baby had kicked. She became instantly coherent. She opened her eyes to see Martin's face mere inches from hers.

"I see you have awakened from your slumber. You should have given yourself into the will of your body and mind." His voice carried a twisted, mocking tone. His torn face had the look of a cat playing with a mouse.

Instead of fright, Deborah felt anger. She violently pushed him away. The rebuff caught the phantasm by surprise. "I am a mother," she hissed. "I don't have the luxury of giving up. Now state your business, get on with it!"

"Very well, Frau… Deborah, I have come to judge the worthiness of your child's life."

The single sentence sent chills down her spine, though she tried hard not to show it. She knew, instinctually, Martin had the power to carry out a sentence.

"Deborah, I can see it on your face. You know what I can do to your unborn. You are expecting, but you might not by the time the sun rises. I have received the authority to judge your child's life. Don't ask me by whom. You should stay away from the seers. The *Der Zauber* you placed on the timepiece; opened a whole other world. I was informed that if I am to carry out this trial, I must offer a blessing to the infant if acquitted. I hold a knife in my right hand and a life of health in the other. Your child will receive one or the other upon decision."

"So, if I don't pass your damned test, you kill myself and my child?"

"No, Deborah, I'm not permitted to harm you. I'm allowed to judge, to…weigh in the balance, if you will, the offspring of my killer."

Deborah's eyes bore into Martin. "Then let this horrible travesty begin."

Deborah's stare dulled Swanger's glee. It held a combination of disgust and contempt that he knew had nothing to do with his face. He suddenly realized that if a pregnant woman from America could be brave in the presence of a phantom, his former country had no chance against its nation's army.

"Deborah," Martin said gravely, "I am required to inform you of the rules. You must answer all questions immediately and truthfully. Any hesitation or deception will result in an immediate miscarriage. Do you understand?"

A concise, cold, "Yes," was her only reply.

"Now, Frau Weston, isn't it true you were once a flapper babe?"

"I don't see what that has to do with my child."

Martin screamed so loud the windowpanes rattled, "Answer me, you stupid *miststück*!"

Shaken to her core, Deborah nodded and sobbed out a "Yes."

"Aren't flapper babes known for their less than exemplary morals?"

"Yes."

"Isn't it true many flapper babes consider it a burden to be with child? Isn't it true that flapper babes often have abortions rather than have children?"

"Which question do you want me to answer first?"

The young woman's response caught Martin by surprise. He knew he had violated a rule by asking two questions before allowing an answer. The pain he felt in his stomach was all the reprimand he needed to encourage him not to repeat his breach of protocol. They would no doubt allow Deborah more discretion as a result of his mistake.

The young mother felt a sudden shift as if she was being allowed more than to answer questions. She didn't know why, yet it comforted her.

"Answer in the order I asked," he finally answered.

"Yes, and yes."

"Is it also true you and my murderer did not want a child because of tacit acknowledgment he may die in the war?"

The question was intended as much to rattle the young woman as eliciting any information. She knew he already knew the answer. The use of *may* instead of *might* expressed a higher probability of her beloved's demise.

The question unnerved her. She closed her eyes, took a deep breath, and held it. As she slowly exhaled, she silently quoted the Bible verse used in the previous week's sermon. It was Philippians 4:13, *I can do all things through Christ who strengthens me.*

"Yes, Martin, we did not plan to have children until he returns from the war."

"Tell me then how you came to become pregnant?"

"We had sex."

The German laughed in spite of himself. Her bluntness reminded him of his own precious Helga. "Describe the circumstances that resulted in your pregnancy."

"Let's not waste the remainder of the night with questions you already know the answer. Let me give a fair account of my child's worthiness, which is translucent to me, yet you have somehow received the right of jurisprudence."

Before he could refuse, Deborah began her child's defense.

"Tell me, Martin, what would you give to have a few more hours with Helga?"

Before he could think, he responded, "everything." It was an instinctual and painful answer.

"Then, you will understand, Jeremy and I received such a gift. Three hours, Martin. Jeremy and I were blessed with three hours more together."

Deborah continued. "It's both funny and tragic if you think about it. How many of us don't think of the time we have until it strikes us squarely in our faces? We go about our lives, taking our loved ones for granted. Oh, we love them deeply. Yet, it isn't until we are faced with separation, death, and living without the persons of primacy that we fully understand, completely feel the depth of our emotions, the vast ocean of our love. Our hunger for any little bit of time together, even a second more, can drive us to insanity. A starving man could not crave food more."

Martin's mind leapt to the fatherland, his family's home, even Max, their dog. He felt his chest well up, although his heart did not beat. Still, he was determined to destroy Jeremy Weston's child.

"Deborah," he barked, "this is irrelevant!"

She roared in response, "No, it isn't Martin Swanger, and you know it! Did you and Helga hold each other that last night together? Did you cling together as if only the other could keep you afloat in a deep and cruel sea?" Before the spirit could answer, Deborah pushed forward. "Martin, I have known you for only a short time, yet, it is evident you love your children and are deeply in love with your wife. There is a common bond we share. We love our spouses and children."

Deborah saw a mixture of grief and rage on the phantasm's face. They warred with each other, both clawing the other for primacy. Neither victorious, Martin's silent heart expressed both emotions in a hopeless, impotent scream. "How dare you!" he sobbed. "Your husband murdered me."

With rising contempt, she glared at her child's accuser. "No, Martin, Jeremy didn't murder you; he killed you in war. Something you would have undoubtedly done to him if given the opportunity. You hypocrite! How dare you call my husband a murderer. Would you want Jeremy's spirit hanging over Helga, threatening Herman and Ingrid?" Silence prevailed in the room before Deborah's emotions boiled over. "Would you?!" she screamed at the specter.

It was quiet once more. The minutes ticked by, each lost in jumbled thoughts and raw feelings. Deborah broke the hush. "Martin, it is now obvious my child was never on trial; it was Jeremy. You thought you had bested him, didn't you?"

Martin started crying. He found himself surprised to have tears. He had never thought of a spirit possessing such a gift. "Yes, Deborah, I was so close to winning the struggle. When he recovers, he will bear a horrible scar for the remainder of his life."

"When? You said *when* he recovers," Deborah said, her voice cracking.

"Yes, my Deborah, he will recover. Still, expect the function of his right arm greatly reduced. His capacity to use his revolver with such an injury is a testament to his resolve. Your husband can no longer wage war. I was his last triumph."

"If you knew Jeremy, you would understand he

wouldn't see your death as a triumph."

Martin looked squarely at Deborah and said, "I forgive him and ask for your absolution as well." With that, he placed the white light on her stomach. "Your child is blessed."

"Martin, I forgive you, and I know Jeremy would too," Deborah said, tears welling in her eyes.

Suddenly, Martin's features changed. Gone were the disfigurement, blood, and filth. In its place was a handsome, young man with Teutonic features. He no longer wore a uniform but was in clean clothes and a cap. He had a gentle look in his eyes - so much different than before.

"Go to your family, Martin. Say goodbye, then go home to God."

Suddenly, he wasn't there. Deborah sat still, stunned by all she had seen and done. She was startled from her thoughts by the chirping of birds and the light of the coming dawn.

Mr. Smith's Neighborhood

A truth revealed costs a price. Why should the telling of this particular revelation be any different? This whole business has a bill. It's a story of what extremes people will do to live in safety. What happens when helplessness and hopelessness invade the human mind? Sometimes there is no right answer to a problem. Sometimes people don't have a just, moral solution to their lives. In the end, what good is a soul if it lives in perpetual fear?

My name is Potter. That is what the people in the neighborhood call me. Potter isn't my Christian name, and I sure as hell won't give you my last name. I'm going to tell you a story, at least the part I know or heard from someone worth believing. It concerns the neighborhood where I live.

Trust me when I say this neighborhood is very, very different than the rest of the city. It might be unlike any other community. I've lived there almost my entire life, and I still don't know if that distinction is a blessing or a curse.

I live in Dawson City. It is one of the most populated cities in Ohio, boasting well over half a million souls. What was once part of the Great Black Swamp was transformed into farmland and city streets and shops.

Dawson City is a great place to live if you don't reside in the old east end. The neighborhood, unfortunately, has all the blight and problems that inflict the most impoverished areas of most major cities. Drugs, gangs, violence, and drive-by shootings are the unfortunate lot of the once-proud community residents.

The old east end was not always the cesspool of misery it currently is now. The area was once a jewel in the golden crown of the city.

What happened to such a beautiful area? It was the same four horsemen that spell the doom of almost any neighborhood: racial tensions, money, politicians, and urban flight. Did I mention politicians?

I will give a description, but I will not belabor the issue with every sordid detail. Needless to say, when the horsemen finished their work, the bloom was most definitely off the rose. The jewel in the golden crown had become the boil on the ass of the fair city.

The area immediately surrounding my neighborhood is like a war zone. If you drive through the community, you will see burnt-out buildings and vacant lots with nothing but rubble in them. The first riots took a heavy toll on the area. They occurred decades ago, but the city did little to clean the mess in the aftermath. It was as if the rest of Dawson City said, "Screw it. If you were so stupid to destroy where you live, you deal with it."

Gangs roam the streets. I have a friend who lives six blocks over. He was walking to the post office a month ago when some gang-bangers pulled up. They hopped out of their Escalade and robbed him of his last forty-eight dollars. If that wasn't enough, they proceeded to beat the crap out of him. He spent four days in the hospital. They would have kept him longer if he had any insurance other than Medicare.

To sum it up, the old east end is full of pimps, prostitutes, drugs, and a hell of a lot of violence.

At times I reflect on this part of the city's history. The area possessed elegance. The people who led and served it once made this neighborhood their home. The houses were majestic. But there is no doubt, the current crop of old east enders shits where they eat.

But, inside all this waste is my neighborhood. It's radically different from the surrounding area, who lives there, and how my neighbors' act.

There are no abandoned or burnt-out buildings. A resident owns every piece of real estate. All contracts stipulate that if the property owner moves an inch out of the neighborhood, they must put the property in a collective trust until someone in the community buys it.

The neighborhood insulates itself from outside influences. There will be no developer from two states away purchasing even a clod of dirt in Smithville. Smithville. That is what the other old east enders call our neighborhood. We are named Smithers. They call us Smithers with equal amounts of jealousy and fear. Smith is the name of the family that originally owned the 200 acres that encompass the neighborhood.

You won't see gang members set up shop or even pass through the neighborhood. There are no prostitutes, crime, or violence in Smithville. Domestic violence, cranking music, and roaring cars are also not tolerated. While police patrol the area, they're rarely needed; we settle our problems.

Everybody takes care of their property. Neighbors genuinely care for each other. Nobody seems to give a damn about the color of a person's skin. Every year there are block parties, or as we call them, festivals. When these events take place, the city blocks off the streets to keep traffic and outsiders away.

You are probably wondering how there could be such a patch of Eden in a jungle of thorns. I can give you the one and only reason - Mr. Smith.

The reason the area is named Smithville is all part of the story. I want you to understand the whole story, the entire history. As I said, in the neighborhood, there lived a family named Smith.

***

The family first occupied the land just after the war of 1812. The young United States government gave Jebediah Smith two hundred acres of land as part of his army pay. Jebediah thought receiving two hundred acres plus his army pay was fantastic. He should have looked at a map.

After being mustered out of the army, Jebediah immediately headed to Pennsylvania to collect his family. Apparently, the man never thought to examine the land before he headed east. The government told him that after he cleared the property, it would make excellent farmland. He must have been naïve enough to believe that the government wouldn't lie to him since he fought for his country. Let me tell you, the property was on the southern border of the Great Black Swamp. The same glacier that created Lake Erie made that damn swamp. That wretched thing was one of the worst areas to raise a family within a thousand miles.

Jebediah's wife, Katie, was less than thrilled when she found her two hundred acres of paradise included rattlesnakes, bears, wolves, large cats, malaria, and enough mosquitoes to fill a continent. To top it off, the rains would flood the fields every spring, making planting next to impossible.

Three years into the prospect, Jebediah and Katie had lost two children to that two hundred acres. One died in quicksand. The other of cholera, the result of a spring flood contaminating a stream from which she drank.

In the summer of the fourth year, their youngest, Rebecca, had to have her left arm amputated from the elbow down due to a rattlesnake bite. Katie never cried, yelled, or screamed as she had for the deaths of her other two children. She was most likely grateful Rebecca was alive, but it was apparent the land had broken her. Their oldest, Caleb, wrote that his mother would stare off into space for hours on end. He said she would often wake in the night calling the names of her dead children.

When Rebecca was well enough to travel, Katie told Jebediah she was *going home*. By that, she meant her parent's residence near Philadelphia. Katie took her two surviving children, one of the carriages, and two of their five horses. She and Caleb loaded their belongings and, with Rebecca, left. They had packed their things and left in complete silence. In his journal, Caleb wrote he had never seen anything as sad as his father's face as they rode away.

Four years later, Katie remarried a tailor in Philadelphia. By all accounts, he was a kind man. Caleb wrote his stepfather treated him and Rebecca as his children. Caleb wrote he and his sister felt the same love for him. With her second husband, Katie had two children. Caleb wrote that for the remainder of her life, he did not once hear his mother speak of his father or her deceased children. Neither Rebecca nor Caleb ever returned to Ohio.

Jebediah hadn't attempted to stop his wife and children from leaving. He most likely was grieving as hard as his wife. He also, no doubt, felt guilty for bringing his family to that particular patch of hell.

***

After his family left, Jebediah became a recluse. At that time, with so few neighbors, it was much easier than today. But his neighbor's, what few he had, said he began to act strangely. They observed him walking through his fields at night, talking to himself.

People said Jebediah's solitary rants sounded as if they were directed at someone specifically, although no one was with him. He asked if she had enough, if he had not been faithful to her in spite of the suffering she had caused.

People assumed he was delusional; the grief and

solitude had snapped his mind. His neighbors believed Jebediah was holding an imagined conversation with Katie. He wasn't.

Jebediah wasn't talking, imagined or not, to any person. He had a secret. By the time Katie left with the children, he belonged to that two-hundred acres. The dirt was just as permanent on his soul as it was under his fingernails. He blamed it for killing his children and driving the rest of his family away. Despite this, he could not separate himself from the soil. At the time, he didn't know something else connected itself to the land.

It seemed under the water and mud; there was a heartbeat. It was as if something in the land had longed for someone with whom it could connect. Through the eons of ice and water, it had waited. It had wanted a companion. It found one in Jebediah. There was no way it was going to share him with another.

Jebediah died an old man. He would have lived longer but for the excising of the water from the land. After all kinds of experiments to deal with the swamp's water, someone thought of a simple solution - drain it into Lake Erie. That is why you see ditches on the sides of a great many of the roads; they must remain open, or the land will return to swampland.

What had been useless mud then became prime farming land. Jebediah's net worth skyrocketed as people continued to look for suitable soil to produce crops. But this brought him no peace. A complex series of ditches and canals sucked the life from his companion. After the waterways dried the soil, Jebediah died.

A group of hunters found Jebediah's corpse when they stopped at his cabin to ask permission to hunt in his woods. What they discovered horrified them. One hunter instructed the other two to remain while he alerted the sheriff. They informed him they had no intention of staying on that land.

The three hunters arrived the following morning in Fremont; only then it was named Lower Sandusky. They told their story to the sheriff. He was not as skeptical as one might think. He had seen more than one person go mad in the isolation of the area. However, the sheriff thought their story likely exaggerated; their observations were fueled more by fear and liquor than facts.

That afternoon, the hunters, accompanied by the sheriff, a doctor, and the local Methodist Church minister, started toward Jebediah's cabin. The Sheriff asked the physician to travel to the Smith farm if medical help, or more likely, an autopsy was required. The sheriff requested the minister join the party to officiate a short graveside service if Jebediah was dead. They arrived by mid-afternoon the following day. The hunters would not go within two hundred yards of the cabin but agreed to stay to answer questions as needed.

The sheriff entered the cabin first. He came out coughing two minutes later with his eyes the size of saucers. He told the minister he would not go inside again alone. The physician was puzzled. He knew the sheriff had seen a lot of death and gore over the years. He steeled himself and went inside. He returned less than a minute later with eyes just as large as the sheriff's. The physician said he would not go back inside without the minister.

The minister looked at both of them quizzically but decided not to repeat the experiment. So, the man of God, with the man of the law, and the man of healing entered the cabin as a trio. The minister made a written record of what he experienced. For him, what he saw had little or nothing to do with a man's mind snapping. It was Jebediah's soul that had gone insane.

First, the minister noticed the stench. The smell of rotting flesh was overpowering. He remarked they all had to hold handkerchiefs over their mouths and noses. It was evident that something substantial was decaying. The cabin had few windows, and the light was low. It took time for their eyes to adjust. The minister recorded in his journal, in the typical nineteenth-century, flowery prose, he wished his eyes had been seized from his face rather than seen what was in that cabin.

Aureate composition aside, it was ghastly by anyone's

standards. The young minister went on to be an army chaplain during the civil war. He later wrote that the Smith cabin scene was worse than any battle site he had seen, except Antietam.

There were only two rooms in the cabin. A sizable table occupied the middle of the large room. It connected to a roughly constructed pipe, driven into the ground. It was connected to the bottom of the table, forming a drain. How deep the tubing extended no one knew, and none of them were eager to investigate. The table and pipe appeared fashioned from a plow blade and other farm machinery.

The cabin was a den of death. It wasn't just Jebediah Smith's body. There were corpses everywhere. There had to be at least six humans, several deer, two dogs, and even a bear cub. The horrible part was the cause of death. A dead dog, strapped to the table, told the manner of their demises.

The dog and the other victims, human and animal alike, must have suffered a terrifying death strapped to that table. Once immobilized, the dog had received a series of slashes. The dried blood by the opening of the drain told the rest of the story. The blood ran onto the table. It then drained down the pipe into the ground. Mixed with dried blood were pieces of wildflowers. Grotesquely written throughout the property's structures was the explanation why Jebediah committed this horror. You see, Jebediah had written a diary. But, he wrote his macabre memoir on the walls of his cabin, the table, the hayloft; hell, he even penned it on the inside of the outhouse.

To their utter disgust and amazement, they discovered the journal written in blood. The minister later said he only copied what he thought was most important; the stench was just too much. He remarked there was more than just the smell of decay. Something beyond a rancid odor reached his brain. Years later, he wrote that, unlike the battlefield, there was what he described as a sort of soul stench. The whole area felt as if something was decaying that should have died long, long ago. He described it as sensing the land had exacted a terrible price.

The gist of Jebediah's "journal" was the land was the home of a spirit. This thing waited for some other being to be its companion. For what reason, God only knows, the entity chose Jebediah Smith. First, it drove his family from him. Then, when he was alone, crushed, it came to him.

I can't tell you if the spirit had a gender, but it presented itself to him as a woman. He wrote that one night, while he was walking in his fields, she approached him. She told him she had waited since long before the giant ice for someone just right to be her companion. She informed Jebediah he was that person. He wrote that she never told him the specifics. Only that he alone, of all who had walked the land, had the exact balance of life and death she desired.

Some think they know why Jebediah had a unique balance this thing needed or wanted or whatever the hell. He had killed men in the war. He had spilled the blood of other thinking beings. Next, as a farmer, he tried to bring life. In one hand, Jebediah offered the land blood; with the other, he brought life.

The minister went on to say Jebediah wrote the spirit had no tangible form; still, he could feel a genuine sense of affection flowing from her to him. At first, he thought he had gone mad. But she kept coming to him. He was afraid but desperate for emotional warmth. He finally gave himself to her, and she responded in kind.

Jebediah wrote they were very much in love. He would tell her stories from his youth, his time in the army, and read the Bible. She would tell him fantastic stories of high mountains of ice, cats the size of bears, and things that looked like elephants but had thick fur.

This relationship went on for years. Jebediah grew very old. Then the water started to be drained from the swamp. The loss of water was a death sentence for the spirit, at least in this world. He was desperate to keep his love alive, but there was no way to stop her death. She grew weaker as the water flowed from the land.

One day she told him before she died, she wanted to be his Sarah to her Abraham. Jebediah wrote he didn't initially understand what she meant. The spirit informed him that while she was not physical, there was a way to give him a son, even in her old age. A child that would rest inside the ground until there were no other of his descendants alive. Then their son would take ownership of their home. The land that had for so long held her spirit.

The spirit told him what must be done for them to have a child. At first, he said no. But as she grew ever weaker, Jebediah Smith, wracked with grief, knew he had a horrible decision to make.

She told him there must be both human and animal blood. The human blood would give the child intelligence and cunning. The animal blood would provide him with strength, speed, and instinct. Some of the blood had to be his, for she would only have his son. She instructed him to mix the blood with wildflowers. The flowers would give their son a sense of beauty and compassion.

The minister wrote the evidence of Jebediah's decision was everywhere. He went on to note that no child could be born of that nature and be human. I wonder if the pastor ever realized how accurate his observation was.

The minister finished copying Jebediah's grotesque journal. At least, all he could stomach. He met the physician and sheriff well away from the cabin. The lawman had long since sent the hunters on their way. The pastor recorded feeling sick and empty inside. The sheriff had a dazed expression on his face, and the physician looked as if he had vomited several times; maybe he had.

Each man said nothing, apparently caught in his own thoughts. None of them moved for about ten minutes. Then, without comment, they went about burning every structure on the farm. He said it was as if God himself had compelled them to destroy any memory of Jebediah's existence. They watched the fire well into the night. The buildings burned well. The smell was horrible, but they had to see this place of blood and pain destroyed.

The minister wrote that when the cabin collapsed, the area was almost entirely flat. The lone exception was the table and pipe, still intact. He penned that when they saw its hideous form, glowing orange from the heat of the fire, they turned away - sickened by the sight of the monstrosity.

The land lay fallow for over six decades. No one who experienced the horror of the events ever discussed them with others. The man of God's copy of Jebediah's insane chronicle was the only evidence the incident ever occurred.

The minister's great-great-grandson knocked on my door one sunny day. He looked very old and walked with a cane. He introduced himself and handed me his ancestor's journal. He said it belonged to the land on which we stood. He steadfastly refused even to enter the foyer of my home. He told me he would advise me to burn the place, but it was evident from the journal fire doesn't work.

***

By the start of the twentieth century, Dawson City had already shown it would become a city of some size. People came pouring into the growing metropolis. Pollution was an issue, so was overcrowding. The city needed more land to address these issues. So, in 1911, the Smith land was annexed into the city and zoned for residential use like the immediate area. The whole of the old east end remained zoned that way for over sixty years until some light industry was allowed in an effort by City Council to bring jobs into the area.

The following year, 1912, the last remaining descendant of Jebediah and Katie Smith moved to his ancestral land. Darrell Smith arrived with his young wife. He accumulated a decent inheritance when his father died young in the Spanish-American war. All the Smiths seemed to have early deaths. The estate was placed in a trust until he reached the age of twenty-one years and one day.

Living modestly in a hotel in the oil boomtown of Wayne, young Darrell divided the land he inherited. Given the high-end residential area, land prices were steep. Fortunately, there was an ever-increasing professional class growing along with the city.

Darrell sold every parcel in thirteen months, save one. He kept this specific lot for him and his wife. The outline of his ancestor's cabin was on the plot. He and his wife fully intended to live and raise a family in the neighborhood. He wanted to build their home on a lot on Shelby Street. However, his wife, Julia, thought it would be quaint if they constructed their home over the original cabin's site. She told him it would bring them good luck.

Three years later, Julia became pregnant with Darrell's child. She was quietly proud she would help continue the Smith family name. She didn't know someone else was also helping the cause.

One night Julia arrived home early from a church function. She heard sounds in Darrell's den. She opened the door to find the maid bent over Darrell's desk. Darrell, in turn, was hunched over the maid. He was giving it to her good, and it was apparent the maid was thoroughly enjoying the experience.

Julia screamed in rage and pain. Darrell and the maid looked up but showed no indication of uncoupling. The maid sneered at her and said, "Did you think you were the only one carrying his child?"

Julia ran to their bedroom. She sat on the bed, thinking and crying; her world crushed. In her mind, it was over. She walked to Darrell's nightstand, grabbed an item from the drawer, then calmly walked back to the den.

She arrived to see them getting dressed. "Are you going to fire me?" the maid taunted.

"No," Julia. "I am going to fire *at* you."

With that, she shot the maid in the head. She was dead before she hit the floor.

Darrell looked at his dead lover in disbelief. He then turned and charged Julia. Darrell was almost on her when she shot him squarely in the crotch. He lurched backward and fell to his knees. Blood soaked his pants. Julia calmly walked to him and put a bullet through his temple, thus ending his crotch pain.

She then began to tremble and cry. She couldn't believe her home; her dream of a family shattered so quickly. So irrevocably. She gently rubbed her bulging belly as she placed the pistol in her mouth. With a flash of fire and the smell of gunpowder, the Jebediah and Katie Smith family line ended.

***

As you would suspect, the autopsies, including the

symbolic shot to Darrell's crotch, filled in the basic idea of what happened. The deaths were big news at the time. The scandal wasn't some case of low-life domestic violence. A member of one of the upper-crust families had eliminated three people in a murder-suicide.

The owner of the *Dawson City Times* lived two houses down on Weston Street. He ran to see what had happened. Later, he printed a four-part expose′ entitled *Tragedy in Eden*. He dug up a considerable amount of dirt on a lot of families. Given the class of people affected, he was encouraged not to run the article, or at the least, not reveal so many skeletons in the closets. He published it anyway. The public lapped it up. People were like they are today. They loved to see someone famous or wealthy fall.

The long and short of it, the house was cleaned of the gore and went on the market. A realty company poured a lot of money into selling that beautiful house. There was no way in hell anyone was going to buy it. There had been a murder-suicide in the home. There were also old tales of an insane farmer that had once lived on that exact spot.

My grandfather lived across the street in the carriage house of a home belonging to a wealthy attorney. He was their groundskeeper. One day, while he was planting rose bushes in the front yard, a fancy car pulled into the Smith's driveway. My grandpa knew it was Solomon Dorse, the owner of *Dawson City Realty*. His chauffeur drove him.

Mr. Dorse inspected the yard and then walked across the street to talk to grandpa. That was an era when men would

remove their hats when a rich, *white* man spoke to them. So, my grandpa put his shovel down and removed his cap when Mr. Dorse hailed him.

He asked Grandpa if he had seen anyone looking at the house. Grandpa replied that only the people who viewed the residence with morbid curiosity. Mr. Dorse didn't seem to like the answer because he huffed and walked briskly back to the Smith house. He took out a set of keys, put one in the front door lock, and entered the house. Grandpa had the idea Mr. Dorse had tired of not selling such an exquisite home and was going to inspect it himself.

He told me Mr. Dorse came out of the house about forty minutes later. He stumbled across the street to him. He looked shaken, his eyes as large as saucers and trembling all over. Then it dawned on grandpa Mr. Dorse's face revealed an emotion beyond rattled; terrified would more accurately describe him.

He handed Grandpa the keys to the Smith house. Grandpa smelled something pungent. He looked down and saw piss was running down Mr. Dorse's pants. He looked at Grandpa and said, "He wants to see you alone."

"Mr. Dorse, sir, who wants to see me?"

"Mr. Smith."

"Mr. Smith is dead."

"Don't you think I know that?" He said in an irritated, trembling voice. He is a... I don't know. A different Mr. Smith."

"I didn't know there was another Mr. Smith."

"Neither did I," he replied. "He said you are to knock, then enter."

"When does he want to see me?"

"Now. Oh, I emphatically urge you to say a prayer before you go onto that property."

With that, Mr. Dorse stumbled back across the street. He ripped the "For Sale" sign out of the ground and put it in the back seat beside him. Grandpa said he heard him tell his chauffeur to take him home.

Well, Grandpa walked across the street and up the steps of the Smith house. He knocked, took off his hat then entered. When Mrs. Smith was alive, the residence was sunny and felt welcoming. The dwelling looked and felt very different. It was dark due to the closed blinds, but he could see well enough. He said he had the feeling he was being watched, studied. He felt uneasy. He wished he had uttered that prayer.

Grandpa called out, "Mr. Smith?"

He said he heard only one word, "Come."

The voice that had given that command was like a

drawn-out whisper. Close but not quite a hiss. It was coming from, of all places, the den. Grandpa said the thought of entering that room filled him with dread. He realized why Mr. Dorse peed down his leg.

Grandpa obeyed the command and walked into the den. He was scared shitless. He saw a chair in front of Mr. Smith's desk.

"Sit down."

So, Grandpa sat in the chair. He knew someone or something was in a chair, set back from the opposite side of the desk. He told me, and from my own experience, I can tell you, no one ever has had a good look at Mr. Smith. At best, I could see a form that was human-like but hazy and pitch black. Grandpa once described it as a place where light goes to die.

Well, there was my grandpa, sitting there, wringing the hell out of his cap. He half wanted to turn on a light. Something in his brain told him that would be worse than the darkness. He listened to that voice and sat tight. He said it felt like hours passed, but he later realized his entire time in the house was less than thirty minutes. He knew he was the object of study by whomever or whatever sat in that other chair.

Finally, it said, "You are Leroy."

"Yes, Mr. Smith."

"I will require your services from time to time."

"For what, Sir?"

"To maintain my property."

"Sir, I'm just a groundskeeper. I'm no electrician and a damn poor plumber."

"You will maintain my grounds," the voice responded. "You will be my agent when I require other services."

"Sir, I already work for Mr. and Mrs. Neese. I don't think, no disrespect, they will allow me time to take care of your property, as well."

"Leroy, are you familiar with the story from the Bible concerning Moses and the burning bush?"

"Yes, Sir."

"You sound like Moses arguing with God about leading the Israelites out of bondage. You have only to wait. Mr. Neese will come to you. You will plant several species of wildflowers on the property. They are to receive your utmost care."

"You will purchase a padlock for each fence gate. As my agent, you will keep one set of keys. You will knock, come into the house ten feet, lay the other set of the keys on the floor. You will then turn around and leave. You will not look back. Mr. Neese will give you the funds to purchase the items."

Then, he quietly said, "You may leave."

Grandpa said he didn't need to be told twice. He damn near tripped over the chair getting out of the den, then hustled out of the house. He said he was almost struck by a passing car while running across the street to the Neese's. Two days later, Mr. Neese came to him. He told Grandpa he was Mr. Smith's attorney, and Mr. Smith's requests would take priority.

Nearly a year passed with no sign of the reclusive Mr. Smith. Then one June day, just before the official start of summer, he was collecting fallen tree branches from a recent storm when he heard a quite audible, "Come." His heart sank, but he was too afraid to disobey.

When he entered the house, he said it looked the same as the last time, from what he could tell. So he had a thought that he should enter the den. The chair was in the same place.

He said he felt like fainting, then heard, "Sit."

There was an uncomfortable silence. Grandpa told me he had a lot of nervous energy and no cap to wring this time. Then Mr. Smith began to speak.

"Leroy."

"Yes, Sir?"

"I need you to perform a service."

"Yes, Sir."

"You will go to the East End Veterinarian office. You will ask for Dr. Wells. He will be expecting you. You will take the travel bag he gives you. You are to proceed with haste to my yard. You will pick wildflowers."

"You will take the travel bag and the flowers to an area by the cellar door. You will then mix the contents of the jar in the travel bag with thc wildflowers. No metal is to touch the mixture. The unused wooden bowl in your upper left cabinet will easily hold its volume. Use the wooden spoon in the second drawer by your stove."

"After completing your task, you will immediately leave. You will not look back under any circumstances. Wait two days and then return for the bowl. You are to keep the bowl and spoon clean and separate from other objects until it is required again."

"Mr. Smith, what's in the jar?"

"Blood."

Grandpa said he shuttered and said, "I don't think, no disrespect intended, I can do this. I have a weak stomach."

"Oh, my Moses, if you only knew why I'm ordering you to complete my command. The alternative would be far harder on a great many stomachs."

So, Grandpa completed the gruesome task. By then, there was no way he wasn't going to follow Mr. Smith's commands.

What scared him most, the thing that gave him many sleepless nights, was Mr. Smith's intimate knowledge of the carriage house. Mr. Smith had known what and where things were in his home. He also knew about his life. He knew the wooden bowl was unused. Grandpa slept with the lights on until he moved to a retirement village near Fostoria. That was decades.

The years passed. Grandpa said that he only entered the house when instructed. He regularly maintained the grounds.

He also said he was always nervous around Mr. Smith. It felt like being in a cage with a tiger. I can tell you from experience that it is a good analogy. Despite this, Grandpa had the feeling Mr. Smith wanted fellowship. No one who spent time with him would ever say he was human; his voice was as human as a snake's hiss or a dog's growl. But something about him gave me the sense that part of him is human.

Grandpa said that over the years, he and Mr. Smith developed a warmer relationship. Mr. Smith would ask Granddad to talk about himself and his life. He was initially reluctant to share his experiences with what appeared to be a predator that was self-aware.

Mr. Smith told Grandpa he would not harm him. So, he told stories of his life, travels, and loves to whatever sat on the other side of the desk. Grandpa said he felt, yes felt, Mr. Smith already knew much of the stories; but he would quietly listen all the same. Occasionally, Mr. Smith would tell my grandpa things. He seemed to have intimate knowledge of the circumstances of Mrs. Smith's murder-suicide.

One day, Grandpa built up the courage to ask Mr. Smith a question. “Mr. Smith, may I ask you a question?”

“Moses, you just did. You asked if you may ask me a question.”

“I mean about you.”

“You may ask, but be careful, my Moses. Think hard before you enquire. You possess only a rudimentary understanding of me; you only see the smallest of a sliver of my being. You might receive your answer and wish you hadn’t asked the question.”

My grandpa said he knew Mr. Smith was deadly serious. He thought for several minutes while silence pervaded the gloomy den. Then, looking across the desk, he asked, “Are you a vampire?”

Grandpa said Mr. Smith made a sound. It was the closest thing to a human laugh he ever heard from him.

“No, Moses, I’m not a vampire. I’m no animated corpse. I am most certainly alive.”

“Then, why the blood? And what about the flowers?”

There was silence. Grandpa knew Mr. Smith was staring hard at him, even if he couldn’t clearly see him. He wondered if he was about to die in the same den as the others had so many years before.

Then, Mr. Smith spoke. “Moses, Mrs. Neese asked you this morning to weed their vegetable garden. You should do that now.”

Grandpa said that he poured all of his fear and nervous energy into that small plot of vegetables. It was a hot day, but Grandpa remembered a cold sweat soaking his clothes. He said he had goosebumps on his arms, and despite the day's heat, he shivered, feeling chilled from a sick fear. He never asked Mr. Smith another question.

***

When grandpa entered his early sixties, Mr. Smith told him to pick a replacement. After much thought, he settled on my dad. He had watched Grandpa perform his tasks for years.

The Neeses told my grandfather of their intention to sell their property and move to Florida. It never made it to the market. Two weeks later, a title agency called. The clerk said my grandpa needed to come immediately to their office. Arriving there, he found Mr. and Mrs. Neese. They completed the necessary papers and handed grandpa the title to their property. During the transaction, Grandpa saw the amount of the sale; it was above market value. The paperwork stated the property's purchase and subsequent title transfer as payment for services rendered by Grandpa to one, I. Smith. Taxes to be paid, on condition of family ownership, by the same. Grandpa had a mortgage and a tax-free home. My family has lived there ever since.

Grandpa knew never to enter Mr. Smith's house without being invited. He stood just before the front porch steps. Grandpa cried and thanked Mr. Smith. Although he never heard a reply, he knew Mr. Smith had listened to his outpouring of gratitude.

The decades rolled on. My father grew older and neared retirement from the city. He chose me to be Mr. Smith's next agent. It seems to have become a family legacy.

I was young when I became Mr. Smith's agent. I was only twenty-three and less than a year out of the army. I had a job at a stamping plant. I was a late-in-life child - the result of a combination of a Caribbean cruise and a little too much alcohol.

Being an agent had become routine. Well, as much as interacting with Mr. Smith was ever going to be. Then came the event.

***

By the time I became the agent, the ever-increasing ghetto was advancing toward Smithville. It began to press against the neighborhood. It was like a swimmer testing the water's temperature with his toe before diving into the pool. Everyone knew Mr. Smith drove it back. Scared drug dealers and prostitutes were a testament to his protective presence.

We formed neighborhood block watches. We tried to be proactive, but we all knew there would be a time when a more forceful repulse would be needed to maintain our way of life. It came two years later.

Chloe Simms was abducted by a local gang while walking home from school. They planned on transporting her to Detroit and selling her to a pimp to be tricked out. She was only thirteen years old. Some men find that arousing. I have never understood why. I hope I never do.

Chloe's parents were frantic. Their daughter was missing, and they feared the worse. Her father called the police. They came and wrote a statement, but they could only search. The police knew what was happening to the girls; they just didn't know where the gang held their captives until their departure to Detroit.

The neighborhood was in a frenzied panic. People were outside, standing in groups, talking. We had all heard the stories of what the gangs did to these girls. Suddenly, I heard Mr. Smith say, "I will bring the child home." No one else seemed to hear his words. I told the people I heard Mr. Smith say he would rescue Chloe. Most people seemed dubious. Scaring prostitutes and drug dealers was one thing; saving Chloe from a vicious gang was quite another. I had no doubt he could do it.

The gang held Chloe in a small, abandoned factory about two miles from Smithville. She was blindfolded and placed in a cage for psychological effect. They wanted to break her will. Even without being able to see, Chloe felt the cage bars and began to sob.

The van arrived that would transfer Chloe to Detroit. It had no back windows. There were shackles attached to a steel bar bolted to the floor. The pimp padded the walls to suppress the sounds of screams and crying. These people were far less human than Mr. Smith. They certainly had less compassion.

The pimp from Detroit inspected Chloe. As he and the gang were haggling over the sale price, they were interrupted by a voice. “I will say this only once. Let the child go, and you will live.”

They turned to see something in the form of a human. But the features were fuzzy, and it was very black. They didn’t know what they were viewing. Their response was to aim a variety of firearms at it.

Mr. Smith told Chloe in that drawn-out hissing whisper, “Leave the blindfold on, and cover your ears.”

They directed a hail of bullets at the vague outline. Chloe told me many years later, she followed his instructions but still heard screams of absolute agony. She told me the sounds of bones breaking were so loud that they were audible above the decreasing gunfire. The shooting finally stopped. Then she listened to a single set of footsteps running. They suddenly stopped, followed by a sickening sound that brought to her mind that of a piece of meat torn apart. Then there was silence.

Chloe said the stillness lasted almost a minute. Suddenly, the door of the cage was violently ripped from its hinges. She screamed in fright. She heard, "Child, leave on your blindfold. Give me your hand." She said she knew she was going home. She also knew it was Mr. Smith.

Chloe held it out and felt it gently gripped by a hand that seemed to hold immense strength. She said it felt human, yet in a way, it wasn't. She went on to say she never quite understood why and had long since given up trying. Chloe vaguely remembered walking home. She knew Mr. Smith led her. The next thing she knew, she was standing on her front porch. The blindfold was gone.

Chloe told the police of the gang, the pimp, being blindfolded and caged. She said she heard gunfire, vaguely remembered walking and finding herself home. The rest she left out. Police theorized a rival gang attacked during the negotiations. Somehow, Chloe exited the cage and, in fear, only remembered part of her ordeal.

The police might not have known how Chloe escaped her captors, but Smithville knew. Two days later, the police found the building. They dismissed the earlier theory of a gang fight. They couldn't determine what or who killed the gang members and the pimp. They did, however, know how they had died - gruesomely. The degree and type of wounds indicated a predator of some size. A lion or a bear, for example. Yet, the killing was very methodical. It had earmarks of human intelligence. It also seemed the line of attack meant to draw gunfire away from the cage.

The cage itself was impressive. Police agreed its construction and strength were equal to any local jail cell. What possessed the power to rip the door from its hinges baffled them.

Chloe's parents went that very night to an area just outside of the Smith house gates. They dropped to their knees, sobbing, and bowed before the house for over an hour. They thanked and thanked Mr. Smith for saving their daughter from those monsters.

The neighborhood was quiet for three days. It was trying to deal with the terror of Chloe's kidnapping. It also came to grips with the realization of the power and care of its benefactor. Then, on the evening of the third day, there was a knock on my door. Several men and women were on my porch and yard. They said they needed to talk to me.

We talked for hours. Chloe's kidnapping showed us the police and our block watch weren't going to protect us. We felt scared, even worse, vulnerable. Several of the group cried. They knew they could not hold back the ghetto. The fear and grief I saw on their faces were heartbreaking. They felt hopeless. So did I.

We all knew we were only going to be genuinely protected by Mr. Smith. The question was what he required in return. They urged me to ask him to forgive them for doubting his power to save Chloe. They said they knew he would only talk to me. I told them I could only enter his house if invited.

I knew Mr. Smith heard our conversation. *Nothing* happens in his neighborhood in which he isn't aware. Still, I heard nothing from him for days. The community began to stress from the silence. Had their great benefactor abandoned them? They watched me, seeing if he had summoned me to his house. One afternoon I was reading *Tom Sawyer* when I heard, "Come, bring pens and many sheets of paper."

People stood outside the gate and watched as I knocked, then entered the house. Two hours later, I exited the property. I told the people waiting to gather the adults in the vacant lot by Mr. Smith's estate.

***

Forty-five minutes later, just about every adult in Smithville was standing there. Someone was there to represent every family. A hush fell over the crowd. I began to discuss the substance of my conversation with

Mr. Smith.

"As you know, Mr. Smith called me to him this afternoon. He has heard your cries for protection. He knows you're scared. He told me he wishes to make the land of his ancestors a place of peace." There was a general sigh of relief.

"He has agreed to enter into a pact with you, the residents of Smithville. There are commandments he requires to be continuously obeyed by everyone. If you follow them, Smithville will not only be safe; it will be at peace. Mr. Smith said to sear them into your heads and hearts. We are to teach these to our children."

"You will keep your property clean. You are a separate neighborhood, apart from the area around you. You must show you are different by the way you treat your homes."

"You will not pollute the land of my ancestors. You will not defile my land with chemicals and trash."

"You are not to act like those who live in the ghetto. They vomit their peace onto the ground in favor of a banquet of chaos. You are not to play obscene music. The volume must be low, so you don't disturb your neighbors. You are not to have loud arguments. There is to be no violence between my people. You are not to be drunk or high outside your homes."

"You mustn't miss the offering of blood and wildflowers. It allows me to tolerate your presence on my land. You will offer it every summer solstice when the sun is highest. You will then hold a festival that night in remembrance of our pact."

"You will annually plant vegetable and herb gardens. I want you to taste the fruits of my land, but you must give offer me a small portion of the very best of every year's harvest. You will do this on the second Saturday in September, at noon. That afternoon, you will hold a festival in honor of autumn until the sun sets."

"Only my agent is allowed to enter my home. He alone will present your offerings. He will place them by the cellar door."

"Do not provoke the fools of the outside world. Do not test me by seeking trouble from which to be saved."

"My land is not to be sold to outsiders. We are a neighborhood unto ourselves."

"You are to show compassion for your neighbors. You are to live in peace. You will show mercy, as I have shown you mercy."

I looked up from reading Mr. Smith's commandments. I half expected people to roll their eyes and walk away. Nobody left. I Then spoke the terms of consummation.

"Mr. Smith said if you agree to these terms, *all* of these terms, you are to prick your finger on this knife. You are to spill a drop of blood over the fence onto his property while saying, *I agree, Mr. Smith*."

I raised the knife above my head so everyone could take a look. No one spoke, and I was getting ready to put it away and go home when Chloe's parents walked to where I was standing. Her father silently held out his hand. I handed him the knife. He studied it. It looked to be old, perhaps from the nineteenth century. Then, he and his wife walked toward the fence.

Stunningly, without words, every last person formed a line behind Mr. and Mrs. Simms. They all performed the consummation ritual. I was the last.

After that day, Mr. Smith made a statement to any criminal element with designs on his neighborhood. Any trespass into Smithville, even to merely pass through, was not tolerated. He dealt with each incursion with absolute, ruthless brutality, reclaiming the original two hundred acres and its residents as his own. He was commanding the ghetto and all it brought with it to stay out. They understood the message. Even during the second riots, no one came into Smithville. It would have been a death sentence.

It seems only appropriate this happened in America. A land where the children of immigrants have achieved great success. Parents have always wanted their children to reach higher, be more than they were. Did Jebediah and the spirit want any less for their child? A thing born of blood and flowers. The land its womb. Isaac to his parents

Abraham and Sarah. This thing, neither spirit nor human but containing something of both. Now Mr. Smith has given his land and his people peace. Though no one would utter it, he has become more than Smithville's protector and moral guide. On the very land his parents had resided, he achieved more than they could have imagined.

Mr. Smith has become a god.

I Tell Them Who They Are

"What a lousy, shitty morning!"

James Lucius looked up from his paperwork in time to see Detective Elizabeth Sipe slam a stack of paperwork on her desk. However, when he looked at her face, it exuded a look of resignation rather than anger. Finally, Lucius stated what he thought was the cause of the outburst. "I heard about the Detro trial. He was found innocent on all counts."

"Not innocent," Sipe tersely shot back. "Not guilty. I told the prosecutor she was handing that sixteen-year-old girl, the only witness willing to testify, on a silver platter. They should have prepped her better. The prosecuting attorney should have fought harder when the defense started harassing the poor girl. Why did they put a woman who passed the bar only six months ago on a triple homicide case?"

"Because Elizabeth, the district attorney's office, like our own, is stretched threadbare. Still, you are right; in a case like this, they should have more thoroughly prepped both the witness and the prosecutor."

Beth sighed, then plopped into her chair. She let out a long breath of air. "Over a year and a half of investigation. We busted our asses on that case. He was dead-to-rights guilty."

"Reasonable doubt, Beth. All it takes is for one jurist to have reasonable doubt. Anyway, I have been waiting for you. Captain Willard wants us to interview a man by the name of Matthew Jade. He's linked to several deaths."

"How many is multiple?"

"Seventeen."

"Jesus almighty, which interview room is he in?"

"He isn't. I called him. He's waiting for us at his home."

"Are you telling me we are going to interview a man, suspected of seventeen murders, in his home?"

"Mr. Jade isn't a suspect of any murders," Lucius stated.

"Manslaughter?" Beth asked.

"Possibly, we're not sure if that even applies."

"How did the victims, I mean, the deaths occur?"

"Suicide," Lucius stated bluntly.

"Suicide? Did he encourage them to kill themselves, you know, Jim Jones kinda thing?"

"No."

"Then what the hell is there to investigate?" Beth growled. "And I don't remember hearing of seventeen suicides, combined, in Dawson City."

"Homeland Security asked us to investigate."

Sipe rolled her eyes. "Great, the Feds."

"They said, because of the unusual nature of the case, they will allow us to interview Mr. Jade. If we decide more investigation is warranted, we will turn over our information to them."

"Of course, the Feds want us to do their work. What do you mean by *unusual*?" She asked.

All seventeen were telemarketers. They lived all over the country. The common denominator is that they all talked with Mr. Jade within a week of doing the deed."

"Good Lord," replied Sipe.

Lucius shrugged. "As you would imagine, telemarketing is a stressful, thankless job. So, no one should be surprised when one of them takes the plunge into eternity."

"Why doesn't Homeland just check him out?"

"They have already investigated him and found nothing. They probably want a double-check."

"To see if we uncover something they didn't?" Beth asked while dismissively shaking her head.

Lucius shrugged and said, "More likely to cover their collective ass in case our Mr. Jade turns out to do something decidedly anti-social and ISIS looking. They can say the local hicks, that's us, screwed up the investigation. We can be framed, blamed, and shamed."

"When is our appointment with this guy?"

"We have to be out of his house by 3:00 pm," Lucius said, looking at his watch.

"Why?"

"He said that's when *The Guiding Light* comes on TV."

"Well, Mr. Lucius, let's go eat, then visit the enigmatic Mr. Jade," Beth said, gathering her things to head out the door.

***

"Jeez, I love *Gino's* pizza," Sipe said while simultaneously wiping tomato sauce off her face with a napkin and climbing into the driver's seat of her Ford Fusion.

"Beth," Lucius responded, "I don't know how you do it. You make us come here every week, and each time you act as if you hadn't tasted pizza in months."

Grinning, Beth said, "Come on, Jimmy, learn to appreciate the finer things in life. A good pizza is a gift from God; savor the delicacy."

"Savor my ass. You eat so much, so fast, it's embarrassing. Let's go see Mr. Jade before you explode."

They pulled into the driveway and parked the car, but Beth didn't turn off the engine. She left the car running in case there was any sign of trouble. Leaving the car running could mean the difference between life and death. Almost by muscle memory, they both scanned the property and surrounding area. They looked at each other. Lucius nodded, and he could see the agreement in his partner's eyes. She shut off the car.

The house did not scream money. It was small yet well maintained. It had pleasant landscaping that started in the front of the lawn and continued to the house, which sat well back from the street. Sipe thought, *If he is a terrorist, he does a hell of a job hiding it. The place looks very nice.*

Pressing the doorbell produced a Winchester chime. The door was opened a few seconds later by a thirty-something-looking man. He had brown hair parted to the side. He dressed in light, summer clothing that wasn't formal but was a couple of notches above casual. Sipe's impression was of a librarian, yet there was something more. She couldn't quite identify what, and that bothered her.

Both showed their badges. "Mr. Jade, I am Detective Lucius, and this is Detective Sipe. Thank you for agreeing to speak with us. May we enter?"

Smiling, he shook both detectives' hands. "Of course, please follow me to the back. I want to talk there if you don't mind?"

"Of course not," replied Lucius.

As they walked through the house, Sipe noticed it was immaculate yet not in perfect order.

Turning his head back to Sipe, Mr. Jade again smiled. “Yes, detective, I like to keep things in order, but no, I’m not OCD.’

How did he know I was thinking that? Sipe thought.

Opening an old-style, wooden screen door, Jade said, “Here we are. I hope you enjoy the scenery.”

Lucius and Sipe stepped onto a wooden deck that allowed a full view of the back lawn. Both detectives involuntarily inhaled; it was gorgeous! Sipe, originally from Los Angeles, had never seen anything like it. The scene reminded Lucius of his grandma’s backyard in Weston. Only, for all its beauty, his grandmother’s flower garden was only a pale comparison to Jade’s. The setting so enamored Sipe that Lucius had to elbow her to remove the detective from a trance.

Jade motioned them to laced, metal chairs arranged around a matching table. In the center sat a pitcher of lemonade and three glasses filled with ice. It occurred to Lucius that neither the pitcher nor the glasses showed condensation on their outsides despite the warm weather. It was as if their host knew the exact time they would arrive. That bothered him. As if reading his thoughts, Jade answered the question before Lucius could ask.

“Detective Lucius, let me put your mind at ease. I saw you arrive. While you were scanning the area, I placed the pitcher and glasses on the table.”

"Mr. Jade, were you once a law enforcement officer?" inquired Sipe.

Jade just smiled. It wasn't sad; nonetheless, it didn't seem to have the desired effect if meant to display happiness.

"Now, please, detectives," Jade remarked as he poured them each a glass of lemonade, "we all know you ran my profile, as well as queried FBI records. So let's not take up a beautiful afternoon asking questions that we already know the answers. And yes, Homeland Security interviewed me several weeks ago; however, I doubt they gave you their findings."

Lucius once again admired the landscaping.

"I see you like my backyard."

"It's just beautiful, Mr. Jade. I can't quite describe it, but it seems…." Lucius let his words fade.

"I think of my yard as Thomas Kinkaid with Monet's pastel colors."

"That is an apt description," said Lucius. The detective again scanned the yard. He received the impression that it was almost perfect. There was something off, but he couldn't pick it out. His silent assessment was not a slight. He knew he was in the presence of a landscaper who was a master artist.

Jade poured them each a glass of lemonade. Sipe, who had been staring at the yard again, turned to see a full drink sitting on the table in front of her. “Mr. Jade, we are not allowed to accept any gifts.”

“Please, Detective Sipe, it’s a simple act of hospitality. I expect no differential treatment, and you can rest assured the drink contains only lemons, sugar, and water. I would feel more at ease if you accepted.”

Reluctantly, she took a sip and was stunned. Like everything else, it was damn near perfect. *Is there anything this man does that’s not incredible?* She thought.

Lucius, as the lead investigator, started the line of questioning. “Mr. Jade, there have been seventeen suicides that have the distinction of being connected to you. We find that more than a little odd.”

Jade smiled grimly and looked the detective in the eye. “I don’t.”

Sipe was incredulous. She interrupted Lucius’ next question. “What do you mean you don’t? Seventeen people who you talked to are now dead, and you don’t find that strange?”

Lucius watched Jade’s reaction to Sipe’s outburst. She had a bad habit of interrupting. Most times, it irritated him. This time, it allowed him to gauge Jade’s body language. Lucius took a sip of lemonade. *Holy shit, that’s good stuff,* he thought.

I didn’t say it wasn’t tragic, just not odd,” Jade shrugged.

Sipe was about to respond, but Lucius beat her to the

punch. "Mr. Jade, would you please elaborate on your view."

Jade looked Lucius in the eye. It was not a mean expression. Still, it indicated, even if he did not consciously intend to, he controlled the conversation. The detective felt a certain shiver of fear. He knew, in his heart, despite the man's genuine warmth, their host was solidly in command. Something about Matthew Jade felt different.

"Detectives, we're inundated daily with telemarketers. They harass each person, with a phone, well over a hundred of these calls every year. It wears a person down. It is dehumanizing, degrading."

"If a customer feels that way, there is the FCC No Call List. There is also software to stop unwanted calls," Lucius pointed out.

"Detective Lucius, I wasn't speaking of the persons receiving the solicitations; I was referring to the telemarketers."

Scrunching up her face, Sipe asked, "what do you mean, the telemarketers? They want to get someone on the line."

Jade vigorously shook his head. "No, Detective Sipe, having someone answer that call is the last thing they want. Most telemarketers dread the thought of talking with someone."

"But why wouldn't someone want to make a sale? It's what they do," Sipe responded incredulously.

"Because they know what they do is dishonest. Most of these salesmen, and I use that title loosely, are afraid of being ridiculed and rejected. By the time most of these people reach telemarketing, they have already been emotionally crushed. They have no confidence left. The world has told them they are too skinny, too fat, ugly, a loser, will never amount to much. So phone sales are usually the last station of a long and dreary journey."

Jade continued. "These people are souls in pain. Then they are handed a script and told to read it with *enthusiasm*. Some, of course, make it - even thrive. Still, for most, telemarketing only brings out all the insecurities and doubts they already have in themselves. Sadly, it reveals their own deepest reflection to the light of day. Telemarketing is their ultimate mirror."

"So," said Sipe, "you encourage these poor people to end it all - suicide."

Jade again emphatically shook his head. "Detective Sipe, I didn't tell or encourage one of those seventeen to hurt themselves in any way. The NSA told me they possess recordings of eight of the conversations. In them, you will not hear me say anything of the kind. I only told them the truth."

"What is the truth?" asked Lucius.

Jade smiled, apparently amused by the question. "You know, a certain first-century Roman Governor of Palestine, Pontius Pilate, asked Jesus the same question. Humans certainly search for the truth. But for the seventeen, they did not like the answer they found. Detective, I told them who they were. I tell you candidly; I said nothing more or less."

Sipe started to ask another question, but Lucius stopped her with a motion of his hand. They locked eyes. Lucius subtly shook his head.

Rising from his chair, Lucius reached out his hand. Jade gripped it firmly, yet not meant to hurt. "Mr. Jade, thank you for your time and hospitality. Here is my card. Please call me if anything comes to mind."

Jade took it, smiling benignly. "Of course. Detectives Lucius and Sipe, thank you for gracing my home with your presence."

Driving back to the station, both were silent. Finally, Sipe spoke. "There is something not right about our pleasant host."

Lucius nodded yet did not speak. He knew his partner was right. Still, he couldn't figure out what *it* was.

***

Lucius was about to knock when the door opened. He

looked into the face of Jade.

"Detective, I have been waiting. Please, let's go to the deck. I think you will find the backyard even more pleasant in the night hours."

Lucius stood on the porch, undecided as to enter.

"Mr. Lucius," Jade said, slightly cross, "you came to me. You know I am not a danger. Please, enter or leave me to enjoy the evening in peace. The fireflies are starting to come out." He then, again, gave him that pleasant, almost perfect, smile.

Lucius exhaled a big breath and entered the home.

Again sitting on the back deck, the detective was astounded by the scene in front of him. There were lights strategically situated around the entire backyard. Not too bright. Again, almost perfect. "Mr. Jade, you were again uncannily correct. I do like the garden even more at night."

"Yes," was all he said. He then produced two elegant crystal glasses and a bottle of liquor.

Lucias stopped gazing at the garden and stared at the malt-colored liquid inside the clear bottle. Looking at his host, "Mr. Jade, you must realize I cannot drink while I am on duty."

Jade's eyes bore into him. Again, James felt he had lost control. He knew he probably could not regain it. Then it hit him like a stomach punch; he had never been in command while in Jade's presence.

"Mr. Lucius, we both know you are not here professionally. As with this afternoon, the evening is much too fine to engage in pretense. After you left, I pulled this bottle from my collection. I knew you would return this evening. If you take the time to search your soul, you know you did, too."

Lucius nodded in resigned agreement.

"Mr. Lucius, you, like many others, enjoy scotch. In my hand is Bowmore, a twenty-five-year-old, single malt. When you relax, you tend to drink without ice. I agree this scotch is far too fine to pollute it with anything else." Jade poured each of them a little more than a dram, though not an excessive amount of the exquisite liquor.

Lucius took a drink and smiled. "Dear Lord, man, this is the best scotch I've ever tasted."

Jade nodded and explained, "the smokiness of the peat used to heat it gives a counterbalance to the citrus, pecan, and other undertones. Allow it to sit on your palate and tell you its story."

Lucius took another drink and held it for several seconds. He did this with his eyes closed. For the first time in his life, he listened to the liquor.

"Thank you for the scotch and the suggestion."

"You are most welcome," he replied, a soft countenance touching his features. It was evident to the detective his host had meant for him to enjoy the experience.

It became quiet. Lucius held the glass in front of his face, deep in reflection. For Jade's part, he sat quietly, occasionally sipping his scotch while admiring the fireflies.

After several minutes, Lucius looked up from his glass. "Who are you?"

"Why, I am Matthew Jade. Thirty-three years-old. I own this small property. I received a sizable inheritance which allows me to indulge in my hobby, landscaping."

"Mr. Jade, the evening is too fine to engage in pretense."

"Touché, Mr. Lucius. I will tell you; nonetheless, this conversation must never leave this deck. And no, I have committed no crime, so that need not cloud your thoughts. I will tell you the truth, but you may not like it. Think hard, for when I complete telling you who I am, I will tell you who you are."

"I need to know," was Lucius' instant, concise response.

"My name is Matthew Jade - for now. I have used countless over time. My ability to know your thoughts isn't reading your mind in the sense of hearing every word you think. It is more like receiving impressions. We have become good at… what is your idiom… connecting the dots."

"You said *we*. There are others like you?" Lucius asked.

"There are none exactly like me; still, others received

the gift. By now, it should be evident."

"No, it isn't."

"James Lucius, you are an outstanding detective, yet your thinking is two-dimensional. Stop examining who I am and start investigating *what* I am."

Lucius looked at Jade. He was trying to take the instruction and sift his words through his brain. Suddenly, his eyes riveted on his host. "You're not human."

"No, Mr. Lucius, I am not."

"Alien?"

Jade chuckled. "No."

"Evil or good?"

"That, Mr. Lucius, is a very western question. It is the basis for a fact-based, empirical life. That sounds appealing to you, doesn't it?"

"Yes, of course. It's how we make sense of the world."

"That is how *you* see the world. Did you know there was a time when most people saw the world very differently? Western thought looks at God and the devil, good and evil. It's very focused on one extreme or the other. That's not how it works." Jade said, almost reflectively.

Lucius shot back, "It has to be; logic is the foundation of our world."

Jade looked at him intently. "James, that is not how the cosmos, the universe, was formed. It isn't about good and evil, but order and disorder. The Aztecs understood this. Why do you think they sacrificed so many people, usually from other tribes? Don't sacrifice, and the world, the cosmos, slips back into chaos. Of course, they were brutally wrong; human sacrifice neither adds nor detracts anything from the universe's larger order. The Mesopotamians also understood the concepts of order & chaos, and behaved accordingly."

Lucius asked, "Are you telling me there should not be any laws?"

"No, there has to be some moral guide. Still, there are three forces, order, disorder, and me - non-order. I am not good or bad. I am the lack of an ordered universe. In the time before time, there was only disorder. Remember Genesis? The earth was void and without form - disorder."

"Where do you fit in?" Lucius queried.

"What would be a good example?" Jade asked himself. "I know," he suddenly stated. "Think of me as a desk containing everything you need, just not always in the right places. That is why I was in the garden."

"What do you mean, the garden?"

"James, I was in Eden, which, by the way, was much older than six thousand years ago."

"You were the one that tempted Eve?"

Jade's eyes flashed with anger. "I never tempted Eve! I told her the same thing I told those telemarketers."

"And what was that?" Lucius almost roared.

Jade snapped back an answer, “I told her who she was. A woman without wisdom, without a clue to the bigger picture. I never told her to eat the fruit.”

“The apple?”

“It was a pomegranate.”

Lucius spat out bitterly, “Now, there is death in the world because of her and Adam.”

“James, there has always been death and suffering. It existed in life and with humans, long before Adam and Eve. When God saw, *It was Good*, He didn’t mean the lack of sin. He had removed chaos. He was stating there was a balance.”

“And, by the way,” Jade continued, “their names weren’t Adam and Eve. Those are Hebrew names. That culture and nation came much, much later.”

“How can you be non-order?” Lucius asked. “Everything you make, from lemonade to landscaping, is incredible.”

Jade smiled sadly. “Trust me, Lucius, there is better. People’s view of these good things is so high because of how low their expectations have become.”

Lucius was quiet for a moment. When he spoke, his voice was calm and measured. “Thank you. I believe you.”

Jade silently examined Lucius for almost a full minute, then asked, “are you ready?”

"Yes."

"You, James Lucius, are a man who believes in justice, an ultimate good. You want your work to matter, to make a difference. Still, you know deep inside yourself, it doesn't. You see the signs almost every day. This world is spinning back into chaos, to disorder. What you have to decide is if you want to spend it alone."

"What are you talking about?" Lucius asked.

"You are in love with Detective Sipe. You have been for some time. You want to be held and told the world will be okay. It will be a lie; still, she would be by your side as the world gets worse."

"To be honest," Lucius responded, "that would be nice, but Elizabeth is so caught up in her work she has no time for a relationship. She's always at the office."

Jade looked exasperated. "James, why do you think she spends all her time there? She wants to be near you. Go to her! She won't, *can't* make you complete, yet, she can give you what you lack."

"And what is that?"

"Hope."

Lucius felt sadness flooding over him like a tidal wave. He felt grief like he had never known before, even when his father died. Jade had, with surgical precision, destroyed his emotional defenses in just a few words. He started crying. It quickly became a sob. "I want the pain to end."

"Mr. Lucius, unlike those seventeen telemarketers, you have someone to whom you can turn. Someone to make the chaos, the increasing disorder, bearable. Unlike them, you don't have to extinguish your flame to find peace. Go to her now. She pines for you as we speak."

"Thank you again."

"Don't thank me. I am not for, or against, you. I am amoral. I have only held a mirror to your life, allowing you to examine the reflection. Like everyone with whom I have held this conversation, I only revealed the truth. It is your choice which of my sisters you choose."

"Sisters?"

"Yes, Order and Disorder." Then, Jade motioned with his hand for Lucius to leave. "Goodbye, James Lucius. We shall not meet again." The last site he had of Jade was of him pleasantly smiling while sipping scotch and admiring the fireflies.

Driving, Lucius's mind was a blur. He believed in ten hours; he had experienced what few had - ever. He silently thanked God for the opportunity given to him. He had decided which sister to follow before the question even rose to his consciousness. After a moment of hesitation, he knocked on Sipe's door.

The Longing

For a few minutes, the man stood motionless. He was trying to control his breathing, attempting to calm himself before he began. He wanted to enjoy every second.

In his left hand, he held a small, razor-thin data storage unit. It was approximately the size of the cards used in cameras in the first half of the century. However, this wisp of plastic and metal stored exponentially more information than even the largest SD camera card ever could. Though covered with manufactured titanium, he held onto it as if the object was china. He knew perfectly well it was backed-up in a dozen places. Still, the sudden thought he might be showing carelessness or callousness caused his breathing to become erratic again.

He looked around the room one last time. He wanted perfection. Finding it correct, like every other time, he walked to the machine in front of him. He cocked his head at the blob of material inside the large glass case, which never failed to fascinate him. It was pliable yet durable. In its unformed state, it held the consistency and texture that reminded him of the *Stretch Armstrong* action figure he found in his great-great grandfather's cycle-sealed storage box. He forgot to put the toy back in the case and disintegrated when he remembered it a few days later.

He had touched the substance only once on a field trip in the fifth grade. Then, they were only beginning to understand how to transfer information into the material. He remembered the plant manager proudly showing them a car's fuel injector made from it. They were each allowed to handle some of the substance before placing the material in a production chamber. He recalled how he had wormed his way toward the front of the class so that he could see better. They watched in awe as the machine manufactured another fuel injector, a perfect copy. The material's texture and strength correctly fit its purpose.

He wished he had never felt the stuff. It was like going to AA then relapsing. No matter how much fun the bar was, there was still the knowledge it wasn't real. The joy wouldn't last. Likewise, even in his most ecstatic moments, when he thought his heart would burst, a mustard seed of reality would creep into his conscious mind. Most times, he could tamp it down, but on other occasions, he couldn't.

The technology had advanced well beyond the initial goal of a more efficient form of three-dimensional copying. Now it was possible to have the material interact, receiving and use the information in incredibly complex ways. The substance could, in effect, act as if it were alive. This advancement allowed the rise of the illusion market - where memories of the past and dreams that never would be - became sensory. Since all humans were required to have one, and for a cost, pets could also receive a memory chip, it recorded every thought, action, and physical feature. The replication, down to personality and minor scars, could be duplicated. Combining the production machine, material, and information could reproduce damn near anything, including different times of a person's life.

He looked at the plaque mounted next to the slot to insert the information card. On it was inscribed: *Then the Lord God formed man from the dust of the ground. He breathed the breath of life into the man's nostrils, and the man became a living person-* Genesis Chapter 2, Verse 7.

He placed the card into the slot and pushed the glowing green button.

Almost immediately, electrical arcs began erupting inside the glass enclosure. After about a minute, the blob started to stretch. A couple more minutes, and the mass took on a humanoid figure. Then the machine began adding details - eye and hair color, skin tone, etc. When the process was complete, there were several seconds of silence, then the thing in the glass case opened its eyes.

Upon seeing him, it smiled broadly.

"Hi, Sweetie," said his wife, who was quite dead.

***

"Babydoll," he said.

He ran to the case and opened the door. The replica fell into his arms, and they passionately kissed one another in that way only those in love do. He picked her off her feet and carried her to the bed beside the open hotel window.

Later, she slipped out of bed, keeping quiet so as not to wake her husband. The bride wrapped herself in the light robe she had bought just for the night. She walked onto the balcony and leaned her elbows on the high rail, letting the ocean air caress her face. She felt a hand touch her arm, and she smiled.

"Did I wake you, my love?"

"No, Sadie, you didn't."

She wrapped her arm around his, opening her eyes. He stared at her faint smile. Just like he remembered, she was enjoying life. It caused a thread of doubt he was quickly able to dash in the afterglow of making love.

"Oh, David, you were so right. Virginia Beach is the perfect place to honeymoon."

"Only because it's with you, my forever love."

She smiled brighter, "Good answer, Hubby, good answer."

They watched the sunrise over the Atlantic. Before surpassing the rim of the world, the king announced his imminent arrival with fingers of orange, yellow, and pink gripping the sky.

***

Dave sat at his parent's house, eating a bowl of cereal. He was dressed in a shirt and tie for his first day back to work after his vacation. He visited them every Monday morning for breakfast. It was less of a family gathering than a weekly inquiry merely to confirm they were still alive.

His mother sat across from him, working on the morning paper's crossword puzzle and swinging her leg absently, not even realizing she was doing it. She had not said a word to him about his vacation. She hadn't given him so much as a welcome back. She had red hair, like Sadie, yet it was artificial-looking like a poorly designed wig. Though it was her hair, she had lost her natural pigment years before. What replaced it was straight from a bottle. He never understood why his mom chose that color. She easily could have had any shade she wanted. At times, it seemed to him that her hair was like many things in her life, a box to check off through her life. Though not lazy, she had given up doing more than necessary to fulfill the minimum expected by society.

His father sat to his right, appareled in his usual attire, a tank top shirt, and striped boxer shorts. He lit a cigar, tucked his left calf under his right thigh, and proceeded to rest his other foot on top of the table. He wore a pair of brown wingtips and white socks that went to his mid-calf. He had curly brown hair and a large nose. He told everyone he was Jewish. He didn't have a Hebrew bone in his body.

He slightly rocked back the light brown, spindle back chair, just to the point the front two legs were off the floor. He leaned his head back, blew out a large puff of smoke, and asked in a conversational tone that belied his sarcasm, "So how was your fuck session with a piece of silly putty *this* time?"

"Dad, why do you do this every time? What is it to you?"

"Son, you are living in the past. Sadie has been dead for what, seven years?"

"Six," he quickly retorted.

His mom interjected with a question, "What is a three-letter slang word for the breast?"

"Tit, Beth, tit," his dad said with some exasperation.

“Oh, now I have five down too - Titanic,” she chirped. She was seemingly oblivious to the argument going on, only inches away.

“As I was saying, you are living in the past. You have to move on. You are still young, handsome, and have a good job. At least go after a piece of ass that is alive.”

“That’s it - ass! Another word for donkey. Today I completed the whole puzzle in under an hour,” his mother said with a real sense of pride.

David barked back, “Don’t you tell me about living in the past! You wear those damn wingtips every day.”

“What the hell is wrong with that? They’re my work shoes.”

“Dad, you haven’t worked a day in over twenty years. Remember, you got shit-canned for going to work drunk and pissing into a tomato soup vat.”

“I wasn’t drunk!” he adamantly retorted. “It was the medication I was on; it affected my judgment. That’s why I won full retirement.”

“Oh, bullshit! You got lucky at the review board, and you know it.”

His mother folded the paper, laid it on the dining room table, and scowled at the two men. “Okay,” you two, that’s quite enough. Son, if you want to be intimate with polymers, that’s your right. And Farrell, if you say you weren’t drunk when you urinated into some child’s school lunch, we should all let it go."

Sighing, Dave rose from his chair and kissed his mother on the cheek, getting a load of cigarette smoke for his trouble. He nodded at his dad as he left.

After the door slammed shut, David's parents absently stared at the table for several minutes. Finally, Beth interrupted the heavy silence. Tears formed in her eyes as she looked at her husband.

"Farrell, what are we going to do? Our son is living in a black hole. He has to let her go."

"Beth, I'm torn. Part of me is proud we raised a son who could love that intense and wise enough to find someone who could love him the same. But, Beth, we failed David. We equipped him to do these things; still, we never taught him how to say goodbye."

"Must you taunt him?!" Beth cried out miserably. "It will only ruin a chance to be helpful at a later date."

Farrell thoughtfully chewed on his cigar a few seconds before answering. "You're right. I thought by pushing Davie. I might shock him into seeing what he's doing to his life. I admit I've become sarcastic." He dropped his cigar in an ashtray, shaking his head, confused as to how to help his son.

***

Relaxing on the couch, Dave leaned his head back and closed his eyes. His feet propped on the coffee stand, a trait he learned from his father, though he would never admit it, even to himself. He was nursing a Jack Daniels on ice. He was not much of a drinker, yet the first day back to work was always the hardest. Everyone asked him if he enjoyed his vacation. He told them the same thing every time, "It was good."

If pressed, he tells them he went to the ocean. He offers no other information and makes it clear, albeit nicely, that's the extent he's going to discuss the issue. His time with Sadie is golden, and he's not about to share it with anyone. He received four weeks of vacation a year, plus ten days off for major holidays. He was going to spend every second he could with her.

He moved to the recliner, refilling his drink on the way. He knows he'll pay for it the following day but frankly thinks, *screw it! I need the helping hand of ole Jack.* He grabbed the chair's handle and slightly reclined.

Dave stared at the amber liquid, turning the crystal glass reflectively in his hand. He is mesmerized by the way the light and glass combine to illuminate the bourbon. The ice cubes only enhanced the effect. For an instant, he believes there are little spirits alive in the elixir. Then the moment passes, leaving him feeling pain. *If they are alive*, he thinks to himself, *that's more than Sadie.* Feeling cynicism and the ubiquitous hurt, he began to sing along with Fleetwood Mac album playing on the stereo.

Sadie, he smiled in remembrance, *boy did she ever love the classics. How many times did we sing along to the 'Rumors' album? Hundreds, if not thousands.*

His mind wandered, flittering here and there before landing on Susan, the woman in the legal department at work. He wondered, not for the first time, how a person with such an effervescent personality could be a tax attorney. He likes her - a lot. He knows she feels the same - the glances she gives him and the way she plays with a strand of her blonde hair when they talk.

Their interactions never fail to cause inner conflict. Part of him wants to ask her on a date. He has little doubt she would say yes. Still, the very thought of another woman produced a sense of guilt that inevitably brought him to tears. How could he betray Sadie? The accident, the damn accident! *IF* it had never happened, he would be quite sober, holding Sadie in his arms.

An automated semi-truck hit a wet spot. Usually, automatic safety devices are triggered. Contact with other vehicles is unheard of since the advent of intuitive driving. The crash was the first resulting in a human fatality in over a quarter of a century. It was a fluke, a one in fifty-two billion chance. That's what the insurance company called it. The micro-chip and both back-ups failed to deliver the warning, thus, never engaging the safety controls.

Sadie lived another day before her body collapsed under the devastating trauma of her injuries. The doctors could fix the wounds, but not her. He talked with her for a few moments, right before she slipped into a coma. She told him to be happy. He had begged her to live. She told him she wanted to be with him, but she didn't have any strength left in her to fight. They each said, "I love you," kissing as her eyes closed. They would never voluntarily open again.

Singing the lyrics to *Dreams*, he shuffled off to bed.

***

Farrell had sat in his living room chair for three days, thinking of his son. The haze of Pabst Blue Ribbons and cigars brought him through a pile of useless thoughts and into a plausible solution.

"Beth, we need to talk."

"You're drunk," she responded dismissively.

"That I am, but I have an idea to help Davie."

"That's it - idea, a four-letter word for a concept."

"Damn it, Beth, forget the puzzle! Please, listen to what I have in mind."

Forty minutes later, Beth was staring squarely at her husband. The crossword puzzle laying on an armrest, forgotten, replaced by stunned silence.

"Farrell," she said slowly, "are you insane? We want to help him. I can't believe you, of all people, could think of something so cruel."

Farrell, hands intertwined throughout his explanation, half pulled them apart as if in supplication. His eyes slightly drooped before reconnecting with his wife's.

"Beth, our son is caught in a whirlpool of grief. He will eventually go under and not resurface. That's not the worst of it; he wants to."

Beth's lip began to tremble and tears formed in her eyes, threatening to spill out. "What if this doesn't work? He may never speak to us again. I don't want to lose our son."

"Honey, we lost him the day they pulled the sheet over his wife."

The ringing woke Dave out of light sleep. He had been dozing for about an hour. He stretched and grabbed his phone. "This is Dave."

"Davie, this is your dad."

"Hey, Dad, what's up?" The two had not talked since that morning in his parent's house. He expected a phone fight. Instead, he received an invitation.

"Son, your mother and I want to go to the holodecks and relive a trip. Do you recall when you were fourteen, we went camping at Yosemite? Remember, a bear almost ate your mom. God, that was funny. Nonetheless, we're camping for the whole week. Your mother and I would like you to come Friday night. You don't have to stay all week, maybe just Friday night. Please, Son, spend some time with us."

His tone sounded desperate. He didn't trust his father's motives; still, he was sure of the man's love for him.

"Sure, Dad," Dave said. "I will be there about 8:00 Friday night."

"That's great, Son. I will tell your mother. Holodeck fourteen on Glendale."

"I'll be there."

"Oh, Son."

"Yes, Dad?"

"I love you."

"You too. See you on Friday."

Farrell ended the call. Looking at his wife, he said, "this will either free our son or kill him. I sincerely believe there is no in-between."

Thursday evening, Dave packed outdoor-style clothes to wear to the holodeck. He felt a sense of anticipation that only preceded his times with Sadie. Still, this felt different. He didn't have grief hanging around his neck, knowing he was always doomed to the separation. The illusion was going to be the reliving of a great memory. There was no emotional tinge connected. It possessed no mental oracle of inevitable pain. He would come home directly after work, eat a small meal, then head to the holodeck. He absently wondered if they would use the formation vehicle. He thought it might be fun to see what his parents concocted.

***

Dave was getting ready to leave his office when Susan stopped by. She had an eager look in her eyes that made him feel uncomfortable.

"Hi, Dave, how is it going?"

"It's going well, Suze…I mean Susan. Sorry about that."

"You don't have to be sorry," she said as she twirled a strand of her hair. She was a naturally happy person, yet in no way shallow or ditzy. "Do you want to see a movie with me? They remade *Salem's Lot*. In the prologue, Sarah King, Stephen King's great-granddaughter, speaks about him. She also discusses her great-grandmother's inspiration for the book's rural setting. It's tonight. We could grab something to eat afterward."

Surprisingly, especially to himself, he heard his voice say, "I would love to, Susan, but I promised my parents I would spend the evening with them."

She looked disappointed, yet happy he would enjoy her company. It was an odd combination of facial features that clearly outlined her thoughts.

"Okay," she said, lightly placing a hand on his shoulder. "Next time?"

"Sure," he said less than confidently. "Next time."

He quickly headed for his car and drove home.

***

Two hours later, he entered the station that held the holodeck cubes. It was similar to the one he often used for his time with Sadie. Ports equipped each holodeck

He hit a console button outside the cube. Through the speaker, he heard a voice that was distinctly his mother's.

"Sweetie, is that you?"

"Yes, Mom, it's me."

"Thank God you're here. Your damn father keeps playing the bear scene over and over. Get in here before I ram the memory card up his ass."

Before he could respond, the light beside the door went green, and it opened. With a smile, he walked into the cube. The scene that greeted him was one he had largely forgotten. Parked between two trees was a small camper. A fire crackled inside a stone pit, and the unmistakable scent of pine trees filled the air. His mother hugged him. Over his shoulder, he saw his dad in a khaki bucket hat, different colored fishing flies stuck in it. With a wave of his hand, his dad motioned for them to sit with him by the fire.

"I have the stuff for s'mores," Farrell said while simultaneously grinning and waving his marshmallow stick back and forth. "C'mon, you two, let's live a little."

"What the hell," said David. "One or two s'mores might be fun."

"That's the spirit," Farrell answered cheerfully. "Do you remember how to make them?"

"For crying out loud, Farrell," said a perturbed Beth. "It's a s'more. How hard can it be?"

"Dad," Dave said happily, "why don't you show me how you cook 'em."

Farrell looked over David's shoulder and stuck his tongue out at her. Beth folded her arms, yet she had a content feeling she hadn't experienced in years. She began to doubt whether they should go through with the plan. They were having so much fun together. She didn't want to taint the experience.

Hours passed. The parents knew their plan might sever their relationship with their only child. They were soaking up all the good they could get. Finally, his mom and dad knew they could no longer hesitate. To wait would mean a loss of nerves, as well as opportunity.

They sat, looking down, on the other side of the fire from their son. His father was poking the embers in an aimless, peaceful way that preluded going to bed. With identical sighs, his parents raised their eye level to look directly into his. Their expressions surprised Dave. There was concern written on each of the faces staring back at him. He was about to say something when his father held up his hand. It was slightly shaking.

"Son, I hope you've enjoyed this evening. Your mother and I will treasure it forever."

"Mom, Dad, this is the most fun I've had in years."

"Listen to me, Honey," his mother said. "Your father and I love you more than life. I want you to promise me one thing, and then I will ask no more."

With a feeling of uncertainty, he asked, "What is that?"

"Walk into the camper, Son," was his father's response.

Confused but willing, he walked into the camper. It looked like any used camper from twenty or thirty years prior. "Okay, I give up. Is there something I'm missing?"

He heard his mother's voice, echoing off the camper walls, "Close the door, Davie, close the door."

He shut the door, and instantly the scene changed. It was no longer the camper but Sadie's deathbed. The spectacle before Dave caught him entirely off guard, and he swayed under its emotional impact. He turned to leave. That was it; he was through with them. He almost had his hand on the door when he heard Sadie's voice call out to him, "Dave, don't leave."

A sob exploded from his throat as he turned to face her. "I won't leave you," he said instinctually. He ran to her, and they embraced. Hot tears spilled over the lids of his eyes and washed down his face.

After a few minutes, she placed his face in her hands and held it before her. She looked so sad. "Dave, I've talked with Farrell and Beth. Is it true I have been dead for six years?"

Tears still streaming, he nodded and said, "Yes, my love."

"What is one of the last things I told you?"

Before he could answer, she did. "For you to be happy.

"Is it also true you spend all your free time reforming me and reliving our honeymoon?"

A simple nod was all he could do in the way of a reply.

Do you think this is what I would have wanted for you? Do you?"

"I miss you so bad. I can't live without you." Dave could barely say the words over his sobbing.

"I loved you," Sadie said, tenderly stroking his cheek. "And I know you loved me, but our time together is over.

Treasure our memories, but move on, and be happy!"

The scene flipped, and it was just a camper again. David briefly considered the possibility that Sadie's words were a ruse, but that brought no comfort. He knew if Sadie was alive, that is what she would have told him.

He walked with his head down to the cube door and into the night.

***

The week passed slowly for his parents. They had considered going home, but Beth had insisted they stay and at least try to have fun. Friday was their last night. They had to be out by noon on Saturday.

They were sitting quietly around the fire when the light indicated there was someone at the door. Knowing he had to sign the exit paperwork, Farrell sighed and hit the door activator to let the groundskeeper inside. Instead, there stood David.

Farrell caught entirely off guard, stood awkwardly, not knowing what to say.

His parent's exchanged glances, hopeful.

"Do you have any stuff left for s'mores?"

"Of course we do, Son," said Farrell. His voice choked with emotion.

Beth started to walk, almost running to her son, then

suddenly stopped.

As Dave rounded the corner, they could see he was holding hands with a young woman. She was a pretty girl with a happy face.

"Mom, Dad, I would like you to meet Susan."

Bone of Contention

Author's Note

Anthropologist Jared Diamond has written several books. Among them is one entitled, *The Third Chimpanzee*. I don't think it takes a lot of guesswork to figure out we, Homo sapien sapiens, are the third chimpanzee.

Diamond spends a great deal of time discussing the supposed unique features separating us from all other animals. As it turns out, our problem-solving, communication and cultural skills are ones of degrees rather than absolutes. Our genetic make-up is nearly identical to our chimp cousins. Therefore, the changes that turned us from simply another large mammal into our planet's dominant species must be small, indeed.

Primarily the story is intended for entertainment purposes. Yet, hopefully, it will cause you to pause somewhere in the bustle of daily life and question what it means to be you.

The man was watching the Ohio State vs. Iowa football game. He had just about given up, it was an early blowout, and he was already checking the scores on the bottom of the TV screen in hopes of finding a more entertaining contest. The man had just about settled on the North Carolina – Virginia Tech match-up when his brother burst through the door; his eyes were practically bugging out of their sockets with excitement.

The excitement wasn't unusual for his brother, and he assumed he had bagged a big buck. Bobby caught *buck fever,* something fierce. It was a running joke for Stephen to tell his little brother, "Don't catch a cold in the woods."

Leaving the television on, Stephen heaved himself off the couch to inspect the deer. "Alright, Bobby, how big is the Whitetail in the bed of your truck?" But Bobby vigorously shook his head.

There was a fear Stephen had rarely seen in his brother's eyes. Bobby had seen some brutal combat in Iraq, and upon his return to the states, the family worried about PTSD. Bobby came home shaken. Still, he had quickly adjusted back to civilian life.

Bobby looked at Stephen and blurted out, "I didn't shoot no deer."

"So, you missed the deer. We've all missed the big one on occasion."

"I didn't miss, but it was no deer."

His brother's statement, combined with his visible anxiety, caused a germ of fear to form in Stephen's stomach. Talking slowly, in a calm voice, he asked his brother. "Bobby, what did you shoot?"

"It was big…massive, and had black fur."

Stephen thought of what large animals, other than deer, were in northwest Ohio. He knew wild boar and black bears inhabited the state, yet none close to their area. He pressed further. "Bobby, tell me more about this animal."

Bobby looked at his brother for a second, then, his voice crackling, vomited out, "It walked on two legs."

Stephen felt his face flush, then rapidly drain of blood. "Oh, dear God," was all he said as he ran to get his jacket and boots.

***

Bobby expected Stephen to hammer him with questions. Strangely, his brother was silent. The quiet unnerved him more than being peppered with inquiries. At least an interrogation would take his mind off that thing lying on the forest floor.

Stephen sat in silence as they drove toward the woods. They were one of the few families in northwest Ohio to own a large, unbroken tract of woodland. Though economically impractical, their grandfather had insisted the land not be clear cut for sale of the wood nor plowed for farming.

As a child, Stephen once overheard his father complaining about the misuse of the land. One day, when they were alone, walking through the woods, he had asked his grandpa Horace why he didn't want to cut down the trees to make more money. His response was typical of his grandfather. "Why Stevie," he said, "where would all the animals live? We live in houses, and the animals live somewhere amongst these trees. How would you like a deer tearing down your house? We have more than enough farmland. Let's not get greedy with God's gifts."

With that, he recalled his grandfather ruffling his hair and saying, "Come on, Stevie, let's see if that roast in the oven is done. After a short mental calculus, he decided his grandpa was the wisest man in the world.

That walk lingered in his mind, a golden memory sliced from the wheel of time. He could still smell the autumn leaves and see his grandfather's Springer Spaniel playing ahead of them. He could call to mind the vibrant colors of a cock pheasant, as it erupted from a thicket when the dog kicked it up.

Stephen's grandfather had shown him and Bobby how to read a game trail and where the best fishing spots were along the creek. He and his brother had caught and released a great many frogs and crayfish from that slow-moving water. In the midst of his reminiscing, Stephen remembered a quote from George N. Wallace, *The heart of [This] hunter looks for a piece of Eden. It feels right to hunt in a place where the land is healthy.* Their land, creek, and woods were healthy.

Stephen was lost in his memories when the truck suddenly swerved, sharply cutting through his nostalgia. Bobby had veered to miss a rabbit crossing the road. "I didn't want to hit the little guy," he said sullenly.

When Bobby first came back from Iraq, Stephen invited his brother to hunt rabbits with him. Before the Marines, Bobby had loved to hunt them. His brother had politely declined. Stephen remembered Bobby saying, "After duty in Fallujah, it doesn't seem fair to them." Since then, Bobby had been all over the North American continent, ever searching for a more challenging and dangerous game.

At the time, Stephen thought Bobby was capitalizing on the skills he learned in the Marines. The training and conditioning were undoubtedly world-class. Why not use them? Today, though, his brother was unnerved. It had reminded Stephen of how Bobby sounded when he called him from Manitoba, saying he had killed a large black bear. He remembered how his brother said it was his first prey that could have killed him. Stephen thought it odd; still, his brother wasn't the first to say something similar. Like skydivers, some hunters are adrenaline junkies.

Stephen quietly sat as something was trying to sort

its way through his mind, just out of reach. It was like tumblers that were turning yet not quite aligned. Then, just like that, the thought rose to the surface. It was another quote, this one by Ernest Hemmingway and much darker than Wallace's, *There is no hunting like the hunting of man, and those who have hunted armed men long enough and liked it, never care for anything else thereafter.*

Dear God, Stephen thought, *what if Bobby had turned bad while in Iraq? What if hunting more lethal prey was his way of satiating some bloodlust? What if, after being in battle, he only wanted to hunt armed people?*

He pushed those ideas away with an almost physical effort. *No*, he thought, *this is your brother, damn it!* Nonetheless, he was comforted by the feel of the .357 long barrel resting in his large jacket pocket.

Bobby glanced at his brother. He grimaced and said, "you think you're going to find a person dead in those woods, don't you?"

Stephen was startled by his brother's ability to divine his thoughts. Still, he answered truthfully. "To be honest, Bobby, the thought did cross my mind."

"How can you think that about me, your own brother?"

"Bobby, I'm not saying you murdered someone, but you did say it walked on two legs."

"Listen to me, Stephen," Bobby choked out. "I didn't get blood lust while serving. I'm so sick of people killing other people I can't even watch *Law & Order*. I'm telling you, what I shot was an *it*, not a person."

Stephen looked at Bobby and could see he was beginning to cry. "Alright, little brother, let's go see what you bagged."

***

Stephen and Bobby were walking through the woods toward the game trail on the western edge. It entered the trees from the south and went almost straight for about a quarter of a mile, then made a sharp turn west and ran a hundred yards into a field. The wind usually blew northeast, which kept the hunter upwind from the entire trail. I placed the hunting stand about fifteen feet off the ground, up an oak tree, about fifteen yards northeast of the path.

"Bobby, tell me what happened?"

"I had been in the stand for about two hours. I didn't see any deer, but there were squirrels and birds everywhere. It was a great time. Then, all of a sudden, the woods grew quiet. I mean total silence. I have never experienced anything like it. The closest I've seen was when a pack of coyotes had come through. You know, we shot a couple, and the rest bailed."

"This felt different. Whatever drove the animals to

cover must have enough presence to scare things from a distance. It reminded me of how the streets would clear before an insurgent attack. The civilians knew something bad was coming long before we did. It was the same thing. That's when I heard it."

"Heard what?" Stephen asked.

A bunch of things running. It sounded like several animals coming north along the game trail. At first, I saw two does, and I thought a buck was chasing them. They are in rut, after all. A buck came charging right behind them. Then it got weird."

"What do you mean...*weird*?"

"The deer were getting ready to make the turn that leads to the field when there was a sound. It was deep and loud enough that both the deer and I heard it. The deer stopped so fast they ran into each other. I thought it might have been another buck in the field, snorting. Then came a whistling sound. I was raising my twelve gauge to shoot the buck in front of me. He was a nice size, with a good rack. That is when they all looked up at me. Their tongues were hanging out of their mouths. It became evident this was more than the rut; something was chasing these deer to exhaustion. They laid down at the base of my tree, right under my stand. I was thinking, *what can be so dangerous that they would pick a hunter over it?* Then it hit me; whatever made that sound did so just when they were about to turn toward the field. Someone or something wanted to drive the deer into the tangle of downed trees, negating their speed."

"Bobby, why would anyone want to do that? It would have a hard time chasing them down."

"That's what I realized; there was a third predator already waiting among the fallen trees."

Bobby stopped talking, yet it was apparent to Stephen his brother still remembered the event in vivid detail.

"Bobby!" Stephen snapped. "What happened?"

"I saw it walking up the path, behind the deer. Stephen, it was friggin huge, I mean massive. It wasn't just big. It was tall. He was every bit of nine feet."

Bobby saw the skeptical look on Stephen's face and returned it with a scowl. Still, he continued. "Stevie, he walked by our old treehouse, and his head was less than a foot below it."

"Impossible!" Steve blurted out. "Grandpa set it ten feet up that oak tree."

"How the hell do you think I measured its height!? At first, I thought I was looking at a huge guy in a ghillie suit. Then, I thought it was a gorilla. Then, it dawned on me that gorillas only walk on two legs for short distances, and they are vegetarians. It didn't make sense."

"It saw the deer, and Stephen, I swear I saw it smile. It puckered its lips as if to whistle, then stopped. You could see the wheels turning in its head. He was scanning the area. It was as if he knew it was too easy. He checked at eye level for a few seconds. Then he looked up. My tree stand is about seventeen feet up. He finally saw me."

"Then, you shot it as it ran?" Stephen asked.

"Ran? He didn't run away. We were sizing each other up. He was the biggest animal I had ever seen outside of a zoo. The tiger we saw at the Toledo Zoo was close to six hundred pounds. This thing had the tiger beat by about two hundred."

Stephen gave an involuntary look of dubiousness, flexing the muscles in his forehead.

Bobby saw his brother's expression and was instantly angered. "Don't believe me, you asshole. Just wait until you see the body, then you'll shut your pie-hole."

Stephen held his hands out in deference. "I'm sorry. What did he, I mean *it*, look like?"

"It had black hair everywhere except his face, and I think, the bottom of his feet. His jaw stuck out slightly, you know, kind of like a chimp's. But not quite as far. The arms hung so long, almost to his knees. He had hands, fingernails, and all. He even had a thumb, I think. I didn't linger too long on that part of him. Stevie, his feet were massive; still, they looked like ours."

"When our eyes met, its face went from concern to straight-up pissed off in about a tenth of a second. It opened its mouth and roared. It wasn't just loud; there was something else to it. It felt like my insides were being pulverized, just like when the armored personnel carrier I was in went over a roadside bomb in Iraq."

Stephen's head snapped around. He looked hard at Bobby. "You never told us you went over an I.E.D."

Bobby didn't answer. In truth, the admission had just fallen out of his mouth. He hadn't meant for anyone stateside to know. He didn't address his brother's statement but instead finished his story. "I couldn't even move for a couple of seconds. I did notice he didn't have any fangs, but he did have big-ass teeth."

Despite himself, Stephen felt drawn in by his brother's tale. It was fantastical. He made a mental note that if this all turned out to be a joke, he was going to beat his brother's ass. "Well, don't belabor the thing; finish what you have to say."

"I noticed out of the corner of my eye the deer didn't move. When he finished his roar, he charged. I knew he would have no problem, with those long arms, reaching my tree stand. The Marines trained me well because I pumped two slugs into his chest before I knew it. It was all muscle memory."

"Then it died?" Stephen asked, instantly feeling stupid for asking the obvious.

"No, it didn't, but it did stop its charge. It stumbled back a couple of steps. I don't think the thing saw it coming. Before the Marines, I probably would have frozen from fright. Not having to think about using my weapon, just shooting it, saved my life."

"After a couple of seconds, he righted himself and took stock of the damage. The left side of his chest, where I placed both rounds, was torn-up. He was bleeding pretty good, still, not as bad as I had wished. While he was doing that, I reloaded the twelve gauge with more slugs. I was hoping he would call it a day and walk away. It didn't happen."

"After he looked himself over, he turned his attention back to me. I could see it in his eyes; he was smart. At least smart enough to want revenge. I've seen that look in Iraq. When a platoon lost someone, they would want payback in the worst way. This thing had the same expression. I knew one of us was going to die in these woods today."

Stephen couldn't talk. He swallowed hard, moved by the raw emotion of Bobby's story. Doubt was no longer a consideration.

Bobby continued, "I took a breath and slowly exhaled while I aimed. The thing saw the shotgun and knew the damage it had already caused; it still charged. I believe by that time, the thing was in a blind rage from his wounded chest and…."

"And what?!" Stephen asked, his heart racing like a

greyhound.

"Pride. I think I wounded the things' pride. Anyway, he reached twenty yards, and I put a single slug in his throat. He staggered a couple more steps forward. I had already chambered another round and was about to fire again when he dropped to his knees. He had a hand pressed to his throat, but blood was pouring all over it. He was swaying back and forth a little bit, then after about half a minute, I think, hell I don't know, he fell backward. His hand fell away from his throat, and his eyes emptied. He was dead."

"I saw the deer take off the way they came, making a wide berth around the corpse. I almost started to laugh. You know, the release of tension. But then, I heard a deep growl from the deadfall behind me. I whirled around and saw something was behind two big trees that had fallen on top of each other."

"If it had been summer, the leaves on the bushes would have completely concealed it. I could see about three feet of black fur through the branches on the fallen trees. I didn't wait for another charge. I aimed the best I could through the gap and pulled the trigger. There was a scream that was obviously from pain. Something tells me it was a gut-shot."

"I climbed down that ladder as fast as I could. I was down two steps before I remembered to unbuckle my safety harness. I was constantly checking my six." Bobby stopped talking upon seeing a confused look on his brother's face. "Think of it as standing on a giant clock, facing twelve. Your six is directly behind you."

"Got it," Stephen said.

"I saw movement in the brush, between me and the field. It was a slight change, yet by then, I was hypervigilant. If I weren't already looking for them, I wouldn't have seen the dark patch of fur. It was moving quickly, trying to cut off my exit. I fired and heard a loud yelp. Before it pulled back into the brush, I saw something dangling. I think I got him in the shoulder."

"Bobby, what did you do next?"

"I got the hell out of there. I made a controlled but hasty retreat. I was back at my truck in twenty minutes. As far as I could tell, nothing pursued me." Bobby finished his account of the morning's event.

During their walk, Stephen couldn't see anything unusual. However, when they were about a quarter-mile from the tree stand, he could feel something different. He stopped for a moment and listened. Bobby was about to ask him what he was doing when his brother held up a single finger, indicating he should be quiet. After a minute, he turned to Bobby.

Whispering, Stephen said, "Bobby, can you feel it? There's tension about the place."

And Bobby could.

He had never felt so uneasy in all the years he had been on this land as he did today. "Yeah," Bobby responded in a hushed tone. "This isn't right."

Still, there was no real thought they could attach to the situation. It was so foreign to those woods. They had always felt at peace. For the first time, they felt unwelcome – interlopers, and yet neither could tell why.

***

They continued up the trail and rounded a slight curve, bringing them to the stand. When Stephen first saw the thing lying dead on the ground, his jaw just dropped. He, like Bobby, couldn't decipher what he was staring at. On the forest floor laid by far the largest animal he had ever seen in the wild. Its musculature was unbelievable! It looked like a bodybuilder in his prime. Stephen thought Bobby's choice of words was correct, massive.

Both brothers skirted the thing, circling it, trying to get a full view. Neither said a word; awe had swallowed conversation. After a while, the two stopped but continued to stare at the dead animal. Bobby finally broke the silence. "The body has been moved."

"What?" Stephen asked, obviously surprised.

"The body has been dragged a couple of feet."

"I don't see any tire tracks, and no one on foot is going to pull that thing out, even on a sled." Stephen's tone was somber yet measured, like a detective on a crime scene.

"I bet they tried to take the body with them but couldn't because of their wounds. Look at the black blood around the corpse and then head northwest. I was right; it was a gut-shot."

"Brother, animals don't usually move their dead."

Bobby quietly considered his brother's statement. "But people bury their dead." His reply caught Stephen by surprise.

"What are you saying?"

"I'm not convinced they aren't part human."

"What frigging part would that be?" Stephen angrily retorted. "What you shot looks to be some form of great ape."

"Stevie," Bobby responded sadly, "the expressions it made looked human. On its knees, it was trying to stop the bleeding, like we would by applying pressure. When it fell backward, it had a look of peace. It accepted its death. I'm not saying it's exactly like us, it obviously isn't, but it isn't like a gorilla or a chimp either."

"Then, what is he, little brother?" Stephen snorted. "Is he a human or an animal?"

Bobby stared reflectively at the giant before him. "I think he is both and neither."

Stephen hissed, "Listen to me, you little shit. You were the one who said it was a thing and not a person."

"I know what I said, but now, I'm not so sure."

"Robert Hayes, you shot a charging animal, not a human. There are animals, and there are us. There is no gray area. I have no relationship to that thing lying dead on *our* property! Now call the cops!"

"Hello, this is 911; what is your emergency?" The dispatcher asked in a nasal voice.

"This is Robert Hayes. I am with my brother, Stephen Hayes. While hunting, I was charged by a huge animal that I can't identify. I shot and killed it. I believe I also wounded two others like it?"

"Are you injured?"

"No."

"Where are you now, sir?"

"In the Hayes family woods, two miles northwest of the Wapakoneta Road and Route 6 intersection, Bobby responded."

"And where is the animal?"

"A yard from my feet."

Can you give me the best directions to your location?" The 911officer asked.

"Take Wapakoneta Road to Poe Road, go west a tenth of a mile, then take the dirt road on the right. Go north about two hundred yards. There will be an obvious trail on the right. Our pick-up is there. We are about a mile and a quarter into the woods."

"A sheriff's deputy will soon be en route. He will arrive at your location in about forty minutes." The dispatcher, trained for emergencies, said in a soothing voice.

"There are still two wounded animals; I suggest no one walks the woods alone."

"Can you meet the deputy at the entrance of the trail?" She asked.

"Yes."

"Can you give me a description of the animal you killed?"

"Extraordinary."

***

"I am calling the Ohio Department of Wildlife Incident Team. Region Four is located in Findlay and should arrive within two hours." Those were the first words deputy Mendez said upon examining the body. He, like the brothers, was in shock upon first seeing the thing that lay under the sparse, autumn canopy.

"Deputy," Bobby said, "the sun is going to be down in about two hours. I think, if we are to hold this position, we need high-intensity lights, facing not only on the body but also outward."

"Mr. Hayes, you sound like you were in the military?"

"Yes, the Marines." Then almost as an afterthought, he said, "Fallujah."

"Jesus – and I thought I had it bad in Afghanistan. Still, Fallujah…" With that, Mendez called for reinforcements, and several high-intensity, battery-powered crime scene lights.

"I asked for what you requested," Mendez said to Bobby, "yet you might be slightly paranoid. I know this was traumatic. Hell, how could it not be? Yet, nothing is going to stick around. You killed one and injured two. Anything left will high-tail it the hell out of here."

"Officer Mendez," Bobby said, "we are unsure of what we are dealing with. I shot three; there is no indication there couldn't be more."

The deputy nodded his head in reluctant acquiescence. He and Bobby talked about the thing's features for a while longer. It began to dawn on them Stephen hadn't said anything in a long time. He appeared reflective, his arms folded, staring at the animal before him, yet not quite seeing it.

"Stevie," Bobby asked, "you're awfully quiet; what's on your mind?"

"You said you think animals were hunting. I have no doubt that is what they were doing."

"What is so important about that?" Mendez asked, not

taking his eyes off the body. "I mean, it's interesting, still not groundbreaking behavior. Animals hunt all the time. It's how they feed themselves and their young."

Bobby's eyes grew wide. Stephen silently stared at Mendez, waiting for the point of his statement to register. Suddenly, the officer turned sharply toward Stephen. Fear rushed into his dark brown eyes.

"Oh my God," Mendez gasped. "They were hunting for their family, and it ended catastrophically. There could be several of these things. Where are they?"

"I don't know," said Stephen. "But I will bet this…they are getting hungry.

***

By sundown, several deputies and the sheriff herself came to the sight. If there were any other primates in those woods, they most likely had retreated to the far side.

The kill site was bright with high-intensity illumination. Several patrol cars at the woods' entrance had their overhead lights on, giving the whole area a surreal look. Trees, thickets, and farmland had blue and red lights flashing on them in alternating hues.

Poe Road, which never received much night traffic, was now amid a flood of gawkers. Automobile after automobile drove down that lonely stretch of pavement.

That chunk of road hadn't seen such excitement since Harry and Jim Darnel had a drunken screaming match, in the middle of the lane, over what kind of animal they had just run over. Harry said it was a fox, while Jim swore it was a coyote. Harry became enraged and shot Jim in the foot. They were both arrested. A deputy later identified the animal as a very large possum.

With so much traffic in an unanticipated and rural area, the Sheriff's Department became stretched of manpower. The sheriff, smartly assessing the situation, requested assistance from the Ohio State Patrol. They responded by blocking all intersecting roads.

The Wildlife team arrived just before eight that evening. Lisa Welcher, a woman in her early fifties, headed the group. She introduced herself to the sheriff, the Sergeant of the Highway Patrol, Mendez, and Stephen with quick hellos and cursory handshakes, ignoring the rest. When Lisa reached Bobby, she stopped and stared at him. He had the feeling she was taking the measure of him. He decided to return the favor.

Looking at him with a completely neutral face, she asked, "Mr. Hayes, are you studying me?"

With his expression just as deadpan, he replied, "Yes."

"Why?"

"Force of habit."

"What do you see?" She asked, curiosity heavy in her

tone.

"Someone is studying me."

"That's true," she chuckled.

"Why?" Bobby asked.

"Force of habit." Then she smiled. "I like you; you are observant. I hope your memory is good because I'm going to ask you a million questions from a thousand different angles. Got it?"

"Yeah," he said while simultaneously sighing, "I got it."

Placing on medical gloves, she studied the body carefully. Again, her face and body held no expression. She stood back and took several photos with her smartphone. It looked to Stephen as if she was texting before sending them. Bobby knew the event just went at least a step up on the ladder of authority, probably several.

She stood back and silently stared at the animal in front of her. After about two minutes, she received a text. Simultaneously, the sheriff's and Highway Patrol Sergeant's phones started ringing.

The woman raised her arms in the air to garner attention. Two latex-covered hands waved back and forth in the bright light. "Everyone, listen up. My name is Lisa Welcher. I am the supervisor of this region's Wildlife Incident Team. Those phone rings you just heard are from the Secretary of the Interior. By federal law, until relieved by a higher-ranking officer, I am now in charge of the incident site. That means everyone will do what I say when I say it. Any questions relating to my authority?"

Other than police chatter coming over the walkie-talkies, there was silence.

"Good. Alright, first things first, no one other than team members is to go within twenty-five feet of the body. Sheriff, I want deputies forming a loose ring around these woods. I want to keep people out. If you see any more of these animals, you are to avoid a confrontation if at all possible."

"You heard her," said the disgusted sheriff. Stay in groups of at least two *always*. Carry large-caliber firearms, but for heaven's sake, do not use them unless you have no other choice."

"No!" Said Welcher. "No more of these animals are to be hurt…period!"

The sheriff stared at Welcher and calmly said, "You heard my orders, large caliber."

The deputies immediately complied with their boss.

Welcher looked into the sheriff's face and saw unrelenting firmness. She knew, at the end of the day, she needed her support. Welcher's face acquired a sour look. Still, she relented. "Alright, Sheriff Thompson, I'll concede this, but don't push me. These animals are not expendable."

The sheriff instantly replied, "neither are my deputies."

***

After securing the woods, Welcher ordered her team to take samples and pack the animal in ice. However, the size of the thing necessitated more. She sent her agents to area carryouts for additional bags. The protocol called for complete secrecy, yet, they discovered news travels fast in small communities.

At one establishment, on the corner of Route 235 and River Road, a teenage girl asked the agent if it was true they had found a crashed flying saucer in Hayes Woods. The agent stared hard at her for a few seconds. The girl looked nervous, unconsciously clutching her Otsego High School sweatshirt. The agent looked back and forth as if checking that no one else could hear her reply. Then, she leaned over the counter and, in a hushed voice, asked, "Can you keep a secret?"

The girl nodded her head and said a meek, "Yes."

"Don't tell anyone, but we have captured a vampire."

The cashier involuntarily swallowed her *Juicy Fruit*.

As the agent left, she stopped at the door, turned around, held her index finger to her lips, and went, "Shhh."

The wide-eyed girl nodded again, this time vigorously.

The agent smiled as she pulled the ice out of the freezer. She knew the cashier was probably already calling everyone she knew. The agent chuckled and thought, *What the hell? It worked for Roswell.*

***

The incident team debriefed Stephen, Officer Mendez, and several others. However, Welcher kept Bobby close to her. Unbeknownst to her, the Marines trained him to answer questions during debriefings, so he was relaxed, giving concise and direct responses. The ease with which Bobby responded to questions didn't pass Welcher's observation, though she didn't broach the subject of where he acquired the skill. She wanted him to concentrate on the details of the case.

"Come on, Bobby," Welcher said. "Let's take a walk."

The night was warmer than usual, and Welcher had rid herself of her jacket, though her badge was still prominently displayed from the lariat on which it hung. The hooded sweatshirt which she donned was oxford gray and thick. In large, scarlet letters, on the front read *Shelby Whippets*, with a sleek dog between the two words.

"Alma mater?" asked Bobby.

"Yep," replied Welcher. "You know, once a Whippet, always a Whippet, and so on."

They walked northwest following the blood trail. It continued along that course for about a half of a mile, the blood drops becoming more frequent. The gait was uneven, with tracks beside the trail. Unlike the others, the blood was red yet increasing in frequency.

"What do you think?" Welcher asked, already having formulated her conclusions.

"Well, both sets of tracks are unsteady. It reminds me of those of a wounded soldier and someone helping him. The ones on the left are probably those of the one I shot in the arm. In the beginning, there was no blood coming from that second animal. The wound had probably clotted off. The blood becomes more frequent and pronounced as the trail goes along. I would assume this was the result of the strain of trying to support the other surviving animal."

Welcher nodded yet said nothing.

Bobby looked at her and said, "But you already knew that, didn't you?"

"What makes you say that?" She replied although it was true.

"Because this whole walk has been a debriefing. You are gauging my ability to reason out the signs; if I can fill in any gaps, you might come across."

"I told you I'd ask you a lot of questions from many angles."

"That you did," Bobby replied.

As Bobby and Welcher rounded another bend, they came upon an area where it looked like a large animal had thrashed on the ground. They ran to it, shining their flashlights on it. There was a lot of blood, very dark. “This is where it hit the dirt - the end of the line,” Bobby said sadly.

Welcher looked him in the eyes and asked, “Then, where is it?”

“Good question,” he said as he unholstered his .357.

“We don’t need that,” she said, now whispering.

“Maybe *we* don’t, but I do. Call it a pacifier.”

Welcher started to protest again and stopped. She knew if he felt unsafe, he would clam up. He would be through as far as a conversation. “Just don’t start shooting everything that moves.”

“I don’t intend to shoot anything if it’s not a threat. We passed two does about three hundred yards back, and I didn’t make Bambi an orphan,” Bobby retorted.

“I didn’t see them.”

“You were busy reading your NSA interrogation manual.”

“You use dry humor to deal with stress.”

“Good grief, woman, stop playing Freud and help me find this thing.”

With that, she stopped talking and shined her flashlight. She started to break away, to circle to the left when Bobby shook his head. "We stay together," he whispered, "no matter what. If we separate, we are easy pickings."

She nodded but said nothing. She spotted a blood trail heading east and pointed to it. There was only one set of footprints, not as deep as earlier. They knelt, looking at the impressions. Bobby stayed silent; he could see she was deep in concentration. She pointed to a large, dark-red blotch that littered the ground. Her mind told her it was time to start looking for a corpse.

Welcher stood up, sighing as she did so. She flipped on her walkie-talkie. "Davidson, this is Welcher. It looks like the more severely injured didn't survive. I need a couple of agents to come up here and help us find the body. Walk three-quarters of a mile along the trail until you see a great deal of blood. Then hang a seventy-five degree right. You will see our flashlights about fifty yards away, next to a large downed tree. Be sure not to compromise the area. She heard a response that to Bobby sounded more like static than words. She involuntarily nodded her head and said, "10-4, over and out."

"Now," she said, "we wait for help."

***

"I found it!" shouted agent Gomez of the vampire story. She waved her flashlight, signaling her position. The distance wasn't far, and the rest of the team was there within a couple of minutes.

They stared at the corpse before them, tucked into a hole made by an upturned tree. The animal stared at the search team with eyes only the dead can possess. It's a look they carry into eternity. There were branches and tree limbs over the body. One massive hand grasped one of the large tree limbs, obviously looking out at the world. They were all thinking the same thing, asking the same silent questions. *What were this animal's last minutes like? Could he have realized his imminent death? Was he afraid?*

Bobby choked out, "I feel so sad. To die alone - abandoned, even out of necessity, had to be a crushing blow."

"How do you know he died alone?" asked the sheriff.

"Look at his hand; it's pulling back the branch. The other animal hid him when it became apparent he wasn't going to live. He covered the hole to conceal him from other animals, specifically us. He wouldn't have covered an area over his face if he was with him."

"Mr. Hayes," asked Gomez, "what do you think he was looking at, you know…in the end?"

"The animal wanted to see one of his own as it walked away, or maybe look at the woods, stars…I don't know. It didn't try to conceal itself; I don't think it cared." Bobby's voice was quiet, reflective.

"Agent Gomez," Welcher said, with a hint of terseness, "what makes you think Mr. Hayes is an expert in animal psychology?"

"I don't know, commander; he seems to be doing well so far. I haven't thought of anything better."

Welcher sarcastically asked Gomez, "Are you trained in animal behavior?"

"Commander, I am. My undergrad and master's degrees are in zoology. I worked with several different animals for over five years, three with great apes. Animal behavior is one of the reasons I joined The Ohio Department of Wildlife."

The sheriff started laughing. "Don't sweat it, commander. We all miss things in the personnel files. I've been torched a couple of times, myself. A bit of advice I learned the hard way, never publicly grill those you command. It kills morale and sets you up to look dumb."

Welcher was no longer thinking of the body lying on the forest floor. She had to maintain control of the situation. Welcher considered firing Gomez on the spot but knew that was petty and vengeful. Reluctantly, she decided the sheriff was right.

"Touché, Officer Gomez," was all she said. It was her smile that eased tensions.

"You know what this means," Welcher barked, "more

ice. Move your behavioral ass, Officer Gomez." The woman instantly had a mischievous grin that was a mystery to the rest of the group. She had already decided she would tell the cashier it wasn't a vampire after all, but a downed weather balloon.

***

By 5:00 am, two helicopters landed on a field by the woods. One was an Uh-Y1Venom. The other was a Ch-47 Chinook. The first person to exit the Venom was a man in a camouflage shirt and pants. Like Welcher, his badge hung from a lariat. The glint from the light bouncing off it told Bobby it was highly polished. He could tell right away; this man loved his job and possibly the authority that came with it. He thought of Carmen from the cartoon series *South Park*. Next, three men came out of the chopper, each carrying a case. Bobby could only suppose it was for taking further samples.

The first man, obviously in charge, was met by Welcher. Her deference to him was apparent, even above the hum of the propellers – it was in her body language. Bobby watched as she directed the man toward him. He was a good 6'2" with a toned yet not muscle-bound build. Bobby noted his eyes reflected not only authority but intelligence.

He walked to Bobby, stuck out his hand, and shook it. Hands still clasped, the man introduced himself. "Mr. Hayes, I am Daniel Bloom. I am a senior advisor with the Department of the Interior."

"Nice to meet you. Hey, that isn't our field you landed your Yankee and transport on."

"Yes, I know, it belongs to David Barnes, age fifty-eight. You used the slang term Yankee for the Viper – oh, yes, that's right; you were a Marine."

Bobby, not being sidetracked, responded, "You're crushing a lot of his soybeans."

"We'll pay for them."

"You're lying," Bobby quickly retorted.

"Normally, I would agree. Still, if it eases your mind, we'll pay for the damages. Fair enough?"

"Yeah, what do you want to know?"

"Mr. Hayes," asked Bloom, "what makes you think I came here to ask you questions?"

"Because you had Lisa bring you to me first."

"Fair enough," Mr. Bloom responded.

"You use that term a lot," Bobby remarked.

"What term?"

"Fair Enough."

"Fair eno. . ." Bloom caught himself and started laughing. "I'll have to watch that."

"Mr. Bloom," Bobby said.

"Yes."

"I haven't slept or eaten in a long time. While you question me, at least in the beginning, can I sit somewhere and have a snack?"

"I'll get you a sandwich, and we can sit against those oaks. Is that alright?"

Bobby looked Bloom straight in the face and suddenly grinned. "Fair enough."

***

Bobby was leaning his back against a large oak tree. He had finished his peanut butter and jelly sandwich, forcing himself to eat slowly, despite his hunger. His mother had instilled in him that table manners were always appropriate, even in the forest. He drank the last couple of ounces from his bottle of water, tipping his head back in an attempt to capture every drop. After succeeding in his task, he looked at Bloom and nodded his head. He was ready to be questioned.

Bloom was sitting opposite of him, propped against a similar-sized arbor. They were seated about three yards apart. He thought this was a good distance for an interview. He was far enough away not to crowd Mr. Hayes, yet close enough to be within easy talking distance.

Bloom appreciated that the young man didn't string

him along or avoid debriefing. “Mr. Hayes, I read the report Ms. Welcher submitted. I am not going to make you rehash every detail.”

The exhausted hunter exhaled in palpable relief. He knew more questions were coming; he just disliked repeating the same answers over and over again.

“Mr. Hayes, you were a Marine.”

“I am a Marine; Once a Marine, always a Marine.”

Bloom almost said, *fair enough*, but stopped himself. “With your military background, you understand the difference between tactical and the big picture, which is strategic.”

Bobby nodded, so Bloom pushed on. “Give me your impressions of what you shot.”

“At first, it was hard for me to register what I was seeing. I walked these woods thousands of times and never saw anything like it. He was *so* massive; it took me a few seconds to recognize that what I was looking at wasn’t something distorted by the sun or background.”

“What were your impressions after your mind confirmed what you were seeing was factual?”

“The first thing I noticed was its gait. Even though the thing walked on two legs, it walked differently than us.”

“How?” Bloom’s brows scrunched together in curiosity.

“I don’t think its knees ever locked. You know, when a person walks, his knees will lock in place.” Bloom nodded but said nothing. "Second, his feet seemed to bend in the middle. It seemed like it had a break in its feet. I don't mean a fracture. I get the impression their feet are more flexible than ours, an extra joint in their arches. Maybe that's why they are so silent in the woods."

"How did it stand?" Bloom asked.

"It walked almost upright."

"What do you mean by almost?

"He was bent over, just a little. It was like the good Lord stopped just before he had him all the way vertical. That hunch didn't stop this thing from being incredibly muscular. I had little doubt his long arms could reach my deer stand, and if he grabbed me, I was going to die."

"Mr. Hayes, I want to come back to the confrontation later, but I want you to give me your impression of him from the shoulders up."

"His head came to a point. I think they call it a sagittal crest. Dogs all have small ones, the bump on each of their heads. His head looked like a Conehead with fur."

Bloom chuckled at the reference. "You talked about how it seemed to move silently. How fast did it move?"

"When the first one I saw charged me, it moved quickly. I didn't have time to think; I just reacted. Looking back, it amazes me how fast an animal that large, on two feet, could move. Maybe the thing was that fast because he had energy left. He had to be going slow before he saw me."

"Why do you say that?"

Bobby explained. "The animal driving the deer wasn't meant to deliver the death blow; he was the one driving the deer. He didn't have to do anything more than push them, wear them down, and drive them toward the kill zone. People have practiced this form of hunting for a very long time."

Nodding slowly, Bloom said, "So, you're saying the field was the kill zone."

"No, the field is too open, too many chances for a deer, even an exhausted one, to slip by them. That is why when the deer started to make the turn on the trail, the second one, stationed between them and the field, started making a whistling sound. It stopped the deer in their tracks."

"So," said Bloom, smiling, "the third animal, hidden in the deadfall, was intended to deliver the death blow."

"Yeah," replied Bobby, "the deadfall forms a semi-circle, just beyond the trail's turn toward the field. They were trapped."

"Well," Bloom replied, "we now know which one was the hunter - the one you shot in the stomach."

"Sir, you are wrong," replied Bobby.

Bloom looked at him quizzically. "How's that?"

"They were all the hunters."

"But, only number three was going to kill the deer."

"Mr. Bloom, there is more to hunting than the kill. There

is the work put in beforehand. They must have done some recognizance of the area before starting the hunt. They picked a great spot. It's the same reason I selected it. I had checked it out beforehand. They all participated in the hunt. It was well thought out and coordinated."

"You know what you're saying? You're telling me they exhibited advanced cognitive skills."

"Yeah," said Bobby reflectively, "I know."

Bloom looked at the young man before him, at one point slightly tilting his head. Bobby stared at the ground and said nothing.

"Mr. Hayes, you're not telling me something. Son, it's time to come clean."

Bobby sighed, raising his head, locking his eyes with his benign inquisitor. "You're looking for them in the wrong place."

Bloom's eyes narrowed. "It's obvious when the one was dying they tried to reach the rest of their group to the southeast."

"Mr. Bloom, may I ask you a question?"

"Of course."

"Say you knew something was hunting you, and while attempting to reach other people, you realized you were going to die. Would you lead the hunters toward your home and family or try to throw them off the trail?"

The agent stared hard at the young Marine for a long

second before grabbing his walkie-talkie. He was trained not to let emotions enter his decisions, yet Bobby had brought up a fundamental behavior. It had required the young man to empathize with the animal to understand its actions. He pressed the microphone button and spoke. "This is Bloom. These things are trying to dupe us. The remaining one is most likely headed northwest, towards its own."

***

To Bobby's relief, they never found the rest of the group. Welcher told him later the search crew discovered the things' had sheltered under an overhang by the Maumee River. At that site were simple, shaped tools, multiple hair samples, bones of several deer and small animals, and a lot of scat.

News and pictures of the corpses got out. There was no way to hide the fact. The government, in a rare instance, gave *almost* full disclosure.

Several months after the incident, there was a knock on Bobby's door. He was wary of who was asking for an audience. He had assumed the reporters would quickly tire of interviewing him. He was, after all, only the guy who shot them. Yet, now and then, someone with a press badge appeared on his porch. He opened the door and was relieved to find Bloom and Welcher.

"Mr. Hayes," asked Welcher, "may we come in?"

"Sure, as long as you don't have a camera or microphone. Come in-pop a squat." Bloom reached in his trench coat and pulled out his smartphone. "What are you doing?" asked Bobby.

"I don't want to trick you. I thought our meeting might possess some import for posterity. I assure you, my intentions are good." Bloom gave Bobby a warm smile.

Bobby replied, "I have told everyone everything I know. What could I possibly offer you?"

"Mr. Hayes," responded Welcher, "we wanted to inform you of some developments before releasing them to the public."

"Why?"

"Because," Welcher stated, "they are culturally shattering. Science and religion are going to have to ask themselves some gut-wrenching questions. People might not like the answers. You are the reason for their self-reflections; they may look at you in a different light than before."

Welcher continued. "We sent tissue samples to the Max Planck Institute in Germany. It's one of the best organizations for using DNA to determine human origins. It mapped both the Neandertal and Denisovan genetic codes and how we were related to those other species of humans. Our best guess is that your discovery, like us, evolved from an early hominid named Homo erectus. We believe that was the last common ancestor between them and us. They branched away a very long time ago and evolved alongside other humans."

"I get you," Bobby stated. "I watched a documentary on the National Geographic Channel. We lived beside other humans before they went extinct thousands of years ago."

"Right," said Bloom. "Pardon the pun, but for a long time, we thought we were the last man standing. There is a little of these others' DNA in some of us, yet they are gone. We took it for granted there were no other types of humans left. Rumors persisted of the existence of large, unconfirmed primates. To most, they were just stories; few in the scientific community took them seriously. To be alone is unusual in our species history. As it turns out, we aren't."

There was a bright look of pain on Bobby's face that hurt his guests. They had grown to like the young man. He closed his eyes, and when he opened them, there were tears. "I didn't kill animals that day, did I? I killed humans."

"Mr. Hayes," replied Bloom, "you have to understand, you did kill animals – we're all animals, primates."

Bobby murmured. "Why do you think they're human?"

"Mr. Hayes," but the young man cut him off.

"My name is Bobby. Please, call me Bobby." His tone held a note of self-torture.

"Bobby," continued Bloom, "several animals use stones as tools. They utilize them for everything from cracking open nuts to swallowing them to help in food digestion. To our knowledge, only humans possess the ability to take stones and shape them, to form them for a specific purpose. In the bedding area by the river, we found crafted stones."

The senior agent went on, "there is also what is called the Encephalization Quotient. It measures brain size compared to the weight of an animal. The bigger the animal, the more brain it usually needs in order to function. A sperm whale's brain can weigh over eighteen pounds, yet they are not as smart as us. Humans, or Homo sapiens, if we go by our scientific name, have a quotient of roughly 7.4. The next on the list was dolphins at roughly 4.1-4-6, depending on the species. Amazingly, chimps are only at 2.2-2.5."

"You said *was*," responded Bobby. "Dolphins were the next. Did our newly discovered cousins take their place?"

"Yes," replied Bloom. "We only have two samples, but they both came in roughly 6.9 on the quotient."

Bobby sat back in his chair, blowing the air out of his lungs in one long sigh.

"Bobby, please understand that not all brains are the same. Dolphins, for example, have brains developed for sonar, although their cognitive intelligence is undeniable." As Bloom went on, he explained, "Our newly found relatives possess highly developed brains in the areas that allow for sight as well as smell. Your report, their riverside campsite, and the autopsies demonstrate they are reasoning beings. I wouldn't, however, place them at our level."

"We have no evidence they produce, let alone think of, expressing themselves with art. The language center in their brains also indicates some speech ability, although we doubt they can utilize anything remotely close in complexity to our languages. If some of the recordings on the internet are correct, what they possess could be called a proto-language at best. Their throat and mouth structures don't allow for the ability to speak certain consonants and vowels."

He continued, "As you know, they are very muscular. Their strength is a plus in defense and hunting. Still, it's not always a positive."

Looking confused, Bobby asked, "how so?"

Bloom responded, "That amount of muscle requires the consumption of a tremendous number of calories *every* day. I will assume that's why they can't live together in large communities or have a large population as a whole.

Remember, they are competing against other predators for limited prey items."

"The limited type of muscles is also a detriment in another way."

"I can't see one," Bobby responded.

"Well," replied Bloom, "chimpanzees can weigh up to 150 pounds, yet they are approximately five times stronger than the average human. Their power is because they have more thick muscle fibers than us. Like them, our recent find possesses incredible strength, but they don't have many thin muscle fibers. Those are the ones that give us dexterity. They allow us to pull the trigger of a gun, write, paint the Sistine Chapel, etc."

Bobby asked, "If there are all those differences between us and only a few simple stone tools to bind us, what does it mean to be human?"

Bloom's eyes drifted off, and his face took on a reflective tone. It was evident to both he and Welcher that the man was in deep thought. Finally, he came back from his contemplation, looking first at Welcher and then at Bobby."

He slowly shook his head, and in an almost sad tone, said, "I don't know, I truly don't. Maybe that's the question we should have been asking all along – not are they human, but what does it mean to be human?"

Welcher entered the discussion. She had remained

silent out of respect for not only Bloom's rank but also his scientific knowledge. Now, she posed an emotional question. "Bobby, the people at the Max Planck Institute refuse to name this animal. They say the honor belongs to you."

He nodded and gave his entwined fingers, already resting on his lap, a light squeeze. It was a release of nervous energy. "Stephen and I have discussed this a lot. We thought we might have the naming rights. We talked a lot about possibilities, you know - what if? Kind of like what you would do if you win the lottery. Is there anything that has to be in the name?"

Bloom answered, "The only requirement is that the genus Homo must appear first."

"We wanted to name it after someone wise and kind. This man was both and more. He loved the land where we found these things. He taught Stevie and me about respecting nature and a love of being in its presence. So, it is with great pride, I present to you, Homo horace."

The Man in the Iron Box

My name is Sal. I am an officer in the United States Army's Bio-Pathogens Division. Haven't heard of us, then the Army is doing its job. We had signed a couple of treaties stating we wouldn't play with these kinds of toys. When those two towers fell, a lot of what we promised went down with them.

Years later, we are still fighting what seems to be an endless struggle. We tend to kill insurgents at about the same rate they recruit them. Homeland Security and the Army are working on a joint project to introduce pathogens designed to kill specific ethnic groups. The fact that it will also kill civilians is incidental. No one will trace it to us, and the other side doesn't seem weighted with any apprehension about killing our noncombatants.

I work with blood, otherwise known as hematology. It's the only damn area I cover. The entire program is huge.

There are thousands of us working on a multitude of projects. Because of my specialty and security clearance, the army selected me to study this phenomenon, this thing.

I received a summons to report to our complex in western Poland. Poor Poland, it always seems to get the short end of the stick. Seventeen floors underground, I was introduced to my specimen. He hadn't spoken a word since he arrived, and no one could identify him. A guy from Baltimore found him, so they named him Camden, after Camden Yards, the ballpark where the Orioles play baseball.

I reported to General Sykes, the commanding officer of a facility that didn't officially exist. She walked me to the control area. I found that unusual. Usually, a lower-ranking officer conducted the tour. I knew her passingly. She had always portrayed herself as a stern person, but now her mood was different. She appeared somber, resigned. Several times I caught her sighing. It occurred to me that whatever she was about to show me had her shaken.

The specialists in the control room were monitoring a plethora of captured terrorists. The facility housed each combatant in a separate room. They wouldn't bring me to Poland to study terrorists. The man in cell four was my lab rat. Little did I know, this mouse had a vicious streak.

Sykes pointed to one of several high-definition screens and gave me my orders. “Major Rizzoni, that is cell four. Whoever this man is, and what makes him what he is, is the sole focus of your skill, intuition, and perseverance.”

“Yes, Ma’am.”

“Listen to me, Major; this subject is different from anything we have ever seen. There are protocols in place for dealing with him. You are to follow these at *ALL* times. Do you understand?”

“Yes, Ma’am.”

“Captain Tolles will give you a full briefing. The thing is to have the highest priority. I will expect daily updates and immediate notification of any incidents.”

“Yes, Ma’am.”

With that, we saluted, and she started walking out of the room. She stopped at the door and turned around to look at me. Sykes placed a shaky hand on the door frame for support. The general hunched over, a dull look in her eyes. She impressed me as tired and sad.

***

Once the General was gone, Tolles and I got down to brass tacks.

“Major Rizzoni,” Tolles greeted me.

“Call me Sal; I work by the book, but I want to be as

informal as possible."

Tolles exhaled and smiled. "Please call me, Pete." With that, we reached across the table and shook hands.

"Tell me what you know about Camden," I began.

"We had Green Beret in Ukraine, doing recognizance on Russian troop movements. It was about two hours into the mission when they realized somebody was tracking them. At first, they thought it was Russian Special Forces. However, one of the soldiers, a lifetime outdoorsman, informed the officer in charge that this wasn't mere recognizance. Someone was hunting them. Whoever was stalking the berets was toying with them. They tried circling back to the rendezvous point several times but were cut-off at choke points, always at the last minute. It became apparent to the Green Berets that whoever was stalking them possessed intimate knowledge of the terrain."

"Still, the berets were apparently gamer than our Camden realized. As sunrise approached, they were able to get a bead on him. Just before the kill shot, Camden suddenly turned and headed for an abandoned house," Tolles continued. "The berets saw him as a possible high priority target and went in after him."

"They found him sleeping in a basement, under a mound of timber. It was pitch black in that cellar. What they discovered horrified them. It was obvious he was human-like."

"What do you mean, human-like?" I was intrigued.

"He had almost no respiration; nonetheless, he did have a pulse. And his eyes," Tolles gave an involuntary shudder, "do not have pupils. They are solid silver in color. There were human corpses in various states of decay. That cellar was his den. He was bringing them back to feed."

"God, almighty," I whispered under my breath.

"They were able to get a stealth helicopter, like the one that crashed during the Bin Laden raid, to the site. They restrained him and immediately shipped him here. Our captured hunter, by pure coincidence, was held in what we call an: *iron box*."

"What's that?"

"It's our strongest section of cells, thank God."

"Why do you say that?"

"Because, whoever or whatever this guy is, he is strong. I don't mean bodybuilder strong. I mean freakish power. The CIA designed those particular cells to withstand high explosives on the off chance the terrorists have bombs hidden on them that we missed during their intake inspections. We have pressure indicators throughout those cells. When he woke, he was pissed. He hit the door with the level of energy close to three sticks of dynamite. It held but scared the shit out of us," Tolles said.

"So, how do I fit into this case? I'm a hematologist."

"Because there is something different about this guy's blood. We don't know what it is or if it's contagious."

"Also, he drinks blood - only human. It is his only form of nutrition. We give him a pint once every three days. Blood type and RH factors don't seem to matter. We believe he has taste capabilities; he seems to enjoy it."

"Anything else?" I hated to ask.

"He is highly allergic to ultraviolet spectrum light."

"Sunlight?"

"Yep," Tolles nodded.

"Can I talk to this Camden?" I asked.

"Sure, there is a two-way from the control room. There also cameras. You can see Camden, but he can't see you. He hasn't said a word since his arrival. Maybe he can't speak." Tolles looked at a timer on his watch. "He will be awake in one hour and forty-three minutes."

"How do you know?"

"Because that's when the sun sets."

***

Exasperated, I shook my head in disgust. "I've been watching this bastard for three weeks, and it's the same bullshit."

Tolles looked on. "Rizzoni, I told you, Camden's behavior hasn't changed in the six weeks since he arrived.

He feeds on a pint bag of blood every three days, sits and sleeps."

I tapped my fingers on the briefing room table, contemplating something foolish. "I am going into the box."

"You can't. Sundown is in twenty minutes," Tolles informed me.

"I'm going alone," I responded.

"It's against protocol, and most likely, suicide."

"Camden is smart; he is also supremely patient. He's waiting us out."

"And?" Tolles inquired.

"And," I sighed, "he won."

I nervously sat on a folding chair with the overhead lights on. Camden didn't wake slowly. One second he was stone; the next, he was standing, staring at me.

"Good evening, Camden," I said calmly. Years of interrogation training had taught me how to keep my fear under control.

The thing's silver eyes looked much more malicious with consciousness in them. Camden sat on the bunk and studied me with a disconcerting intelligence.

"I have studied every inch of you, Camden, just as you are doing to me now. We both know you just waited us out. We both also know you can speak. I've watched your reactions to our words. It's obvious you know quite a bit about the English language. So, let's cut the deception."

Camden didn't even twitch in response to my bravado. I was wondering if I was soon going to be dead. Nonetheless, I pressed on. "Your mouth samples indicate traces of nicotine. We found a cigar on you. It was machine-processed and unsavory looking. I brought you a gift, a Macanudo cigar. This baby is handcrafted, has quality construction, and emanates a series of complex flavors on the palate. I also brought along one for myself. I took the liberty of cutting them a little while ago. If you want to smoke one, then say yes."

"Yes," he said in a Russian accent.

I was both happy and stunned; we finally, albeit one syllable, motivated him to speak.

"I am going to walk to you and give you the cigar. I will light it with a butane-type lighter. It burns hotter than a normal one and won't leave a lighter fluid taste. I'm not checking to see if you have an aversion to fire."

The thing across from me smiled. It appeared amused. I slowly walked to the thing sitting on the bunk and handed him the Macanudo. After I lit Camden's cigar, I went back to my chair and lit my own.

"Well, are we going to keep calling you Camden, or will we get your real name?"

"My name is Ivan. Why do you call me Camden?" He asked.

"It's a baseball thing," I chuckled.

"You Americans love your baseball. I once saw a game at Yankee Stadium."

I was flabbergasted and didn't do a good job hiding it. Ivan smiled broadly, showing perfect, if slightly yellowed, teeth.

"You have been to America? When? Why?"

Ivan blew out a mouthful of smoke. "You're right; the taste is creamy."

"Ivan, how in the hell did you go to a Yankee's game? It must have been at night."

Ivan stopped smiling, anger flashing in his eyes. I wondered how long it would take for him to kill me. Then, a sort of sadness crossed his face that I could tell was genuine. I also realized the emotion in Ivan lacked something human, though I couldn't quite place my finger on the difference.

"Major Rizzoni, tell me your age?"

"I'm thirty-seven," I answered.

"You are young; you know nothing of life's pain, let alone death's."

"Ivan, I realize my statement, while more reflective than directed toward you, has hurt you. Please, forgive me; I meant no offense."

Ivan drew the last puff, then dropped the stub on the floor. He looked at me almost pleadingly.

With a grin, I brought out two larger cigars. "I was hoping our conversation would last longer."

Ivan smiled at me again. Something was unnerving about it. I knew I would have to study the tape to match his body movements to his emotions. I didn't think the producers of the facial analysis software ever considered a scenario like this.

Before I knew what happened, Ivan had crossed the length of the room, taken the cigar from my hand, and was lighting it. It was all I could do to keep my breath even. "Didn't anyone ever tell you that it's impolite to pull a gift from the giver's hand?" I said.

Ivan loomed over me, staring down at me with that chilly smile.

"Ivan, damn it! If you are going to kill me, just fucking do it."

The smile remained. Still, the thing turned and casually walked back to the bunk.

"I'm sorry, I thought we could have a conversation. It's obvious you don't want any human companionship." I stood to leave.

"I'm not human!" the thing roared.

I could feel the force of it in my chest. I knew I had to answer if there was any hope for further discussions. "But you were once!" I yelled back.

The reply seemed to catch him by surprise. Ivan held

his cigar in his hand - unsmoked. His forehead creased. It appeared to me that Ivan remembered something, which swallowed him in introspection.

He went to take a draw of his cigar and found it had gone out. I walked over and relit it without comment.

When I returned to my chair, the prisoner spoke. "My full name is Ivan Nikovi. I was born in the winter of 1918 on the outskirts of Leningrad. My mother was a seamstress. My father worked on a small collective farm. My older sister, Nadia, took care of me while my parents worked. That is how I spent most of the first years of my life. There was a famine, but my sister would always tell me better days were coming, to just trust in comrade Stalin. The name Nadia means hope, but there were no happier times. Even with my father working the collective, we were starving. Nadia was giving me most of her portion of food. I was only eight and hungry. I didn't know it was for her."

"Nadia became weaker and weaker." Then, Ivan cried out miserably, "I swear to God I didn't know the food was hers." Then, incredibly, silver tears started to stream down his face. "She died just after the thaw in 1927."

Ivan continued. "Two weeks later, we were awoken in the night by the NKVD-the secret police. They told my parents we were leaving for a larger collective in the west. Mama told the police she wanted to stay close to

Nadia's grave; she wanted to be near her spirit. One of the policemen spat in her face and called her a superstitious old hag, and that we needed to give up our belief in an afterlife."

"West meant Ukraine. I worked and went hungry on that collective until war erupted in Europe. I didn't want to fight; I was a farmer. One day, a man in an army uniform hung a piece of paper, by a nail, to the office door. On the note were written the names of men and women drafted into the Red Army; I was on the list. I was part of the defense of the southern oil fields when the Germans invaded in 1941. That is how I developed the scar on my chest you, no doubt, studied. A German soldier shot me with his rifle. He was undoubtedly going to finish me with his bayonet, but when I hit the ground, my rifle discharged. The bullet went through his neck. He died instantly."

"I remember screaming in pain. A sergeant gave me a shot of vodka, then knocked me out with a punch to my face. When I woke, I was in an army hospital, and my left arm didn't move well. I couldn't return to active duty, so I finished the war working in a munitions factory."

"After the war, I returned to the collective, looking for my parents. The survivors informed me the Germans shot them. I never found their graves. I had been a good soldier, so the government paid my tuition, allowing me the opportunity to attend university. I studied the only thing I had known - agriculture. I worked on collectives for close to a decade before accepting an offer to be an attaché to America. I was to study your agricultural practices."

Ivan continued. "I had a chance to travel extensively through your American Midwest. I also visited several of your large cities, including the Kansas City and Chicago stockyards. An American friend invited me to the Yankee's game while I was attending a conference in New York."

Ivan continued. "After my time in America, I was assigned to supervise a large collective, once again in Ukraine. I was there for about a year when people began to go missing. As the highest-ranking supervisor, I was responsible for investigating. The police were drunken most of the time, so they were of no help. People kept screaming that the dead were taking people."

"I began to think it was a large animal, possibly a bear. One night I tracked the thing to an abandoned factory. I remember feeling an incredible impact on my body, and I went unconscious. I awoke, hanging upside down by a rope. The thing bit my neck slightly and began to lick and suck on the wound. I struggled but became exhausted. At dawn, with me securely tied, it crawled under some tarps and was still. I cried out but had no hope of rescue. The factory was bombed during the war and was kilometers from any homes."

"Then, incredibly, the rope broke. I hit my head but remained conscious. I was able to remove the rest of my restraints. I then turned to the tarps and pulled them away. The thing screamed and started to fry like a piece of meat in a pan. It died quickly. I turned and ran. I couldn't believe such things existed. I ran about four kilometers and collapsed."

"I woke after sunset. I remember a thirst like no other. I drank from a stream, but it didn't quench it. I became consumed with a maddening drive. I saw through the darkness a fisherman about three kilometers downstream. He had a small fire. I do not think, Major, I need to recite the rest." Ivan went silent.

I sat back in the chair, deep in thought; my fingers absently played with the long-dead cigar.

Ivan's voice broke my reflection. "Is this where you call me, *poor man*? Are you going to try to comfort me?"

"No. Why would I comfort a tiger for being a tiger? You are who and what you are. I have the who. The *what* is still a mystery." I responded.

Ivan said, "I feel sunrise coming soon. Our conversation must end."

I looked at my watch. "Good grief, the night flew by. It's over so quickly."

"Trust me," he said, "there is more to come. An endless

stream of nights."

***

"Are you nuts?"

I stood, stone-faced and at attention in front of General Sykes. I knew the ass-chewing was coming. Still, I was caught off-guard at the intensity and length of the discipline. It dawned on me that Sykes' world-class dress-down was fueled more by fear than anger.

"That thing could have killed you. In fact, at one point, it looked like a predator playing with its food," she barked.

She finally calmed down enough to let her intellect take control. "Well, since you decided to play with the lion, tell me what you gained from your dumb-ass move."

"His name was…is…Ivan Nikovi. He was born in 1918 near Leningrad. His sister starved to death in 1927 while giving him a large portion of her food. Soon after his sister's death, the Secret Police forcibly relocated him and his parents to a large collective in Ukraine. The authorities mistreated his family during the process. He was injured defending the southern oil fields during Operation Barbarossa. After the war, he majored in agriculture at college. He widely traveled the United States as an attaché, studying American agricultural practices."

"He was reassigned to supervise a large collective in Ukraine. Workers started disappearing. While tracking what he thought was a large animal responsible for the deaths, the thing ambushed him. He was bled but managed to escape. He seems to have remained in the region ever since."

"Anything else?" General Sykes probed.

"He likes fine cigars and once attended a Yankee's game."

"What?"

"He likes good cigars, and he has attended a Yankee's game. The game was before he was changed, of course," I reported.

Sykes then asked the question everyone wanted an answer to. "Major, do you think the prisoner in cell four is human?"

"No, Ma'am, I don't. I think Ivan's attack and subsequent decades of hunting and solitude have fundamentally changed him, both physiologically and psychologically. The thing in that cell is a predator. What's more, I recommend classifying Ivan as a habitual man-eater, albeit human blood. Yet, there is something human left in him. Something in it that identifies with the man he once was. His tears were silver, but I truly believe they were real."

***

Ivan went from dreamless sleep to standing in less than the human heart has time to beat once. He looked down at the bag of blood before him. There were also two cigars. One was the familiar Macanudo. The other was an Opus X. Beside them was the butane lighter and a note. He gulped down the blood in a genuinely grotesque manner. The amount of lip-smacking and the use of his tongue to get every drop highlighted how he wasn't wholly human. It was more akin to watching a hyena eat than a man. Once finished, he cleaned the blood from himself and turned his attention to the note.

Ivan, I do not wish to visit you so often as to be an unwelcome guest. Since variety is the spice of life, along with the Macanudo, I left you an Opus X. If invited, I will visit tomorrow. Enjoy your meal and cigars.

Respectfully,

Major

Ivan put the letter down. He had an amused look on his face. Looking into one of the dozens of cameras placed in the cell, he said, "Please tell the Major it would be rude, after he provided me with food and good cigars, not to invite him to my home. Tomorrow evening would be splendid. Please tell him to bring many cigars; I have questions."

***

Ivan awoke to a comfortable chair beside his bunk and Rizzoni on the other side of the room. The Major had replaced his folding chair, as well, for one similar. A small stand accompanied each chair. Both had several cigars and a butane lighter on them.

"Thank you for inviting me back. While you're technically a prisoner, I want to be respectful of your space."

"I thank you for your consideration," was all he said.

"By your message," I said, "I am assuming you want to ask me about what is happening and your future disposition."

"There is one thing I would like to discuss. What am I?"

"Alright," I answered, "let me try to answer your question. You stalked a group of men. Their debriefing indicated their belief you had an intimate knowledge of the local geography. They also think you underestimated the abilities of your quarry. They were just about to remove your head from your shoulders with an explosive round when you suddenly turned to an abandoned house. They saw you as a high-value target and had you shipped here."

"Arrogant ass," Ivan said reflectively. Then he blew a smoke ring. "It had been so long since I found prey of any competition. The Russian Special Forces were a definite upgrade. I killed a few. I assumed these men were the same. I had just eaten the night before. There was no reason not to study them first. My hubris brought me here. Give my congratulations to the Americans. I would have had them, but they have always been unpredictable. I should have noticed the difference between them and the Russians. My superiors at the embassy were right; your military never reads their training manuals. That makes them too unpredictable."

"No," I replied, "we tend not to read instructions on how to do things, even in the military."

I continued, "As to what happens to you, I don't know. It's unlikely you will ever be released. I also find it unlikely the U.S. government will ever kill you. There is the real possibility of Guantanamo Bay."

"What is this Guantanamo Bay?" Ivan asked.

"It's a detention center where terrorists are confined. It's on an American military base in southeast Cuba. You could have a tropical atmosphere."

"A terrorist prison!" Ivan roared. "I'm no terrorist."

"No, you're not a terrorist; you're a man-eater. You are a predator that toyed with the wrong prey. Your days of killing are over. Either accept it or don't, but that's your reality."

Ivan sat in stunned silence. His silver eyes made reading his train of thought difficult. Finally, he spoke. "You're right. I had long ago become an abomination to the land on which I lived. My instincts don't allow me a choice whether or not to feed. And to be blunt, I don't know if I would want to become human again, even if I could. Still, oh how I miss those blue skies."

I gently inquired, "do you still want to hear about what you are and why?"

"Yes, please tell me. I have wondered for decades why I became what I am." His voice was gentle and eager, almost that of a curious child.

"Well, for starters," I began, "you are not a vampire, at least not in the conventional sense. Yes, you drink blood and avoid daylight. There is no indication of fangs or tooth extension during your feedings… I mean, when you eat. We ran your blood for…."

"Ran my blood?" Ivan interrupted; his brows scrunched together in confusion.

"We examined your blood for the presence of a virus. We found traces of childhood diseases you contracted, measles, chickenpox, etc. We also found the presence of hepatitis A." Ivan seemed perplexed by the last diagnosis.

Sensing his concern, I tried to clarify. "Hepatitis A is not uncommon. A large portion of the population has contracted it and doesn't even know it. Most times, the symptoms are like the common cold. They disappear, but the virus is still there."

"We also tested the contact of your skin to religious icons - crosses, religious symbols of multiple faiths. We even tried holy water. Nothing happened. Whatever you are, it's not spiritual. Your condition is flesh and blood, a real-world phenomenon."

Ivan cracked an almost human smile. I sensed it was genuine, but I don't think his brain, facial muscles, and for that matter, his heart, quite remembered how to come together. "The locals were terrified of me. They would say prayers and throw holy water on me. I was their dark idol, *bete noir*, or boogeyman to use an American name. It's just as well. My mama used to tell me the person who thinks he is God is worshipping a fool."

I proceeded, "What we have found appears to be a form of a parasite. It appears human-specific. It dies in all other hosts - dogs, cats, sheep, etc. It also does not affect them. Do you know about DNA?"

"Yes, I have had a long time to read."

"That you have, my friend. That you have."

Ivan inhaled a deep breath. His silver tears began to flow again. "No one has called me by that title in decades. You consider me your friend." Ivan placed the palms of his hands to his eyes and began to rock back and forth. He openly wept for many minutes. Ivan had cried for his sister, yet that was a memory of his time as a boy. That he became so emotional over friendship cemented in my mind that Ivan had not relinquished all of his humanity. That, however, didn't come close to making him a man.

When he finished crying, including some very human-like snuffles, he looked at me again. "Please continue."

"Well, the parasite locks onto the cells and manipulates the host's, in this case, your DNA. Our distant ancestors were nocturnal. They saw well in the night. They also produced, like many mammals, their own vitamin C. As we evolved, our lineage became diurnal, or simply put, we became active in the day. We gained the ability to see a broader range of colors but lost our night vision."

"You no longer needed to see in daylight, so the parasite triggered the dormant gene to see at night. I hypothesize this is why you have silver eyes. Your eyes are completely silver because it allows your entire eye to receive the maximum light onto your optic nerve. It's a layer much like that of several mammals. It has a shine somewhat like a dog's eyes and for similar reasons."

"Your ability to produce vitamin C was re-activated.

The parasite caused physiological changes that allow you to have a much-reduced diet selection. Your body, for reasons quite frankly we haven't discovered, utilizes blood as the sole nutrient. Most times, when something eats, the body only captures around ten percent of the energy contained in the food. You are utilizing approximately ninety-eight percent of the blood's potential energy. This stunning percentage is largely responsible for your incredible strength and speed. It also explains the radically reduced respiration and blood pressure."

"Ivan," I continued hesitantly, "there are severe drawbacks."

Ivan nodded and said, "Do not hold back, Major. Tell me."

"First, exposure to daylight. The parasite turned on many things but turned off your body's ability to process the ultraviolet spectrum of light. Your body, no longer active in the day, shed its ability to produce melanin. Sunlight, as you know, is a death sentence. The parasite appears to be nocturnal. It wants its hosts to be, as well."

"Also, while your brain looked healthy on a scan we completed, there is one glaring exception. The parasite seems to reduce blood flow, approximately every three days, to the part of the brain that allows you to delay gratification. This suppression coincides with an increase in a hormone named Ghrelin, produced in the stomach and travels to the hypothalamus. Ghrelin plays a large role in feelings of hunger. Thus, the inability to delay the urge to feed peaks every third day."

I continued, "The parasite is so invested in your DNA, it controls duplication integrity. That is why you have not aged. At least, not very much."

"How long will I live?" Ivan asked nervously.

"We ran a computer simulation. If you stay here, with everything remaining the same, another four hundred, thirty-two years, give or take a couple of decades. Of course, all we have is you for a test subject. We could be incorrect."

"But you don't think so," Ivan said. "I can read it in your face."

"No, unless the parasite radically mutates, I trust our estimate is in the ballpark."

"Rizzoni," Ivan flatly stated, "I don't want to live like this for over four centuries."

"I don't blame you."

An alarm went off on my cell phone. "Ivan," I said, "sunlight in ten minutes." Ivan lifted his bowed head and looked at me. The despair in his face was the most unnerving sight yet from the thing across from me.

***

General Sykes, Captain Tolles, and I were watching Ivan on the main screen. He still drank blood. His body wouldn't allow him otherwise. But, the cigars sat untouched on the table. I had replaced them with fresh ones periodically, yet the thing in that cell hadn't smoked since the conversation we had three weeks prior.

"What's wrong with him?" Asked an agitated Sykes.

"He is shutting down," I answered.

"Why?" Sykes asked.

"Why do you think?" I angrily retorted. "What would you do if you were going to spend over four hundred years, the remainder of your life, in prison with no chance of escape or release?"

Sykes sighed, nodding her head. "I would do the same thing."

"I can't think of anything else to do to break his lethargy," remarked Tolles to the General. "We have tried talking to him, pleading, you name it. We had the prison psychologist try talking with him. Nothing has worked. We even stole some of your single malt scotch for him. He refused."

"You stole my scotch?" Asked an incredulous Sykes.

"We had to try something," I responded.

"Did he drink it?"

"No, General," I replied.

"Did you put it back?"

"We drank it," said Tolles.

Sykes sighed again.

***

Ivan woke to me sitting on the other side of the room. On his stand were two Montecristo #2 cigars. He looked at me without a word. He rolled one of them reflectively between his fingers.

"Pack your shit and smoke some cigars," I said, smiling. "You're moving up in the world."

A confused Ivan looked at me questioningly. "Where am I being taken?"

Instead of directly answering, I stated, "That, my friend, is one of the finest cigars on the planet; it's expertly constructed."

Ivan smiled broadly. "In Cuba!"

"Warm, tropical breezes, starlight, and palm trees, all under the *protection* of the United States military," I announced with a grin.

"But, how will I experience these things in a cell?"

"Because we have arranged for a reinforced walking area connected to your cell. You will be allowed nightly walks inside that area. There are fences; nonetheless, you will still be able to see the world around you. Please, cause no trouble, and you should receive none. Oh, I also arranged for you to receive two boxes of fine cigars monthly. You also are to have assistance lighting them. DO NOT pull what you did to me during our first meeting."

"They will have no problems with me. Still, why are you doing this for me?"

"Because, Ivan, we're friends."

"Thank you, yes, we are friends," Ivan choked out.

"You will be flown out after sunrise," I stated. "With the sunrise in Poland first and heading ever west, there should be no problem getting you there before sunset, Guantanamo time. But, just in case, blood will be on board. Once there, you will be processed, then taken to your cell."

"Ivan, I'm not going to blow smoke up your butt. If you become a liability."

"I know," was his only reply.

Time went on, and we talked. All too soon, the alarm on my phone rang.

"Goodbye, Ivan."

"Goodbye, Sal."

We looked at each other a moment longer, both knowing we would never see the other again.

Finally, I stood and signaled the guard to open the door. I was walking through the entryway when Ivan, from the other side of the room, asked, “Rizzoni, tell me something. If Americans are Yankees, then why does so much of your country dislike the New York Yankees?”

I smiled back at Ivan and said, “It’s a baseball thing.”

That's Some Candy Bar

Author's Note

When I finished writing this story, Joe Biden had almost completed two terms as America's Vice-President. Hillary Clinton and Donald Trump were battling for the White House, and it appeared Joe Biden was content to enjoy retirement. I thus created a candy bar named *Biden Bar*. The name snapped into my brain and became a part of the following story. It did not occur to me Joe Biden would become America's President.

"Now, Joseph, you know we have this argument every year; it isn't going to change. You are not getting that candy bar."

"But, Mom," Joseph whined in that unique way only an eleven-year-old can, "why this one? You know how much I love Biden Bars. They're the best candy. Can't

I give them something else?" Joseph's trick or treat bag was bulging, he had knocked the treat collection out of the park, and he knew it. Still, parting with one of his several Biden Bars seemed like cruelty.

Each child would pick one of their favorite candies from their bags to give to the local orphanage children every year. It was a community-wide endeavor that continued generation after generation. The annual votive served two purposes: the first was simple kindness. Secondly, by giving the best of their treats, the children learned there are more important things in their lives. The parents hoped the act instilled a sense of gratitude and empathy.

Joseph was winding up for another round when a glaring look from his mother told him, like every year, the arguing was over. But then his mother did something she hadn't before; she knelt before him, so they were eye level, and softly placed a hand on his shoulder.

"Son," she began. He could see her love for him in her eyes, and it made him wince. "You have a great life. We live in a beautiful home, and you have a family that loves you very much. Tonight you were given a massive amount of candy. The children in the orphanage aren't even able to trick or treat. Every year we argue about giving away one piece of candy. Before, I thought you resisted because of your young age, but now I'm afraid you are becoming selfish. You aren't thinking of others.

"Son," she continued, "in the next few years, you will begin to change from a child to a young man." She choked up as tears formed in her eyes. His mother had always been melodramatic; he also knew she was sincere. "I'm afraid if you can't give away one candy bar now, how will you act when you get older?"

Joseph hugged his mom. "Alright," he said grudgingly, "I guess one won't hurt."

His mother hugged him back tightly, hoping he had a sincere change of heart and wasn't complying to appease her.

"All right, young man, get ready for bed. Do you want me to tuck you in?"

"No, Mom, but thanks for the offer."

Feeling generous in the glow of her son's apparent change of heart, she said, "you can eat three of any candy in your bag before you brush your teeth. Just don't eat that one Biden Bar."

Before closing Joseph's bedroom door, his mother added, "Goodnight, Son, I love you."

"Love you, too," he replied.

As soon as the door closed, he lunged for his trick-or-treat bag. He had peanut M&M's, just like his dad bought him at the hockey games. He also crammed a "Fun Size" Snicker's bar into his mouth. *Fun Size?* He thought, m*ore like cheap-ass candy giver size*. He finished his treat with three, two-bar Kit Kats, which he reasoned added up to one regular size package. When he finished his delicacies, he brushed his teeth without toothpaste because he didn't want to ruin the taste of chocolate with mint flavoring.

***

Joseph was drifting off, hovering in that twilight land between consciousness and sleep, when he heard a gravelly voice say, "Hey, Kid, that's quite the haul of treats you pulled in tonight."

At first, the boy thought he was dreaming and accordingly ignored the compliment.

Seeing no response, the voice became stern. "Hey Kid, wake your ass up. I want to talk to you."

Joseph was sitting up by that time, his mouth agape as he stared at the closet, the door slightly ajar, and beyond, a black void. He couldn't even see his baseball bats. He was about to start screaming when the voice, apparently well versed in children, intervened. "Relax, kid. I'm not here to eat you or anything, just the opposite; I want to help you."

Joseph was still scared, but the fear was slowly melting, giving way to curiosity. "So, my mom was wrong; there is a closet monster."

There emitted a chuckle from the darkness, still in that

voice of a twenty-year smoker. "Well, kid," it stated, "that's not the only thing your mom didn't get right, let me tell you."

Joseph squinted his eyes, his face flushing with anger. "Don't you say that about my mom," he retorted. "I have a good mom!"

"Relax, relax," said the voice, sounding apologetic. "Of course, your mom raised you right. I wasn't saying she isn't a good egg, just a little overprotective."

That word, *overprotective*, resonated with Joseph, and the last of his fright slipped away unnoticed. "That's just the thing I was thinking. But my mom and dad love me."

"Of course, they do," the voice soothingly responded from the closet. "Your parents brought you up to be a strong man, to think for yourself. The problem is that they are having a hard time letting go, knowing they finished their job. Don't be hard on them; lots of parents are the same."

"I guess," responded the boy on the bed, "there is nothing I can do. I'm stuck until I grow up."

"That's just it," the voice retorted sternly, "you are a man now! Time to move on to the next phase of your life."

"Then," Joseph asked, "why do you call me Kid?"

The voice started to fumble a response, then stopped. The boy had the impression the question caught it off guard. After about a minute, the thing responded, "It's just a nickname because while you're a man, you're still young."

"Are you telling me the truth?"

"Of course, I am," said the voice, sounding hurt. "You're still young, your whole life ahead of you."

"My parents are never going to admit I'm a man, so it doesn't matter anyway."

The voice immediately responded, "that's just it, uhm… Kid, there is something you can do, something to prove you're a man. Not in years to come, but tonight."

"What?" asked Joseph, sitting at the edge of the bed, his eyes wide with excitement, "I can prove I'm grown-up now?"

"Sure thing, but you have to act like an adult to be considered one."

Joseph frowned. He had spent so much time wishing people would treat him like an adult; he never considered what would be required to reach that goal. "I don't know what to do," Joseph sighed.

The voice from the closet chuckled kindly, sounding rather grandfatherly. "Kid, there's no shame. In fact, that's common when starting out."

"It is?" a surprised Joseph responded.

"Sure, your ignora…not knowing reveals how much you want to get this adult thing right. That tells me you are ready today to show the world you're a man."

"Wow, you're right; I never thought of it like that. You're, uhm; I don't know your name. I'm sorry I didn't ask before."

"See what I mean? What a polite, young man," it said, ever so slightly emphasizing the last word. If you don't mind, call me Buddy. I don't want the name Closet Monster because that's not what I am. Now back to you, all you need is a demonstration of your independence; give an example to your parents that you are indeed all grown-up."

Joseph thought of how he could show his parents, who other than his teachers were the only adults of consequence in his life, that he was genuinely mature. After a whole thirty seconds, he glumly said, "Buddy, I don't have any ideas."

"Hmm, let me think about this." After a minute that seemed a lifetime to Joseph, Buddy chirped. "I have the answer! Eat the Biden Bar you saved for the orphanage."

"I can't!" exclaimed Joseph, "I promised I would save it. I don't want to lie to my mom."

"Kid," replied Buddy, "may I ask you a question?"

"Sure."

"Did you promise your mom because you wanted to or because she made you save the Biden Bar for the orphans?"

"She told me I have to save it."

"Listen," Buddy said as Joseph leaned forward, giving the thing in the closet his undivided attention. He continued his recitation. "If you promised to give away the chocolate bar without your mom pushing you to do it, I would agree. Joseph, I would tell you that as a man, you need to keep your word. Yes, sirree! But you didn't. Your mother pushed you into the promise. Those kind don't count."

The idea was such a revelation to the eleven-year-old that Buddy could almost see a light bulb turn on above the boy's head. "Buddy, you're *soooo* right!"

A modest chuckle emanated from the darkened closet. "I do what I can, kid. I do what I can."

"Buddy, does it have to be that Biden Bar?"

"Afraid so, Kid, afraid so."

"Buddy," queried Joseph, "does it have to be that candy bar because it has special powers?"

"Get a grip, Kid," replied Buddy, "it's a candy bar."

"Oh."

"But you know," Buddy said, elongating the third word, "I can see where you're coming from. It does have the power to show the world you're an adult. So, like a wizard's wand, it only works if used by a special person."

The thing could see the finish line in sight; he was almost there. The boy's last line of defense was in view, the one he relished breaking the most. It knew he was about to breach Joseph's final redoubt; he just needed to push the right button - pride.

"Buddy," Joseph said, "my mom said that if I ate that candy bar, I would grow up to be selfish."

"You will not be selfish! Did you or your mom trick-or-treat tonight?"

"I did."

"Once the person gave you the candy, did you say thank you?

"Yes," Joseph answered immediately.

"They gave you a good treat. Did you then play a trick on the person?"

"No!" the boy retorted indignantly.

"Then," replied Buddy, "you earned that chocolate fair and square. Your mother could have picked any other piece of candy, even another Biden Bar; why do you think she didn't allow you, the rightful owner, to decide which treat to give?"

Joseph had a blank expression, trying to comprehend all the words that had just traveled across the darkened room.

Buddy didn't give the boy time to answer the question. "Joseph, young man, if you eat that candy bar, you surely will not become selfish. Your mother knows that on the day you eat it, you will become *as* an adult, making your own decisions and controlling what is yours. So the only thing left is for you to decide whether or not you want to become an adult or stay a little boy."

Joseph walked to the dresser and picked up the Biden Bar, staring at the former vice-president's smiling face. He even read the ingredients. The wrapper was smooth but not slick. *Funny*, he thought, *I never realized how good it felt.* He carefully removed it and peeled back the gold-tinted foil of his chocolate idol.

"Joseph," Buddy said from behind him, "is tonight when you grow up?'

Seeing how good the candy bar looked and knowing how delicious it tasted, he took a bite.

"Don't hurry, young adult; enjoy your treat. You *earned* every bite."

Joseph finished and turned around; he didn't see Buddy. "Now what?" He asked.

"Well," replied Buddy, reflectively. He had retreated out of sight, back into the dark closet. "On cold nights like this, adults like to light the fireplace and curl up on the couch with a book. But, you are probably not ready for that."

"I am, too," Joseph petulantly replied.

"Then go enjoy yourself, remember to read an adult book. It will impress your mother and father."

"You got it! And Buddy?"

"Yes?"

"Thanks."

"No problem, now go show the world the man you've become."

Joseph tiptoed downstairs, past his parent's and little sister's rooms to the family room, at the front of the house. The next day was Saturday, and he wanted to impress his family when they saw he had built a fire and was reading an adult book. Not knowing what grown-ups read, he grabbed a dictionary. *Yeah*, Joseph thought, *this will impress the hell out of them*.

Joseph threw a match on the kindling and watched as the fire steadily took hold. He curled up on the couch, just like he had seen his mother do, and started reading. The boy did an admirable job, making it to the word *action* before dozing off.

***

The night passed, and Joseph began dreaming of smoke. The nightmare seemed so real that his lungs hurt. He coughed yet couldn't quite reach consciousness. He felt strong hands grip him and lift him off the couch. He opened his eyes to see flames everywhere.

Joseph heard his sister screaming, crying in fear. He tried to tell the man his sister was in the house, his parent's too, but he could only cough, the acrid smell of smoke silencing his voice, leaving his desperation mute. He struggled to explain to the man with the mask on his face and oxygen tank on his back that he had to drop him and rescue his family. To his horror, Joseph couldn't get the words out.

Then he was laid on a cot, and a plastic mask covered his small face, pumping air into lungs that felt searing pain. The firefighters fought hard. Still, the conflagration was too intense, and further rescue was desperately, heartbreakingly, futile. Joseph overheard the firefighters talking, thinking the boy was out of earshot.

Crying, one of them said, "I tried, but I couldn't reach the rest of them." With that, the man broke down, sobbing.

His partner placed an arm around him and said, "Carl, you saved the boy. You saved a life tonight."

The man nodded, even as he continued to weep. "If the boy hadn't been on the couch just inside the front door, he wouldn't have made it either."

Carl looked at his partner and said, "Dan, I think I know where the fire started. They were using the fireplace, but no one had shut the screen. It must have somehow spread and worked its way up inside the walls."

Joseph laid on the cot but didn't listen to the rest of the conversation. Neither did he hear the kind words the paramedic spoke. His brain wouldn't have allowed him to take notice, even if he had wanted; the memory of his sister's screams rang like clarion bells inside of his mind.

***

Joseph lay on a single-sized bed, constructed of a steel frame and stiff steel springs. His bed was the same as the other nineteen beds in the boy's dormitory. His bedding consisted of a thin mattress, a pillow, two heavy-duty sheets, and a thick, wool blanket. He lay on his back, silently crying as he looked at the orphanage ceiling, painted in a dull, eggshell color.

At that moment, Joseph didn't feel very old or mature. He desperately wanted to tell his mother that she was right; he had a good life. The boy wanted to be held and rocked by his mom but knew he would never see her, or his dad, or sister, ever again. He knew he had killed his family.

The authorities brought no charges against an eleven-year-old boy in what was an accident. Still, Joseph's aunts and uncles knew he was the cause of his family's death. Each of them had their own Buddy, whether acknowledged or not, whispering that to take him into their homes meant their demise. None offered to take custody of the broken little boy, so he became a ward of the state.

As Joseph, the orphan suffered in the arms of crushing

grief, from underneath the bed, he felt two good-natured pokes in his back and an all too familiar voice whisper,

"Hey kid, that was some candy bar."

The Resurrected Atheist

The pounding became more insistent. There was a sense of dogged urgency in the sound of the fist knocking on the door. An older woman slowly walked to the spot of the disturbance. Her movements were glacial in speed. Her arthritis, and health in general, had worsened since her husband's death. She finally reached the source of her annoyance. She opened the door and almost received a blow to the top of her head from a fist intended for the door.

The man stopped his arm in mid-swing, missing the woman's head by two inches. The woman looked at her almost accidental assailant. He was approximately 6' 2", a good foot taller than she was. He had a full head of wispy blonde hair, very blue eyes, and a sheepish look on his face. With him was a woman of apparent Latin-American descent. She had mocha skin, brown eyes and was only about an inch or two taller than herself.

Silence pervaded for a short two seconds before the unintentional host spoke. “Well, a Viking and a Mayan at the same time. The variety God brings to my door never ceases to amaze me. Come in; I guess my dishes can wait a few minutes longer.”

“Mrs. Margaret Gillespie, I am Agent Michelle Rodriquez, and he is Agent Anton Subby.”

“Agents, huh? Are you here about the marijuana growing out back?”

“Mrs. Gillespie!” Agent Rodriguez gasped, clearly surprised.

“What kind?” Agent Subby asked with interest.

“Shut up, Subby!” barked Rodriguez.

“Margaret Gillespie winked then said, “I’ll show you later.”

“No, Mrs. Gillespie, we are agents from the Center for Disease Control. We want to talk to you about your husband.”

“He’s dead,” the old woman replied tersely, her mood quickly turning dark. “Thanks to the CDC and that cursed virus, my Jeremy wasn’t even allowed a decent funeral. Just two men in hazmat suits shoving him in his coffin and burying him before the ink on his death certificate was dry.”

“Mrs. Gillespie,” said Subby, “surely you must understand why they had to handle your husband’s remains in such a manner. The H1N1 virus had mutated into a strain with features never before seen. The virus developed two extra receptors. It became J2H1N1. It is truly a marvel of evolution."

"There is no such thing as evolution," replied Mrs. Gillespie. "We were made from God and descended from Adam and Eve. Death wouldn't have entered this world if they had not disobeyed God."

"Now, Mrs. Gillespie, you surely don't believe in such…."

But Rodriguez cut him off with a glare. It was apparent to Margaret that Rodriguez was in charge. She also had better people skills.

"Mrs. Gillespie," Rodriguez stated, "we do not wish to argue theology. What you believe is your business. We come because we have a favor to ask of you. It is a big favor."

"What do you want?"

Agent Rodriguez felt her stomach tighten. She was the supervising agent; still, she wished she could hand this off to Anton. "We want to exhume your husband's body."

Surprised by request, her green eyes widened, and her mouth involuntarily frowned. It was evident to both agents Mrs. Gillespie was having difficulty mentally processing Rodriguez's appeal. Finally, appearing no closer to resolving her mental gridlock, she asked, "Why on earth would you want to do that?"

"The virus," said Subby, "has certain preservative powers. J2H1N1 dies, like many other pathogens, upon the death of its' host. We have found, however, that the evol… I mean, the mutation, while killing the host, also appears to preserve the structural integrity of the cell, including its DNA."

"Huh?"

"What he means, Mrs. Gillespie is for reasons we don't yet understand, a specific strain of the virus will kill a person, yet also, to a remarkable degree, preserve the body after death. "

Agent Subby interjected with a devilish grin. "Yeah, because of the way it preserves its host, they have nicknamed it the *Trophy Virus*."

"Are you saying you can bring my husband back to life?"

"Oh no, Mrs. Gillespie, what Agent Subby and I are saying is that this virus can preserve human remains to an uncanny degree. It kills the host not by destroying cells but by blocking their ability to function. Once dead, the virus dies, leaving the cell intact. If we could somehow discover how to repeat this process, we might be able to use it to allow doctors to treat patients without fear of damaging the area around the wound."

Rodriguez's exuberance was beginning to show.

Margaret watched as the agent's eyes shined, and her hands spun about, moving in an irregular cycle of going far from one another, then quickly coming back together. It was clear to Margaret that this project was vital to her.

"Mrs. Gillespie," continued Rodriguez, "your husband's remains could help us unlock secrets that may revolutionize the treatment of scourges, such as heart disease and cancer."

Margaret placed her hand over her heart. The woman was slightly shaking. Filled with emotion, she said, "Jeremy always loved the verse: *And we know that God causes everything to work together for the good of those who love God and are called according to his purpose for them.* Romans chapter eight, verse twenty-eight, New Living Translation."

"But, of course," said Subby with a grin.

"I like you, Agent Pothead."

***

They were driving back to the CDC regional office in Cleveland, heading east on the Ohio turnpike. Behind them, the sun was setting a bright red, very different than its usual orange.

Agent Subby pulled a ripe tomato out of a large paper bag and scowled. "That old woman lied to me."

Rodriguez started laughing. After Mrs. Gillespie prayed about her decision for half an hour, she consented. She then took Subby and Rodriguez to her backyard. Subby was looking for marijuana plants. All they saw were tomatoes. Mrs. Gillespie looked at Subby and, with a wicked smile, had said, "Sorry, Agent Subby, I must have given all my marijuana to the Ladies Missionary Society. I guess you'll have to settle for late summer tomatoes."

"Damn, Anton, are you that stupid?" Replied Rodriguez. "She's a Fundamentalist Christian. She made us wait while she prayed and talked to her minister before she consented to allow us to exhume his body. She doesn't do drugs and probably doesn't drink. What did you expect?"

"More than tomatoes. Then the old woman made that snide remark, telling me to call her if I had any problems fitting them into the bong."

With that memory, Rodriguez laughed so hard she swerved their car, almost hitting one of the turnpike's endless orange barrels.

***

The body of Jeremy Gillespie lay on an eight-foot-long, stainless steel table. His corpse, divested of all clothing, looked somehow odd to Rodriguez. The even lines of a farmer's tan showed where his t-shirt had protected his skin from the sun's rays. She was fascinated that even the melanin remained in the skin.

"The damn guy looks as if he is just sleeping," commented Subby, with a combination of awe and disgust. It was the first time he had seen a J2H1N1 victim in person. The giddy, recitative mood in which he calmly explained the virus to Mrs. Gillespie was gone. It had become authentic to him.

"That damn guy, as you put it," snapped Dr. Craven, "is to be treated and spoken of with respect. Do you understand Agent Subby?"

"Yes, Sir," was all the junior agent could get out. Edmund Craven had a reputation for skewering people. He was old school in the extreme.

Each person followed Craven's instructions and, dressed in medical attire, intended to protect someone from MRSA. Gowns, masks, latex gloves, head covering, and protective eyewear were the order of the day. As the field agents assigned to "retrieve" the specimen, they were on hand to answer any questions Dr. Craven or his assistant, Wes King, might have during the autopsy.

"Hey, Doc," asked Subby, "what do I do if I need to use the restroom?"

"Piss yourself," was Dr. Craven's only reply. Rodriguez could see the smirk even under the pathologist's mask.

With anxiety in her voice, Rodriguez asked, "Dr.

Craven, is this level of precaution sufficient to protect us from the virus? Previously, every time I worked with J2H1N1 patients, the protocol required a Hazmat suit.

"Are you questioning my judgment or that of the CDC?"

"No, Sir, but I am, as the Supervising Agent on this case, responsible for Agent Subby's safety."

"Not to worry, Agent Rodriguez, I have already run a viral scan as well as a blood culture. The virus is as dead as Mr. Gillespie."

"Doctor," she asked, "what can you tell us about the state of decompensation?"

"What I can tell you is that there is none. I have run the man through a CT scan, an MRI, about a billion x-rays, and a massive battery of lab work. There is simply nothing, aside from normal wear and tear of a man in his late fifties, wrong with this man."

"Are you going to open him up?" Asked Subby.

"Yes, eventually, but I want to try something first. The human body, like a lot of life, performs many functions through electro-chemical processes. We need a certain amount of electricity. I want to test his body's ability to transmit electricity."

"Why test that?" Asked Rodriguez.

"Two reasons," replied Craven. "First, to see if the virus damaged the electrical pathways. Second, to see if the virus preserves them to the degree that they may be useful in such things as organ transplants. Mr. Gillespie was a southpaw. I am going to place electrodes into that hand. I will send electricity to see if there is any response. The procedure is very much like how to test for carpal tunnel."

"Except what is ailing this guy is a hell of a lot worse than carpal tunnel," interjected Subby.

"You are going to test to see if his fingers and hand moves?" Rodriguez asked, clearly stunned.

"Agent Rodriguez. . . Michelle, if we don't push forward, the spiel you gave Mrs. Gillespie about possibly saving lives is just that, a spiel. We must begin to unlock the secrets and possibilities of this virus. Wes, get me the electrodes."

Twenty minutes later, they were all hovering over the left hand of Jeremy Gillespie. Dr. Craven had inserted the electrodes and was about to flip the switch.

"Dr. Craven," Rodriguez nearly shouted, "Mr. Gillespie has been dead for over three and a half years. Could this experiment possibly burn his flesh?"

"Agent Rodriguez!" snapped Craven. His face was flush with a wave of anger that both she and Subby could see bordered on rage. "I am the chief pathologist in this case and the study as a whole. My decisions are the ones that count. Shut your damn mouth and take my directions, or I will toss your ass out of those doors. Not another word out of either of you two unless Wes or I ask for it. Do you understand me?"

"Yes, Doctor," Subby said meekly.

With a strong sense of discomfort, Rodriguez nodded and said, "Yes, Doctor."

Intellectually, she knew it was just flesh and bones. She had seen hundreds of experiments conducted on dozens of corpses. Still, something in her gut said this was different.

"And for your information," said Craven. "Mr. Gillespie has been dead for three years, seven months, and fourteen days. The electrodes are low amps and should not burn his tissue. Wes, make sure the videotape is running."

Craven gave a quick, last examination of the electrodes, then, without turning, said, "Wes, hit it." The assistant moved a dial to the setting he wanted, then flipped the switch.

Almost immediately, the hand contracted to form a fist. All four stared mesmerized for what seemed like forever. Then the silence was broken by Craven's voice, "Wes, cut the juice."

He complied, and the hand relaxed. Quiet returned to the room. Craven shook his head in disbelief. It was evident by the surprised look on his face he was checking off a box. He never actually thought the electrical pathways were still intact.

Craven gave the order, and Wes repeated the experiment. Once again, the hand contracted. He told the assistant to turn off the connection. They started talking when he turned back to the hand. “Damn it, Wes! I told you to turn off the juice.”

“I… did,” was Wes’s startled reply. They watched as the hand continued to flex back and forth.

“Quick, damn it! Wes, get the epinephrine and the oxygen now! You two, get the EKG machine that’s against the wall.”

“What the hell for?” Asked Subby.

“Because I told you, Asshole,” was Craven’s scathing reply. “We’re going to see if the heart can react the same way.” He said all this while rushing to place the connectors of the EKG on Gillespie’s chest. Craven looked at King and said, “This might be the breakthrough we have been looking for in heart attack victims.”

Wes, clearly shaken, brought the adrenaline to Craven. As the assistant was standing beside the body, the hand contracted around his surgical gown. He gave a high-pitched scream and yelled, “Get it off me! Tell that damn thing to turn loose!”

“He’s dead, Wes,” Craven said disgustedly. “What the hell do you want me to do? Un-pry his hand and get that tube into his right lung. I want there to be an oxygen supply.”

Wes' pathetic look was enough to jerk Rodriguez into action. She ran to his aid. She pulled Gillespie's fingers back, releasing their grip on the assistant's gown. The digits were ice cold. She couldn't mentally process what she was seeing and now feeling. *Dear God*, she thought, *can it get any worse?* She was about to discover the answer was yes.

She heard a slight hissing sound and realized it was oxygen going into the corpse's lung. Wes had recovered his senses and had expertly snaked the oxygen tube into place. *Snaked*, thought Rodriguez, teetering on the edge of control. *Ha, a hissing sound, snaked. They're trying to resuscitate a three-year-old corpse, and I made a pun. Comedy Central, where are you when we need you?*

She stood back, next to Subby, who was even paler than his Nordic skin warranted. Wes quickly cleaned Gillespie's chest area with disinfectant. The syringe was coming down as the assistant pulled the swab away - missing their intersection by a tenth of a second, at most. Craven punctured the heart's left ventricle with the precision of countless previous attempts made as a battlefield trauma surgeon. She was vaguely aware of a bell going off. It was a flatline heart alarm. She distantly heard Craven scream at Wes, "Turn that off!"

Suddenly there was a beep sound on the cardio monitor. Craven turned to his assistant. "Let's see if we can get a normal rhythm. Paddles." Wes squeezed the gel out of a tube and onto one of the defibrillators and hit the charge button. Craven quickly rubbed the paddles together to spread the gel. "Wes, if we get a normal sinus rhythm, start the timer. I want to see how many seconds before total cardiac failure."

"Got it, Doc."

The alarm indicated the defibrillator was fully charged. Craven yelled, "Clear!" It was more from habit than a necessity; no one else was anywhere near the body. The paddles no more than touched his skin when he triggered the charge. Jeremy Gillespie spasmed violently, his upper torso contorted. Rodriguez had seen defibrillators used on television, yet never in life. She was stunned by the violence of the event. Suddenly, there was a beep, followed by another and another. The heart was beating at a regular rate.

Craven was smiling broadly. Wes flipped on a timer. "Wes, damn it, boy, we did it. Hopefully, we can keep a normal rhythm for over a minute."

Then came a sound that no one expected. Dr. Craven's eyes expanded to an incredible size. The corpse did the impossible. It inhaled a breath. It blew the air out, then took in another. Subby turned away and pulled his mask down just in time to vomit. Then Gillespie's face scrunched while the jaw stretched its muscles. Michelle felt unsure on her feet. Her eyesight turned gray. Just before she lost consciousness, she heard Jeremy Gillespie gag on the air tube.

***

"How can this be? How can this be?" Anton Subby kept repeating the question. Rodriguez had the impression he was halfway asking himself, halfway asking the air, and one hundred percent traumatized.

Michelle sat next to him, bent over in an identical plastic torture chair for which hospitals are infamous. She was holding a hospital ice bag to her forehead, a nice size lump forming where her head hit the floor. Although quiet, she felt no less rattled than the junior agent. Visions of multiple incarnations of Frankenstein's monster were dancing and weaving in her head.

Craven had directed them to a private waiting room in a secure portion of the hospital. Staff arrived a few minutes later and unceremoniously stripped them of their protective garments and gave them the cold compress and a little bottle of mouthwash. Through the small, mesh-enforced window, Rodriguez could see nurses and physicians running up and down the hallway. With her head pounding, she slowly rose from her chair, curious to see what was going on, assuming Mr. Gillespie was the source of the commotion. Michelle began formulating the most likely scenario: He was alive yet brain damaged beyond all but basic neural commands. He was being kept alive as a guinea pig to advance God knows what.

Trying to turn the doorknob, she found it locked. Noticing a pad on the wall to the right of the door, she stopped looking out the door window to examine it. It looked like a credit card scanner seen in almost any store. Only this swipe pad verified employees by their identification cards. The light emanating from it was red, no doubt indicating the door's locked status.

With the realization of her confinement, Rodriguez began to panic, temporarily forgetting her headache. Her mind began to race. Rapid, shallow breaths were distorting her vision, causing her to perceive the walls were coming together. She tasted fear, like a copper penny, in her mouth. She was pounding on the door and yelling for someone to open it brought no response. No one even turned their head to check out the source of the commotion. Studying the room, she discovered padding – it was soundproof.

Leaning against the door, Rodriguez closed her eyes, exhaling a deep breath, forcing herself to relax. The pain in her head returned, a throbbing reminder of her fall. Looking for a place to relax, she saw Anton, seemingly oblivious to her outburst, had by this time moved to a semi-comfortable couch, pushed against a wall, laying with his back turned to her. *Bastard,* Rodriguez thought, realizing the only alternative left to the hard chairs was an old recliner. Despite its age, she was pleasantly surprised, finding it comfortable and, more than that, comforting. Leaning back and rolling onto her side, she curled up and fell asleep.

"Get your asses up," came a terse voice. "Rodriguez, it seems every time I see you today, you are unconscious. Subby, how is your stomach?"

"Better, Sir."

Grinning, Craven gave them an appreciative nod. "I can't blame you two. If I hadn't seen the shit I did in Iraq and Afghanistan, I probably would have puked and crapped myself, then passed out for good measure. I helped bring back soldiers I was certain were dead. Hell, we had even triaged some of them as hopeless. But I admit this one takes the cake. No one has ever been brought back after this long. Hell, Jesus was only in the tomb for three days. His injuries, though, if the stories are correct, were catastrophic. Lazarus beat him in length by a day, but Jesus pulled strings on that one, so I'll call it a push."

"I had no idea you were so religious," Rodriguez said.

"I never said I was religious," he snapped. "I am versed in the Bible because my parents were very devout. As a boy, my parents required me to attend church, Sunday school, youth group. When I turned sixteen, they added Wednesday Bible study. When I left for college, I left my well-worn Bible on my bedroom desk and never opened it again. Well, except. . ." his face showed grief, "my dad had written a letter, and my mom gave it to me after he died. He asked me to read, from that Bible, some of the Psalms at his funeral. In all the long years between college and his death, my parents never moved it."

Craven seemed lost in thought, yet only for a couple of seconds. Rodriguez had known him for years and understood he was too disciplined to remain in nostalgia or regret. With a nod of his head toward the door, he started walking in its direction, pulling out the identification card, which hung on a lanyard from under his lab coat. Rodriguez and Subby stood, rooted to their spots. "Well, haul your asses," he barked at them. "You want to see our patient, don't you?"

The three of them rode the elevator to the fifteenth floor. Craven had to use his access card to reach that secure area. Trying to steel herself for almost any scene, Rodriguez was still finding it hard to keep her emotions under control.

Dear God, she thought, wiping away cold sweat from her forehead, *how could we be doing this? Studying reflexes and heart functions is one thing, yet keeping this thing alive is an abomination against not only God but nature itself.* She closed her mouth and breathed exclusively through her nose. It was the only thing she could think to do to keep from vomiting. Still, Michelle knew Craven was a dog that had found a bone; he was not going to stop chewing.

Subby walked with purpose. His initial shock and disgust had given way to a quiet firmness. *I'm not puking again,* he thought with a sense of shame. *This resuscitation is the opportunity to be a part of one of the most significant events in history: studying a reanimated corpse. I'm going to ride this wave right into the history books.*

***

Walking into the room, she found the scene just what she imagined; a man hooked to tubes. Several nurses were moving about Mr. Gillespie, taking vials of blood and monitoring vital signs. One nurse was collecting urine from a bag connected to his catheter. Meanwhile, in the corner of the room, Wes was engaged in an animated discussion with a man.

"What the hell is the matter?" Craven yelled. Red spots were forming on his face.

"Dr. Craven," Wes half screamed, obviously very hot

under the collar, "the dietician has calculated the calorie and nutrient requirements, but Dr. Wessel refuses to insert the feeding tube into Mr. Gillespie's stomach.

"Dr. Wessel, why are you not doing as instructed?" There was a spurious calmness to Craven's voice. He was giving the gastrologist a professional courtesy, a chance to capitulate or make his case. Michelle knew from long, painful experience it better be a damn good argument. It wasn't.

"Edmund, damn it, he's dead! You want me to put a feeding tube into a corpse. The CDC buried it over forty-two months ago. It's sick! It's an abomination against God, trying to keep something alive that's meant to be dead."

"Pious bastard, don't you talk to me of God. I don't give a damn about what you think, and I sure as hell don't give a shit about God! That tube is either going down his throat or around yours, but one way or the other, it will be put to good use."

Closing his eyes, Craven took a deep breath and held it for what seemed to Rodriguez an eternity before slowly exhaling. She had no doubt he learned the relaxation technique while working on combat soldiers.

"Dr. Wessel," Craven said, obviously calmer, "this study could eventually save countless lives. We need you on this team, and we need you to understand that we all must push through our moral qualms. We are not harming anyone. Still, time is of the essence. We need this information before his heart stops. This body is the only one that has shown no signs of decay. This man may be our best, only chance to study the effects of this strain of the virus."

Realizing the gravity and opportunity of the situation, Wessel began preparing the feeding tube. After completing the task, he turned to Craven. "In a few days, if Mr. Gillespie's functions continue, we will need to revisit the tube placement."

"I will make a note of that. And, Dr. Wessel, if you need information or a medical consult, your peers at the CDC will be at your disposal."

Wessel, obviously still uncomfortable, nodded, handed Craven his business card, and said, "if needed, you can contact me at this number. I will recheck the tubing and flow in two hours." He left without waiting for a response.

Dr. Wessel had not left the room ten seconds when the neurologist, Dr. Mazell, entered. Rodriguez thought this to be fortunate. It cut short an uncomfortable silence that was beginning to descend. She thought the nurses were lucky, despite their obvious distaste. They were swamped. She, on the other hand, had time to step back and look at the bigger picture.

Dr. Mazell looked around, confused, then focused her

attention on Craven. "Dr. Craven, I was instructed to perform an EEG and neurologic examination. There must be some mistake; the order said I was to administer these tests on a corpse. At first, I thought it was a joke, and then I saw your name undersigned the order."

"Dr. Mazell, the orders are not a mistake, and they are not a joke. Our cadaver is in that bed."

"That man is not dead. He looks close; still, he sure as hell isn't there yet. You want me to administer these tests right after expiration?"

"No, I want you to perform them right now. Wes will help you administer the EEG. I want you to read the results right here, and I want to know the brain function immediately. Chop, chop Deborah, I want these tests done before he likely expires, again."

Mazell, looking even more confused, began directing Wes where to place the electrodes. Within five minutes, the EEG was printing the brainwave activity. The neurologist read the results with an emotionless demeanor Craven admired. Turning to him, she said, "Mr. Gillespie's EEG results are normal, so was the cursory exam of his reaction to physical stimuli. The brain activity looks like someone who is coming out of very deep sleep."

Craven started laughing hard. When he finished, he had tears rolling down his face. Mazell didn't grasp the significance of her statement. All but the neurologist understood the irony of her words. "Deborah, this man is coming out of a sleep that has lasted years and been as deep as it can get."

"If you tell me the details of his trauma or illness, I might be able to give you a reference as to his prognosis."

"Here are the details, Deb; he was dead."

"If his tests are any indication, they quickly revived hin."

"No, he wasn't. Jeremy Gillespie died of J2H1N1 over three and a half years ago. After death, the Center for Disease Control placed his body into a coffin and dropped it into a vault below the ground. Then, less than seventy-two hours ago, we exhumed his body."

"That's impossible. Don't screw with me."

"Deborah, I swear to its truth. You are looking at the results of the virus. Perfect, and I mean *perfect* preservation. We are reintroducing gastric bacteria, but he should otherwise be fine. Your results were the next to last piece in the puzzle. The only question remaining is, how much of his memory remains intact?"

Mazell found herself staring at her most unusual patient, mesmerized by the thought he had crossed the ultimate veil, then returned. Suddenly, Gillespie's eyes opened, causing her and Craven to rush to him. Wild confusion filled his face, and then they locked on Craven. The disorientation left, replaced with a conscious recognition of another person. Leaning over him, Craven stared into his patient's face, smiling.

"Mr. Gillespie, I am Dr. Craven. You can rest easy. You have had a rough time, but you are doing much better. The nurse is going to give you something to relax."

Gillespie started moving his mouth, trying through the tubes and years, to speak. Then came a single, hoarse word, spoken low yet with immense meaning, affirming a remembrance of his former life. In a single word, Mr. Gillespie completed the puzzle. He said, "Margaret."

***

Mrs. Gillespie opened the door and almost caught a fist on the nose. She looked at Rodriguez and Subby with a reluctance that betrayed a slight annoyance. "What is it with you people and doors? At least it was the short one this time." She turned and started walking toward the living room. As she walked, she sighed and motioned them to follow. "Let me guess; Agent Subby couldn't get his bong to light."

They all sat drinking tea. The moment was somber. It was silent for ten minutes before Margaret, her face turning blush, snapped out, "Good Lord, just spit out whatever brought you back to my door."

Rodriguez and Subby looked at each other, then turned

to face Mrs. Gillespie. “Mrs. Gillespie, we would like to tell you about your husband.”

“What is it?”

“Mrs. Gillespie, Agent Subby, and I were present for the autopsy. Given Mr. Gillespie’s condition, The CDC decided to run a series of tests that are, frankly, unheard of in a normal autopsy.”

It took Margaret a great deal of strength to keep her composure. “It doesn’t matter,” She said casually, trying to convince herself, as much as her guests, that she didn’t care. “He’s not here.”

“That’s just it,” Rodriguez said. “He *is* here.”

Margaret stopped her teacup just as she was bringing it to her lips. She lowered it thoughtfully. “What do you mean, he’s here?”

“Mrs. Gillespie. The virus killed your husband but died as well. It preserved his body perfectly. And as far as we can tell, your husband’s body was in a healthy condition for a man in his fifties.”

“What do you mean, he’s here?!” Margaret almost screamed. Her face had gone from blush to crimson.

“Mrs. Gillespie. We wanted to know how preserved different parts of his body remained. We wanted to determine if any of your husband’s functions might still work. They all worked extremely well. Mrs. Gillespie, they resuscitated your husband. He is alive.”

Margaret Gillespie's face went from red to white, with those last three words. "So, you're keeping him alive, but he is brain dead?"

"No, Mrs. Gillespie, his brain works just fine. Your name was the first word he spoke."

"You are telling me my husband - my Jeremy - spoke?"

"Yes, Ma'am," Rodriguez answered.

Mrs. Gillespie put her hand to the collar of her dress. The fingers absently played with the buttons. Her mouth was open but not agape. She had turned her head slightly away from them, but it appeared to have less to do with her conscious desire and, instead, the depth of her thoughts carrying her head that way.

Subby started to say something then stopped. He couldn't imagine what this woman was going through. Her loved one's absence had easily eclipsed all biblical resurrections combined. And while one could argue those raisings, this one couldn't. The U.S. government currently housed Jeremy Gillespie in a medical facility operated by the United States Center for Disease Control. It occurred to him the Buckeye state had become the empty tomb. He and Rodriguez were the angels telling Mary Magdeline of Jesus' resurrection. As he expected, this modern-day Mary did what her counterpart did two thousand years ago; she ran to the people of God. Margaret went to the phone to spread the news.

Rodriguez reached Mrs. Gillespie before she could finish dialing on her old landline. Laying a soft hand on top of hers, she asked a delicate question. “Mrs. Gillespie, who do you intend to notify?”

“Why, Reverend Miller, of course. He and Jeremy were best friends.”

“How discreet is this Reverend Miller?”

“He is a man of God, held to a higher standard than you or me.” She saw the bewildered look on the agent’s faces. “They will look but not see. They will hear, yet not understand,” she said to herself. “Reverend Miller has listened to decades of scandals, confessions, and accusations. He probably knows more about this town than your NSA, and yet, I have never heard him say a word.”

“Mrs. Gillespie, please don’t divulge information until he is here and has signed a non-disclosure form.”

She stared at the agents keenly. “You know the people do not trust the government. That might have started about the time the government stopped trusting the people. I will call him. I will also say nothing but to come here.”

“Unbelievable. Margaret, it is nothing short of incredible.” The Reverend Robert Miller finished his sentence, then shook his head. “If ever there was a man, other than our Lord, to bring back to us, it is Jeremy Gillespie. Agents, if only you knew the kind of man

Jeremy was, I mean is, you would realize the magnitude of this blessing.

"Reverend, I believe you mean brought back, not given back."

"No, Agent Subby, I mean given back."

"Reverend, with all due respect, God didn't bring Jeremy Gillespie back to life. It was a timely, farsighted medical service, expertly delivered by a coroner with years of battlefield experience as a trauma surgeon. It was a concurrence of random events that led to the procedures. If you want to thank someone or thing, thank science."

Rodriguez's face twisted in anger. "Shut up, Agent Subby, that's an order!"

Quiet pervaded the room. Agent Subby spoke. "Reverend, Mrs. Gillespie, I want to apologize for my outburst. It was conceited. I ask for your forgiveness."

"It's okay, Son. Let's not argue with Aquinas about how many angels can fit on the end of a pin. Nor should we act like skunks."

Subby looked confused by the last sentence. The reverend smiled. "Let's not try to out - piss each other."

Subby just smiled back.

Margaret asked, "when do we get to see him?"

"There is a seven pm press conference scheduled for tomorrow. The two of you need to pack your things. A man from the CDC is already on his way from Cleveland.

I will notify him of Reverend Miller. He will be here in about seventy minutes. He will drive both of you to the facility just east of Cleveland. Roughly a two-hour, fifteen-minute drive, not counting stops. We figured of stopping at the turnpike stop between Fremont and Sandusky and the one in Lorain County."

"Agent Rodriguez," Margaret asked, "you don't think I can go the entire trip without using the restroom?"

Rodriguez felt herself blush. "I am sorry, I just assumed, with your age. I didn't mean any disrespect."

"Well, you're right. Trying to go over two hours without peeing would be torture." She emphatically shook her head. "I'd be floating my uppers."

Subby laughed so hard he dropped his smartphone in mid-text.

***

Rodriguez introduced Margaret and Robert to Dr. Craven. "Mrs. Gillespie, Reverend Miller, thank you for coming on short notice. About this time tomorrow, I, I mean the CDC, will be announcing Mr. Gillespie's resuscitation. It is bluntly one of the two or three most incredible events in human history."

"We are not going to release personal information, but Mr. Gillespie might. If you haven't already, you might consider relocation. I have contacted the FBI. They are prepared to enter you into the witness protection program. I can't imagine there will be any normalcy if you were to return home." The weight of Craven's words only added to the pressure the two were experiencing. Craven immediately regretted mentioning that aspect of the resurrection. "Of course, we can all discuss this later."

"Excuse me, Dr. Craven." It was Reverend Miller. "Margaret and I had a chance to discuss the spiritual ramifications of this, um, event."

Craven kept a neutral face only with effort. "What kind of spiritual ramifications, Reverend?"

"Doctor, Jeremy went home to the Lord years ago. We're worried Jeremy returned an empty shell. His body is working just fine, but his soul didn't return. Has he shown any sign of immoral behavior or demonic possession?"

"Mrs. Gillespie, Reverend Miller, the only spiritual activity I've observed is his request of a Bible."

They both quite audibly exhaled. Smiles and relief touched their features.

"As to behavior," Craven continued. "Mr. Gillespie was administered a full battery of psychological tests and has received an extensive observation for any sign of psychological or physiological issues. By all rights, Mrs. Gillespie, your husband, appears to be a pleasant, kind, and intelligent man. There is nothing to indicate he is any different than the person he was before the onset of his illness three and a half years ago."

After a short prayer, Margaret entered her husband's room. She went alone. She wanted to look upon him as she used to before he died. Her hands trembled.

She whispered to herself, "I can do this. But Lord, I am so afraid." She clenched her teeth, rounded the corner, and there he was, working on a jigsaw puzzle, a lake cabin. She thought, *how Jeremy*. He looked up; their eyes locked. They both burst into tears.

He stood up and started toward her. She took an involuntary step back. Fear etched on her face. But it was the pain on his that caused her to stop. She thought, *he is your husband, your lover, your soulmate. God has given you what He has given no other. Am I to reject this gift?* With that, she ran to him.

"I can't believe it is true. It is you."

"Margaret, I love you. You are on my mind from the time I wake until my head hits the pillow at night. I can't believe they brought me back. Unbelievable."

"We missed you, too. Honey, I have missed you so much since you…."

"Since I died. It is okay to say. Think of it as a medical team giving me CPR for a very long time, and it finally working." He smiled brightly. It was his smile. It was that mischievous yet good-natured smile of her husband. She fell in love with him all over again at that very moment.

They talked another half an hour, holding hands. Suddenly Margaret put a hand to her chest and said, "Good grief, Jeremy. Robert is waiting to see you."

"Bob, he's here?"

"Yes, my love. He came with me."

"They don't want me roaming the halls. Would you please get my friend?"

Five minutes later, Robert entered the room with Margaret. When he saw Jeremy, he stopped, rooted to one spot in stunned silence. He thought, *It's true. Despite everything, I didn't entirely believe it until now. Lord, please forgive my unbelief. I always wondered what disciple I most emulated. I am a lot less like Peter than I thought. I am much more akin to Thomas - the doubter.*

The man before the reverend had been an elder in the church. And more than that, his best friend. He noticed he had a healthy skin tone. None of the sickly pallor he had the last time he saw him through a transparent quarantine barrier.

Jeremy smiled broadly. "Robert Miller, as I live and breathe. Come here and greet your best friend."

Robert practically tripped, getting to the man he loved like a brother. They shook hands, smiling, then instinctually hugged. Bob noticed Jeremy felt warm, his muscles toned. The same man that helped repair the church and countless homes of those in need.

After talking for some time between the three of them, Jeremy asked, "Margaret, I have to ask you a question."

"Sure, my love."

"I wouldn't blame you if you have, but I have to know, did you remarry?"

"No, of course not, Silly. I had no interest in remarrying." Then, suddenly, Margaret stopped. She cocked her head like a dog might and looked at him.

Jeremy was caught off guard by his wife's sudden observation. He knew well enough it was a look that had generally preceded an argument. It was more disconcerting that Bob was also silently inspecting him. He was wracking his brain, trying to understand the sudden change in atmosphere when Margaret answered for him.

"What do you mean if I remarried?"

"Honey, I didn't mean to make you mad. But three and a half years is quite a while. I'm just saying I wouldn't want to interfere in your marriage. That is if you have a new husband. But, I would still like to remain, in some capacity, in your life."

"No, I haven't remarried. The bigger issue is why you didn't already know I wasn't remarried."

"Honey, nobody gave me any information other than you were alive and well. I think they were unsure, until recently, if I was going to stay alive. Then they were feeding me news, slowly. I see the Browns still haven't won a Super Bowl."

"Please, correct me, Margaret, if I'm wrong, but that's not the issue. Jeremy, what we both want to know is why you did not see this while you were in Heaven."

Jeremy slowly swallowed, then looked at his wife and best friend. "About that. Margaret, Bob, I wasn't in Heaven."

Margaret began to cry, and Bob's face became a mask of horror. "Dear God, my friend, what a blessing, released from Hell."

Margaret held him and wept. "Whatever sent you there, we will address it and ask our gracious Lord to forgive you."

He looked somberly at them. "Margaret. Robert, I wasn't in Hell either."

A look of profound confusion plastered their faces.

"Well, where else is there for the deceased?" Bob asked.

"Nowhere. Guys, there is no Heaven. There is no Hell."

Bob, shaken, exclaimed, "Margaret, his soul must still be in Heaven."

"No, listen to me; there was nowhere for me to exist. There was no light, and there was no dark. There was no pain; there was no pleasure. Trust me when I say there is only one thing waiting for us after death, oblivion.

Annihilation is what awaits us. But don't think of it as a bad thing. I was unaware of anything because there was no more Jeremy Gillespie. Only the random mutation of a virus kept my parts intact for science to revive."

"Think of it this way. We need no longer waste time trying to bring people to a god that isn't there for him to save their souls, which don't exist. We can spend our lives helping others without the trappings of religion. We now can see many things we used to consider as sins in the light of truth. We are the result of random evolutionary processes and the natural selection that helps shape us. We can be free."

"So, what," an angry Reverend Robert Miller said, "will keep you from killing, raping, and taking advantage of other people? How many women do you plan to have sex with?"

Margaret, who was quietly crying, started sobbing. "Is that it? You have come back, and you plan to screw as many women as possible? No guilt. Just do whatever feels good, no matter how I feel?"

"Margaret, honey, I wouldn't do that to you. I love you."

"Yeah?" she replied, "Without God, there is no morality in your life."

"That's not true. We've never had God in our lives because there is no God. We have all lived decent lives. Lives of service to others. Bob, *we* give our lives meaning. We don't need something other than ourselves to be moral. We can be good because it is good. No god required."

"Then why did you ask for the Bible?" Asked a disgusted Robert.

"Because I wanted to make sure. How many times did we discuss the Apostle Paul's words in his second letter to the church in Corinth? Chapter five, verse eight, clearly states that to be absent from the body is to be with God. I read and reread that verse and the entire letter to make sure I had the right context. Margaret, Robert, when we die, we will not be with the Lord. There is no Lord to be with."

Margaret, pointing to Jeremy, growled, "and what are we supposed to do? Should we give up our faith based on your testimony alone?"

"Honey, with all due respect, you're not going to find a better source."

Feeling sad, Margaret said. "I hurt so bad. When they told me you were alive and had asked for me, my heart leaped for joy. Now I am crushed. I should let you know; the kids are coming. They don't know anything. Bobby will be here tomorrow afternoon. He is doing mission work in Amsterdam. Kelly lives in Kentucky. She works at a creation museum. She is married. They have a son.

His name is Jeremy. You will have to break the news to them that the grave gave you time to hatch the idea to ditch God."

"I'm a grandpa?" Jeremy said, not hearing the latter part. "They named him after me. I can't wait to see them and then go home. How is the house? Are the gutters still leaking?"

"No, the damn gutters aren't leaking! I had them fixed. I have to think and pray. Goodnight."

"Please, Margaret, Bob, let's not end our first time together in years like this."

"I don't see why not," said Bob. "According to you, you didn't know a thing." With that, they walked out the door.

***

"Please, Kelly, let me hold him. I was able to hold both you and your brother without breaking either of you." His daughter, initially thrilled, became much cooler when her mother announced her father was now godless.

"That's not it, Dad, and you know it. I don't want an atheist polluting my baby's mind and soul."

Jeremy looked hurt and was near tears. "I can't believe all of you. The fact I am a reanimated corpse doesn't seem to be that big of a deal. But my saying I'm an atheist drives you practically to convulsions. I am still me. Please, Pumpkin, let me hold my grandson. I promise not to say a word about religion or God."

Reluctantly, Kelly handed her son over to her father.

"Well, hello, Jeremy. I'm your grandpa. I love you so much. I am so glad to be in your life."

Handing his treasure back to the child's mother, he cleared his throat. "Everyone, I want to apologize. I want to say I am sorry to you, Margaret especially, and you too, Bob. I came on strong last night, and I am sorry. I promise not to bring up the issue of religion or God in front of you again. Who am I to tell anyone what to believe? Margaret, I will support you in your faith. I will be supportive of all of you."

"I will support raising Jeremy in a Christian home. I won't discuss God with him. As for the press conference, I plan to stand front and center."

Bobby cried out. "Dad, people will recognize you."

"Son," said Jeremy wryly, "I think people will notice something is up when they see a guy they buried walking down the street. I think it's only right they get fair warning."

"I can't deny it," said Robert. "That sounds like the Jeremy I knew and loved."

***

At 7:05 pm, Dr. Craven, Wes King, and agents Rodriguez and Subby stepped into the Cleveland CDC Medical Facility press room. Subby held to his steely firmness while Rodriguez was nervous by the number of reporters on the podium's other side. She was most definitely more comfortable in the field.

"Ladies and Gentlemen of the fourth estate, I am Dr. Richard Craven. I am Chief Pathologist at Cleveland's Center for Disease Control Medical Facility. I was also the CDC's chief pathologist concerning the J2H1N1 outbreak four years ago." There was a murmur among the crowd.

"First, I want to assure you; there is no new sign of the virus. The news I want to present is connected to the virus but, fortunately, positively. As you undoubtedly know, the J2H1N1 virus was lethal, killing one hundred percent of its victims within forty-eight hours. What caught our attention were some of the properties in a sub-strain of the virus dubbed J2H1N1-D."

"It killed its victims like all other strains of the virus, but differently. It did not damage tissue. It simply blocked cells from performing their necessary functions. It died with the death of its host. The virus, upon death, decomposed quickly. The decayed virus released a chemical that preserved the corpses to an astonishing degree. We saw the possible medical benefits if we could decipher its process."

"There were few remaining corpses with this strain. Most of the victims required cremation to stop the spread of the disease. There were only four remaining corpses. We exhumed all four, with permission from the families. They were in an incredible state of preservation, even though no embalming had taken place. One corpse, however, stood out among the four. His body was in perfect preservation. Right down to his DNA."

"An autopsy began, but for soon-to-be obvious reasons stopped. The team performed certain, uhm unusual tests. Though dead for over three years, the corpse responded to electrical, then cardiac stimulation. We monitored his neurological and cardiac systems, curious how long they would function."

"Doctor," Bill Dodge of *The Times* chimed in. "How long before they failed?"

"They didn't."

"What do you mean?" the *Times* reporter asked.

"The cadaver is no longer a cadaver but a living organism."

There was an incredible buzz going on among the press.

"Doctor Craven, Mary Grossi Hammer of *The Dealer*.

Are you saying you have a brain-dead man in your care?"

"Not at all, Ms. Hammer. We have a fully functioning, healthy, and conscious man under our care. There is no brain damage. He is quite lucid, intelligent, funny, and retains his memories of life before his death."

Now, there was no sound in the press room, just blank stares. You could hear a pin drop.

Slowly, almost meekly, a reporter raised his hand. "Dr. Craven, Jerod Rizzo, of the *Herald*. What is this, uhm, man's name? Did he describe an afterlife? And when do we get to see him?"

"Mr. Rizzo, I am assuming you meant to ask three questions but asked four. You no doubt are asking what many people are and will ask, is this a man? The answer is an unequivocal yes. He is a man. Any thought otherwise is demeaning to him and what it means to be human."

"As for your other questions, this is what I can tell you; we were going to identify our subject - I mean our patient - as Lazarus II. If you want to know why there is a Roman number two after the name, read the Bible. The team working on this gentleman doesn't want him looked upon as a freak, an oddity to be stared at and scorned. We went as far as to contact the FBI to enter him into the witness protection program. He refused. He is insistent that he resume his former life."

"As to the afterlife, this is not our concern. Not once

have we, nor will we ask him about a possible afterlife. Our concern in this project has always been preserving life, not seeing what lies beyond it. I will turn the microphone over to the CDC Field Agent in charge, Michelle Rodriguez."

"I am Michelle Rodriguez. I, along with Agent Anton Subby, did the fieldwork in this case. Agent Subby and I approached the patient's wife, requesting the opportunity to study her husband's remains. In the interest of improving medical science, she reluctantly agreed. Never, and I mean never, did any of us foresee these events come to pass."

"In a moment, the patient will come to the microphone. He will read a brief statement and then, if he wishes, answer questions. He DOES NOT have to give you his name or any identifying information! Keep in mind that any disrespect shown by the members of the media will result in the press conference's termination. We will not allow this man to be bullied, harassed, or demeaned. With no further ado, I give you Lazarus II."

The press stares at a man that has stepped from around the corner and walked to the podium. He is sweating and nervous; his eyes are darting from the crowd to the medical team.

"Hello, my name is Jeremy Gillespie, or if you like, Lazarus II. If you are surprised, it's no more than me. I was the victim of… please give me a second; my heart is racing. Well," Jeremy said, laughing, "compared to a month ago, I guess that's a good thing."

The reporters started laughing, and that seemed to break the ice.

"You will find out about me, so I may as well tell you. I was fifty-eight years old at the time of my death, approximately forty-four months ago. I once lived and hope to reside once more in my hometown - Dawson City. I was married to my beautiful wife in 1989. I ask that you leave my family out of this matter. You will find the more you do this, the more receptive I will be to your inquiries. I will take a couple of questions."

"Mr. Gillespie, Martin Golden of the *Toledo Sentinel-Tribune*. How do you feel, and how did your family react to the news?"

"Well, Mr. Golden, I feel good, actually terrific. Up until the time I contracted the virus, I was healthy. As for my family, stunned would probably be an understatement. I know people have a natural repulsion to anything dealing with death. Given the number of zombie movies I have heard are now popular, I expect a certain amount of people expressing disgust or a sick interest. I want to assure you; I am as alive as any of you. I hope that in time, people will come to accept me as a person, as someone who wants to live his life out in peace and dignity."

"Mr. Gillespie, Geoff Drennan, *WXXXXL* radio out of Dawson City. I want to ask the question on many people's minds. What was it like to be dead? By that, I mean, what was the afterlife like?"

"Good ole *WXXXXL*. I hope you still broadcast the Browns. As for your question, I can say that before I passed, I was an Evangelical Christian. I only offer this information because my prior affiliation will eventually come to light. I have no comment on what I saw or didn't see. Thank you, everyone."

***

"How could you have done this?" An angry Margaret Gillespie spat out. "You had the opportunity to preach the cross of Christ, and instead, you said, "no comment.""

"What do you want from me, Margaret? Do you want a husband who lies? Enough with this. I have kept my promise; I didn't speak one word against Christianity. I do this out of love, but I have to hide my views if I want to see my grandson. I don't have a choice."

"Grab your bags," Margaret hissed. "We're going home."

***

The stretch sedan pulled into the driveway. Jeremy looked

through the tinted glass at the house before him. It was there, in the presence of his home, the immenseness of his existence hit him squarely in the face. He started crying, placing his head in his hands. Since the press conference, Margaret, who had been cold, put her arm around him and tried to comfort him. To her, this was another opportunity to bring Jeremy back into the fold.

"Honey," she said soothingly, I can't wait for you to come inside."

Looking at the exterior, he said. "You painted the outside red and green."

"What do you think? I know you never wanted that combination."

"I think it looks like a square piece of rhubarb."

"I didn't think you would mind. Being dead and all."

With that, he started to belly laugh. "Well, I can't argue with that." He leaned over and kissed her. "By the way, I had planned to paint the house these colors for you before I, I, well, I became ill."

"I know, baby. A couple of weeks after the memorial service, I found the paint cans in the garage." Now she started crying. "Honey, I have missed you so much. Praise be to God for your deliverance from the shadows."

He leaned over and kissed her on the cheek, and gently squeezed her hands. "C'mon baby, show me what horrors you did with the inside of the rhubarb box."

***

Jeremy and Margaret were home less than an hour when there was a knock on the door. It was agent Rodriguez. She asked to speak to them. The three sat in the living room; the agent sat in a recliner while the couple held hands on the couch. “Mr. and Mrs. Gillespie,” Rodriguez stated, “as the senior field agent, I’m responsible for all continuing research into the effects of the virus. I’ll be coordinating with the regional center in Cleveland and the national center in Atlanta. When further testing such as blood samples or x-rays are necessary, I will be the one making the arrangements.”

Margaret asked, “can’t he have the tests at the Wood County Hospital or Blanchard Valley Hospital? That way, Jeremy doesn’t have to travel so much.”

“I am afraid that isn’t an option. There is concern that outside testing may result in unauthorized examination and leaking your medical condition to the public. Also, the CDC will maintain 24/7 surveillance on both your husband and the house. We have also installed your home and property with a state-of-the-art security system. The CDC has already spent over half a million dollars in the last four months and has budgeted over six million dollars over the next five years alone.”

"Mr. Gillespie, there is also the not-so-minor job of changing a plethora of records to indicate you are in the land of the living. Your job is to relax, get reacquainted with your life, and help us save lives."

Jeremy said, "We will be attending church tomorrow. After services, Margaret and I then usually go out to eat." Jeremy's statement was more of a question, asking if it was safe to do so.

"Mr. Gillespie," Rodriguez replied, "do as you wish. Just let us know twenty-four hours ahead of time if you plan on traveling more than fifty miles from home."

***

Jeremy walked into the church for the first time in almost four years. The butterflies in his stomach were the same as any other. He had always seen the church as the physical structure - the building that held the people of God, the Bride of Christ. There was a realization of something extraordinary and humbling. As a church elder, he knew God charged him to serve and lead his flock. It was a duty he took seriously, but not grimly. Now, he realized those were feelings not based upon the truth. Not lies, just lacking justification. Before he could shake too many hands, Reverend Miller pulled him aside.

"Jeremy," the minister inquired, "can I ask you for a

favor?"

"Sure, fire away."

"I was hoping you could address the congregation. The members of this church love you an awful lot, and it would mean the world if they saw you at the pulpit again."

"I love them, too. I'm truly honored you asked me to speak. I am most certainly humbled. And you needn't worry. I will say nothing. I have never broken a promise I made to you; I don't intend to start now."

Jeremy stood at the pulpit. He couldn't remember how many times he had occupied the same space. It never occurred to him he would ever address the congregation without the hope of God's grace.

"I want to thank everyone for the comforting of my family in my absence. I saw that a plaque, in my memory, was hung by the new baptistery. I'm humbled that you built it in my memory. I can tell, by the paint, Margaret had a hand in it. If I had known she was going to pick that color, I wouldn't have died in the first place." That brought loud laughter from the congregation.

"Hey, Jeremy." It was Dale, a man Jeremy had helped deal with alcoholism and brought him to Christ. "You didn't answer the reporter. Tell us, your friends, what it was like to be with God."

Jeremy started to tear up. How could he lie to the men

and women whom he loved? "Dale, I'll tell you and everyone here, you are commanded to place your faith in God's word, not my statements. The Pharisees wanted a miracle, and Jesus told them they shouldn't need one. No, a Christian should base everything on and against the word of God. Let that be your hope."

Bob put his hand on Jeremy's shoulder and stated with authority, "well said, *Brother* Gillespie, well said."

***

After the speech, the number of people convinced he was soulless or a demon-possessed corpse plummeted. But, unfortunately, the congregation pulled him, unwillingly, back into the life of the church. He was feeling trapped. It was beginning to show. He was trying hard to be nice, but it was getting increasingly more challenging. The protective womb of the congregation, to his horror, was, in fact, a prison from which he felt he could not escape.

The arguments with Margaret became bitter and frequent enough that his medical team recommended marriage counseling. He and Margaret both refused. The pressure from his family and the *good* reverend to become a Christian again was causing stress. It reached the point that massive levels of the stress hormone cortisol, was always in his system. It was beginning to take a toll physically as well as psychologically.

"Listen to me, damn it!" Craven barked at Margaret Gillespie. "Stop hammering him with this Jesus shit. You're going to kill him. Do you fucking understand me? I have seen too many people die in which there was no hope. This hounding is going to stop, or I'm going to file for protective custody due to spousal abuse."

"You listen to me, you godless heathen; you may not care about my husband's immortal soul, but I do." Margaret spat the words out of her mouth like a piece of a rotten apple. "He has a church family. We have kept his atheism quiet, but we will have no choice but to bring him before the congregation for discipline. We love him; still, the church must come first."

Jeremy sat on the examination table, shaking. He had lost almost thirty pounds since he first went home. It had been three months. He experienced bouts of crying, sleepless nights, anger, and depression — classic signs of post-traumatic stress disorder.

"Good God, woman," Craven roared. I saw this shit on the battlefield. He comes out of the ground, and all you and Reverend Fuckhead over there do is grind away at him."

"Jeremy," Robert said, "I tell you now, and in front of the blasphemer, return to the faith. If you do not return to God, *our* God, everything, and almost everyone you love will leave you. We are a Bible-believing church. Margaret and I have been persistent because of our love for you, but as Jesus commanded us, we will knock you as dust from our sandals and leave you to your own life, apart from us."

Craven was glaring at both of them. "Two weeks. I want to see my patient back here in two weeks. If you haven't stopped these threats and abuse, I will knock the shit from his boots. And you two are most certainly shit. I mean it. Two weeks and if the abuse hasn't stopped, I swear by your sky fairy, I will take him into federal, protective custody and turn this over to the state attorney general for prosecution on charges of mental cruelty."

That night, after Jeremy went to bed, Margaret had a long phone conversation with Robert.

The following evening, Jeremy returned from a long walk to find Margaret and Robert, his children, and John, a church elder. Jeremy quickly scanned for his only source of joy, his grandson. He didn't see him.

"Well, hello, everyone. Kelly, where is little Jeremy?"

"Dad, we didn't bring him."

Margaret looked at Jeremy and motioned for him to sit. "We want to talk to you. We need to express to you how your unbelief has affected us." She continued, "Jeremy, I married a man of God. You no longer fit that description. I think it's time we part."

"But Margaret, the Bible states a person is to remain with a nonbelieving spouse. We vowed to marry-until…."

"Until when?" Margaret asked cruelly. "Until death do us part? Been there, done that. I discussed the issue with the reverend and Elder John. It is their opinion I am no longer biblically required to remain with you. They have been kind enough to retain an attorney on my behalf. I plan to stop all legal proceedings to validate our marriage."

"Dad," Kelly said sternly, "we have decided we can't risk exposure of Jeremy to such a destructive belief as atheism."

"But Pumpkin," Jeremy pleaded, "I have not said a word to him about God. I have kept my word."

"Dad, my decision is final. Furthermore, I talked with Bobby. He had an idea. The FBI offered you the opportunity to enter the witness protection program as a special case. We think you should seriously consider entering the program - alone. Your absence would allow us a chance to move on with our lives, spreading the warmth and love of God."

"Jeremy," Robert interjected, "none of this has to be this way. A simple statement to us that you were in error. Proclaim that Christ is the Lord of your life. Do this, and we have agreed none of this will happen."

"Dad, Jeremy can be an active part of your life."

"Honey, our marriage can go on happily for the

remainder of our lives. No need to move. No need to be, be, uh, different."

Silence loomed over the room.

Jeremy looked at his hands; they were shaking. After a few seconds, he looked up at them, with tears running down his face. He had a dazed, punch-drunk look. "None of you ever wanted a husband, did you? Or a father or a friend. I was just a cog in the machinery of your idea of God. Why can't I be different? Why can't I be a friend, a family member, and think differently? I would harm no one. Now I see, I was never in a church family. I was an active, willing participant, a cog in a heartless machine that uses every situation and everyone for a chance to ring up another one for God. To you, people aren't persons with souls. They are souls with persons that happen to be along for the ride."

Jeremy sobbed out, "this is an either-or club. You are either all in or all out. Then I am all out! I won't suck more people into the abyss."

With that, he jumped from his chair and ran to his den. He came out ten minutes later. No one spoke to him, and he made no effort. He had told them all he had to say. He walked outside and found one of the security members. "Derrick?"

"Yes, Mr. Gillespie."

"Will you see Agent Rodriguez soon?"

"Yes."

"I know she sees Dr. Craven in a couple of days. Will you please give her this letter and relay that I asked her to deliver it to him?"

"Yes, of course, Mr. Gillespie."

With that, he handed the sealed envelope to the guard and said, "Derrick, my name is Jeremy. There is no need for someone protecting me being so formal."

"Mr. Gille… I mean Jeremy, is everything ok? Are you alright?"

"I will be. Thank you, Derrick. Thank you for caring about me."

"Jeremy, are you going to go to bed soon?"

"I'm going to sleep."

"Goodnight."

"Goodnight and dreamless sleep to us all." Jeremy smiled, but to the agent, he looked so sad.

Jeremy turned to go back into the house, then stopped, turned around, and spoke. "Stay warm, Derrick. It is a cold night. It matches a cold people." He smiled again, turned, and casually walked toward the door. Just before he went inside, he took in a deep breath of the cold air. He pointed upward and said. "Derrick, look, there's the Big Dipper. Nifty, isn't it?" He walked in and closed the door before the man could answer.

Two minutes later, while Derrick was still looking at the

Big Dipper, his peripheral vision caught a flash of light, immediately followed by the sound of a shot. He pulled his weapon and was calling for backup as he barreled through the door. Hearing a scream on the second floor, Derrick took the steps two at a time. He burst through a small group huddled around a desk. As Derrick pushed his way through, he saw a gun and Jeremy Gillespie's head, both lying on the open rolltop desk. Both void of life.

***

Standing at the pulpit, Reverend Miller stared into space with a grinding sense of disgust, topped to a level he never imagined he could possess. He directed his dark feeling toward Jeremy. Margaret sat with her children in the front pew, silently holding the boy named after her once again deceased husband. The family was grappling with grief and recrimination. How could he do this?

If only he would have returned to the fold. Jeremy could've avoided all of this. They asked Jeremy Gillespie to lie as a condition of acceptance. Now those close to him had decided to live a lie, to feast on the same meal of hypocrisy they wanted him to eat. They concluded it was better to hide the truth. The truth would hurt the kingdom of God.

Robert plastered on a smile and began. "Family, friends, and, most importantly, those who belong to, and in Christ; we come together in grief. We all know the circumstances in which our Jeremy moved, once again, onto eternity. We could see it coming but felt helpless to stop it. While suicide is a grave sin, we must realize our Lord makes allowances. Jeremy repeatedly told us that after experiencing the peace of God, life on earth, no matter how much he loved us, was excruciating. He told me many times how he wished he could return to God. Finally, his desire to be with his Savior was too much. I believe, in reflection, God sent Jeremy to us as a reminder and a lesson. A reminder that God is still working miracles. While Jeremy's methods were wrong, still, he taught us by his daily actions, devotion to God, and our brothers and sisters in Christ that our walk with God should engulf and ultimately enrich our lives."

Dr. Craven,

By the time you read my short message, I will be no more. While I say this out of context, Nietzsche was wrong. When we have a chance to stare into the abyss, nothing stares back. I have hopefully removed enough of my brain that resuscitation is quite impossible. You, per the medical contract, possess my remains. I hope my corpse serves to improve lives and reduce suffering.

While you are certainly entitled to believe what you will, I can assure you we face annihilation. But if there can be a hell, I experienced it in Dawson City. For me, to be shunned by the people I loved the most was pain beyond what I ever thought I could experience. I never saw it coming. The worst part is that for years I perpetuated one of the most exclusionary groups in the world. How could a group be so theologically right yet, scar so many people?

If you are a praying man, offer your petitions for those that suffer in silence rather than give up human warmth - even conditional warmth.

As for the radical elements of the church, Daniel 5:27 aptly applies.

All the best,
Jeremy Gillespie

Laying down the letter, Agent Michelle Rodriguez wiped the tears that streamed from her eyes. "Dr. Craven, what did he mean, Daniel 5:27 applies?"

Smiling in sad resignation, Dr. Craven looked at her and said, "Daniel 5:27 – *You have been weighed. You have been measured, and you have been found wanting.*

Answer to a Prayer

From the deserted beach, I stand and stare at the dead lake. The water that used to harbor such life is now a void. Well, that is not entirely true. *They* are in there, sweeping the inland sea for any remaining semblance of cellular activity. If there is, which I doubt, they will eradicate it.

The area was once Crane Creek State Park. It was part of a chain of wildlife refuges and recreational areas that butted against the southern shore of Lake Erie. It was a great place to swim, fish, picnic, or just hangout. It was part of all that was right with the state. My husband and I brought our daughter here many times. I can't tell you how many sandcastles the three of us built. There were always tiny shells in the sand. There won't be any more shells made. They say the road to hell is paved with good intentions. We built two lanes, both one way.

My name is Rachel Kluber. I worked in the biology department at a university in northwest Ohio. I received a grant to study the effects of invasive species on indigenous populations. Lake Erie was being hammered by several.

Of course, it wasn't just this great lake. Our nation was up to our shiny butts in foreign plants and animals, making life hard on the native flora and fauna.

I worked with the Ohio Department of Wildlife on the Lamprey problem when I was approached by Matthew Burke, Professor of Robotics, in the Department of Engineering. He had been encouraged to engage his project on a real-world problem. He had stumbled across an article about my work while looking for the schedule of the university's hockey team.

Matthew had been one of the world's leading pioneers in the field of nanotechnologies. He solved one of the principal problems with this type of machine: mass-producing something so small. His answer was brilliant - he would have the nanobots replicate themselves.

Engineers initially provided materials for the machines to complete this task. Another breakthrough came when he and his team constructed the component of scavenging. At a microscopic level, the mechanisms could take material left in nature: car parts, old lawnmowers, etc., and self-replicate.

Up to that time, lamprey control was chiefly accomplished using lampricides and sterilization of the males. Matthew recommended a trial of the nanobots.

I agreed to meet him over Flurries at the Dairy Queen. "Dr. Kluber, I would like to join you to engage in a trial experiment. We would jointly supervise."

"What exactly would this trial entail?" I asked while simultaneously spooning in a piece of frozen peanut butter cup and ice cream into my mouth.

"The nanobots can be programmed to do a variety of jobs. I believe they can eliminate the lamprey population in Lake Erie."

Matthew was excited by the thought of using the nanobots. He was so engrossed in the conversation that he twice completely missed his mouth, spilling his gummy bear Flurry down his shirt. I wondered how such a brilliant, thirty-year-old man be such a dork? Still, he had appeal. It was the innocent look that perpetually encompassed his face. It made him look adorable.

I took a sip of Cherry Coke and thought. He continued to talk, but I silenced him by holding a finger in the air. "Dr. Burke, how do you propose to test this hypothesis of yours?"

Matthew immediately replied, "I thought two identically constructed tanks with the same eco-system, including the type and number of lampreys. One will have nothing added to stop them from living and multiplying. That, as you know, will be our control tank. The other will have a small number of nanobots introduced. They will attack and kill the test animals."

"You know, Matthew, this would only be the first of

many tests and peer reviews?"

"Rachel," he said, somewhat annoyed. "I may be a nerd; nonetheless, I am also an engineer. Please, give me ideas, and remind me when I forget something. If I make a mistake, tell me, but don't talk down to me."

I realized how condescending I had sounded. "You are right; please forgive me."

"Hey, no problem," he said with a big grin. There was part of a gummy bear in his beard.

***

The first test was basic. We needed to pare it down more than we initially expected. We worked a lot of long hours defining what characteristics make a lamprey a lamprey. We needed to convert all of that data into a program the nanobots would recognize. We had help from the computer science department. Molly Hart, a young Ph.D. student, was looking for a dissertation. We gave her one - proving a sophisticated program could effectively work with a machine too small to see.

Her accomplishment was nothing short of brilliant. It not only allowed for the downloading of information, but it could also relay data and adapt to new commands. The program allowed us to direct the bots toward a specific animal or plant. We could also aim them at one or more targets, turn the machines off, or put them in a rest mode.

We placed the nanobots in groupings of five thousand. We called each of these a pod. We could direct and track them via satellites. We worked and worked until it became evident to us, it was time to test the little guys.

We lowered the waterproof bag into the tank containing the lampreys. The team had invited members of the Ohio Department of Natural resources and the Canadian Wildlife Service to the experiment. Everyone knew invasive species didn't give a rat's ass about international boundaries. In other words, we would have to convince our neighbors up north that our methods were safe.

We told the press, in attendance, the team had asked Molly to initiate the program due to the work she put into developing the system. That was true - partially. It was also good PR that she had a very pretty face and cleavage to spare. She wore a dress that highlighted that asset without looking slutty. The media ate it up.

"Ms. Hart," Matthew stated, "engage program one of Test Prime. Smiling, Molly hit the enter button on the keyboard. The bag containing the nanobots began dissolving almost immediately.

Matthew watched while addressing the crowd, which had huddled around the tank. "The nanobots are using the bag as energy. Dr. Kluber has informed me many animals in nature eat the embryos that once contained them. As you can see, the bag is now entirely gone. We will now move on to identifying the lampreys. Ms. Hart, engage test two if you please."

The slightest of currents formed. An unseen force moved through the water. On the screen, a small blue circle made a recognizance of the tank. They swept through the water; a single blue dot would leave the pod and attach itself to each of the ten lampreys. Each of these had a number inside of it.

"Ladies and gentlemen," I announced, "each of these blue dots indicates a nanobot that has microscopically secured itself to a lamprey. The numbers tell us how many of the specie were located, identified, and tagged. At this junction, nothing has happened to them. This identification allows us to identify how many are present in a given area. This feature of the software can help us with developing an accurate census of any species, not just ones we want to eliminate."

Nonetheless, the horse and pony show was over. Now came the time to kill a lamprey. Everything before was a leap, a massive jump in wildlife management. Still, an animal was going to have to die if this study was to prove successful. Matthew and I nervously looked at each other. We nodded our heads, and I stepped forward. If this went wrong, I didn't want it hanging over Molly's head.

"Ms. Hart, I will initiate part three of the test. Ladies

and gentlemen, we are now going to instruct the nanobots to kill lamprey seven."

I punched in the instructions, then, after a moment's hesitation, hit the engage button. Suddenly, one of the prehistoric fish went into spasms. The convulsion lasted a mere few seconds before the animal went limp and sunk to the bottom of the tank.

There was dead silence for about ten seconds, and then the Ohio Wildlife representatives broke into applause. They worked on the front line against these species. Everyone else joined in, clapping.

After a few seconds, the applause died down. Smiling, I said, "ladies and gentlemen, we have just turned the corner in the long war to keep our nation free from invasive species." With a clenched jaw and a cold heart, I engaged the, *kill-all,* program. The remaining lampreys were dead inside five minutes.

***

"Damn!" I yelped. "That gel is cold on my belly. I thought there was supposed to be things that heated that shit."

"Just relax, Rachel," said the doctor. "You've experienced enough of these ultrasounds to know how they go."

I laid there as she ran that damn thing over my swollen

belly. I couldn't believe I was pregnant. How did this happen? Well, I know how it happened. It's just the events leading up to the coup de taut. In hindsight, it turned out to be the best screw-up of my life.

There was a celebration after the first test. We were all so happy, so proud. We were doing something to better the world. The drunker we became, the more that thought stroked our egos. My belly bump made it plain to see that wasn't the only thing I stroked that night.

The more alcohol I consumed, the more my, *I want to have sex,* meter went up. I should've been more responsible. My perception of Matthew transformed from a cute dork into a total hottie. Our relationship had become much closer yet still professional. Some sexual tension had built, but it was strictly low-level. In hindsight, I was beginning to notice we did more than work well together; each felt good around the other.

By our tenth drink, we were banging away in the maintenance closet. For a dork, he was good. When we finished, we had some mop talk while still in the closet. At one point, we looked into each other's eyes. We didn't say a word; nevertheless, we knew we would be together for the long haul. We also realized we had to get back to the party before anyone noticed. We walked in casually. I thought we had fooled the room. Drunk people don't usually evaluate things well.

While getting some punch, Molly walked by. She stopped, looked at me, and said, "You and Dr. Burke must have really gone at it. You put your pantyhose over your dress." I ran to the restroom and looked in the mirror at my drunken, laid state. I would have jumped to my death, but our room was in the basement.

"Honey, look at our baby. Isn't she beautiful?" Matthew continued to stare at the screen, telling me how gorgeous our fetus was. He was right.

"Alright, Rachel, everything looks good. I want you to schedule another ultrasound appointment for six weeks. Oh, and Honey, if you bitch about the gel one more time, I'm going to shove the bottle up your ass." That's what I get for having an obstetrician as my best friend.

Six months into my pregnancy, Matthew and I married. It was a small ceremony at the University's Chapel. It was a dry reception.

The pregnancy wasn't a burden; still, it put a crimp on my ability to do some of the rougher fieldwork. My stomach was as big as some of the rocks I was trying to step over. Coordination was not my forte. Ivan, a graduate student from Russia, repeatedly needed to help me navigate the rough terrain. I kept that poor, young man in constant terror during our excursions along Erie's shoreline.

Giving birth was just like Carol Burnett described

it - having your bottom lip pulled over your head. The labor was hard. Eventually, a C-Section was necessary. Matthew was a trooper. He was so supportive. We were proud parents. We knew nothing about raising a child; nonetheless, we loved our daughter. We asked for suggestions and made it through. Since conceived in a building on the university, we decided to name her Frieda, after one of the school's mascots.

I took an eight-week maternity leave. Matthew's paternity leave was a month. By the time we returned, the Ohio Department of Wildlife was anxious to complete the testing. They didn't seem to realize that there were many steps before permanently releasing the nanobots into the environment. If it were up to them, we would work 24/7. That wasn't going to happen. We put in fifty-five hour weeks. No more. They screamed. We drew a line in the sand. Accident or not, Frieda became our top priority. Looking back, I wonder if that is where we made *the* mistake, the one that would kill a hell of a lot more than our reputations.

***

It took a little over three years to complete all the trials. They succeeded beyond our wildest dreams. The Department of the Interior approved the use of a pod to kill one hundred of the lampreys. They had inched their way into the western basin of Lake Erie. Canada did not sign-off on the project. That was not a problem; we could keep them on our side of the lake by GPS.

One of the test conditions was the bots' ability to replicate was turned off. We also had to retrieve all the bots after completion of the test - no exceptions. Another stipulation required completion of the trial in one week.

Matthew trusted the math. He was calm. He was more concerned about damaging the bots during transport. I was a biologist. I knew nature was wrought with unexpected consequences. To little fanfare, we released a pod near Fisherman's Wharf in Port Clinton, Ohio.

From the second the bag touched the water, we were on the clock. At my insistence, we reviewed the system one more time before we turned the nanobots loose. You know, measure twice, cut once. My dad had been a carpenter. Matthew and Molly looked exasperated by my demand. We had reviewed the system three times before we ever placed them in the bag. They silently completed my request. Finally, Molly looked up from her laptop screen. "Dr. Kluber, just like every other review, all aspects of the system check green." I was about to ask for another review when Matthew jumped in.

"Damn it, Rachel. It's time to fish or cut bait."

He, of course, was right. I couldn't let my fear dictate

my intellect. I looked at each of their faces. Ivan was slightly nervous yet excited. His face carried the same look as he had right before he rode his first rollercoaster ride, at the Cedar Point Amusement Park. Molly's face reflected a giddy eagerness to start. Matthew's annoyance was quickly dissipating, replaced by a zeal that closely matched Molly's.

"Fish."

Matthew let out a deep breath and hit the engage button. A second timer automatically started in the program. The bag was *eaten*, releasing the nanobots into the wild for the first time. Sixty-two hours and seventeen minutes later, we extracted them from the lake. It was an unqualified success.

***

The next six months were incredible. The world threw fame, fortune, and dead lampreys our way. We not only cleaned the American side of things, but we also kept it clean. Finding no solace in the Land of the Free, the creatures migrated to the Great White North side of the lake. Ottawa finally cried, *uncle*. Within a year, the inland sea was lamprey-free.

Our next task was to maintain the lake while targeting Zebra Mussels. They came into the lake in the ballast water of foreign freighters. We hit the kill all button, and thirteen months later, Lake Erie was Zebra Mussel free. They were tough little bastards.

While we were picking our next target, we received a call from the Florida Department of Wildlife. They had enough invasive species to start several zoos. What was in their immediate crosshairs were snakes - specifically constrictors. The Python population was going nuts. It was wreaking havoc on the deer and raccoon populations. We did some calculations and transported seventy-two pods to the everglades.

"I have to tell you, Rachel," said Matthew, "I'm concerned about the pods against something so large as pythons. And did our program give enough information to identify the animals accurately?"

"Honey," I replied, "we will just have to wait and see. Everything has turned up roses so far. Let's give the little guys a chance." He nodded, but I could tell he was still nervous. We didn't design the program for an animal with up to twenty-five feet of dense muscle mass.

The wildlife department helped us coordinate where to deploy the bots. Initially, we sent them to gather a census of the constrictors. It was worse than anyone expected. There were thousands and thousands of the things. We deployed an additional fifty pods, and the governor, seeking press, smiled as he pushed the, *kill all and maintain,* program. The first month over two hundred were killed, two of them over fifteen feet long. One had a Labrador Retriever in its stomach. I hoped that one died slowly. I love dogs.

After six months, it was evident the tide had turned. Python corpses were everywhere. The Sunshine State next turned her attention to Nile Crocodiles. Who the hell would release these things? Same result - death. After that, we programmed the bots to eliminate a plethora of invasive species that inhabited Florida.

The long and short of it, we became rich, very rich. And the funny part is, we didn't own a damn piece of the project. Bowling Green Technical University rightfully claimed every nanometer of it. Nonetheless, if they wanted our experience and expertise, they were going to have to pay through the nose. They paid until they bled. That's alright. As wealthy as we were, they were making a hundred times more. We should have taken our fortune and walked away.

***

We were vacationing in the beautiful city of Nice, on the French Riviera, when I received the call. It was Molly, and if her voice was any indication, she was freaking out. "Dr. Kluber, there is something wrong with the bots."

"Molly," I said, trying to calm her down. I had never heard her sound so ruffled. "Just tell me what is going on."

"You know how we have been trying to eliminate the Quagga Mussels in the lake?" She asked.

Quagga Mussels are a more aggressive cousin of Zebra Mussels. They attach to the native mussels in such a way as to stop them from eating. They had been challenging to eliminate, causing us to spend a lot of time battling them.

"Molly, do some of the mussels have some protective feature the bots can't penetrate?"

"No, they are getting through. But, after the bots kill a Quagga, they are tagging and killing the native mussels."

A cold chill ran down my spine. I felt my face flushing.

Matthew, who had been playing in the surf, must have looked back and seen my face. Even at a distance, I saw him frown. I motioned for him to come quickly.

His face had worry written all over it. "Is it Frieda?"

"No, it's the bots."

The look of worry faded from his face, replaced with one of curiosity.

"After killing a Quagga, it is tagging a native mussel and killing it."

He asked for the phone. "Molly, place them in *retreat and rest* mode."

After a couple of minutes, Molly, sounding relieved,

said, "Okay, Dr. Burke. Alright, they are complying."

We looked at each other; this was bad.

Most people might think, *It's a frigging clam, who gives a shit?* I don't think they understand how vital these invertebrates are to the cleanliness of lakes. They were making a comeback after teetering on the brink of extinction.

We packed our stuff and took the next flight to Detroit. Ivan, looking worried, met us at the airport. After grabbing our luggage, we headed down I-75. We talked with Molly on the phone on the way south; however, the reception was spotty. The last we heard, they were still obeying the command.

We hit the control center running. Molly greeted us in tears. The handsome Russian ran to her. She sobbed in his arms. Ivan, who had cried for three days straight when he had watched *Old Yeller*, was almost as distraught as his fiancé.

Prying the two apart, Matthew immediately got down to business. "Molly, what the hell is happening? We need to know now!"

"Dr. Burke, all of the pods complied with the command, except one. Pod fifty-seven initially did the same. But after the first rest cycle concluded, about twenty minutes ago, it did not renew another one. It reactivated and started going after the mussels again. I ordered it to resume rest mode, but it's not complying."

Matthew's face turned red. It reminded me of how he looked when Frieda wouldn't listen. Only he looked a lot angrier. My husband had worked long and hard on this project. Looking back, I think he saw it as a child he had helped bring into the world.

"Molly," Matthew instructed, "turn them off."

"Yes, Sir."

We waited the three minutes it would take to send the command and receive confirmation of their compliance. Our faces turned ashen white as we saw the blue dots still moving. Molly stared at Matthew; her face had a desperate look. "Molly, what makes pod fifty-seven unique?"

"They are not obeying commands."

"We know that, damn it!" I winced, along with the young woman. I had heard Matthew annoyed plenty of times, we all had, but that was the closest to mean I had ever heard him. That dug into my heart, as well as my brain, how serious the situation was.

"Well," Molly half cried out, "pod fifty-seven are all nanobots created in nature."

I remember Matthew rubbing his beard and looking thoughtful. The engineer's brain was at work. Knowing him, I knew calculations were running through his mind. He saw them as machines with either a fault in the programming, the bots themselves, or the delivery system

- nothing else. I was hoping he was right.

"Ivan," he said, "check the communication feed. Run a maintenance test on the entire system. We seem to be receiving information from the pod, yet how accurate is it? I also want to know if they are receiving the correct commands from us."

The young man immediately went to a panel of screens and computers. We waited as Ivan ran a complete scan of every component - twice. In his mind, Matthew was already formulating a decision tree. Forty-five minutes later, the report came back.

"Sir, I have double-checked all of the communication systems. We are receiving accurate information, and they are receiving accurate commands. I can't find a cause for the malfunction."

"Molly," Matthew said, "what is the closest pod with a lab-made alpha-1 bot?"

"Pod twenty-nine has two alphas in it. It is approximately sixteen hundred yards to the west, attacking a group of Round Gobies."

"Send the highest-ranking alpha to pod fifty-seven. Once there, it is to take command of the pod and order it to shut down immediately."

Molly stated, "There will be a little bit of a wait. There is a slight, western current."

I asked, "How long is a little bit?"

Cringing, Molly answered, "not quite two hours." She was afraid of another outburst by Matthew.

"Send the command immediately." Then, looking at the young woman, he said, "please forgive me, Molly; you deserve much better." With that, he left the lab to wait it out in his office.

A few minutes before the two-hour mark, the alpha bot reached the renegade pod. Matthew said, "Alright, everyone, cross your fingers."

The alpha sent a signal indicating it was taking command of the pod and had a new directive. The other bots circled the alpha. It ordered immediate sleep mode. The order seemed to be working; the bots were beginning to power down. We all exhaled a sigh of relief. Then, the unexpected happened.

The pod reversed its shutdown process. It then destroyed the alpha. We all stared in stunned silence. We quickly received a message from the renegade group. "Defective vehicle identified and destroyed. Will now continue to eradicate all invasive species."

Molly didn't wait for Matthew or me to tell her; she sent the command. "Send the list of what you identify as an invasive species.

Pod fifty-seven answered with one ubiquitous, horrifying target. "All cellular life."

"Oh, my God," was all I could say.

Ivan looked up from his laptop. His face emanated profound sadness.

"Molly," Matthew said, "instruct all naturally produced bots, globally, to immediately self-destruct. Instruct all pods in Lake Erie to first contain and then destroy every bot that is, or has ever been, a member of pod fifty-seven."

She pulled up a program titled in red. She punched in piece after piece of information; several times, the program asked her if she was sure before hitting the *yes* entry. The program finally indicated, in flashing letters, that it was ready to implement. Molly didn't hesitate; she hit the engage button.

A couple of minutes later, the bots complied and began to form both containment and hunter-killer pods. The idea was to herd the rebel pod into shallow water, picking off any that tried to cut and run. It was a brutal yet time-tested military strategy, corner then kill.

After eight agonizing days, they cornered fifty-seven. None tried to escape. Then, outnumbering the renegades by a ratio of hundreds to one, we sent the order to destroy the malfunctioning bots. Pod fifty-seven proceeded to annihilate every opposing bot. They lost a little over sixty percent in the battle. They then proceeded to use parts of their *dead* brethren to repair and reenergize the remaining group.

***

We tried electrocution, explosives, corrosives; you name it. We reduced pod fifty-seven to about ten percent of its original size. Meanwhile, they produced over four hundred replicate pods. The only saving grace is that we could finally plant a program commanding them not to manufacture more. It stuck. They wiped out all life in the Great Lake in a little over a year and a half. We contained them from leaving, but Erie was lost. We believe they can last at least another century before the systems are too degraded for them to repair themselves. We could be wrong; it could be a millennium.

***

So, now I stand on the empty beach at Crane Creek. The wind is blowing off the dead body of water. It is a mild day; still, the wind makes it even cooler. We were pushed hard, against our view, by the Department of the Interior to allow the bots to reproduce. That public knowledge allowed us to keep most of our money. Still, our reputations were in tatters. The university escaped with its capital, and rightfully, its honor. We ordered every other bot on the globe to self-destruct. They complied.

Molly and Ivan were married in front of a judge in

his chamber at the Wood County Common Pleas Court. They didn't invite us. Matthew wants to move away, take Frieda, and go.

Yet, I cannot leave. In truth, I don't know why I want to stay, why I visit Crane Creek so much. It is not a penance. Maybe it is because, like someone visiting the gravesite of a loved one, this site brings back happy memories. I remember sandcastles and laughter. A happy family. *My* happy family.

I thought the bots were an answer to a prayer. I should have realized what we put into that body of water. They are what we built them to be, harbingers of death. We should have known better; we did know better. We caved into pressure and hubris.

In the end, it wasn't programming that caused it to all go wrong; it was statistics. We built millions upon millions of these things, then gave them the ability to construct even more of themselves. No matter what item or means of production, the results are eventually the same. A certain amount will end up on the far end of the bell curve, the wrong end. We pushed their adaptability to the point some of them started to choose. Maybe not consciously, but they decided nonetheless.

For a specie to survive and thrive, it needs space. If other species are driven into extinction, it is incidental. The nanobots saw the lake as their habitat. Like the animals and plants we had sent them to destroy, they chose to eliminate the competition.

Charade

My name is Jackson Mack. The first thing you should know about me is I'm a thief. Not anymore, mind you, I'm what you call rehabilitated. Whatever the case, I think it's time to tell you the story of Atticus Crabtree. Yeah, I know, I'm no Morgan Freeman, but this isn't that kind of story.

There are things in this world which are dark, unnatural, and just plain terrifying. Most people don't want to think about what's under the bed or in the closet. To dwell on these aberrations causes them to lose sleep, not hike in the woods or buy a house that is the site of a murder. Without noticing, most of us will block out and avoid these strange and horrifying things.

The world runs on order. Even planes flying into buildings and South American coups, while bloody, are explainable. The ultimate gut punch is chaos. Trust me; I understand people's aversion to becoming personally involved in macabre and mayhem. It's one thing to watch on TV a group of people walking around the woods declaring every strange noise is a squatch. It's quite another to see an unknown great ape standing beside the hiking trail. I would have joined the vast horde of humanity, mentally blocking out the strange - except I couldn't leave. We became prisoners, not just to the justice system but also trapped with something much different than a human, yet every bit as smart, or more.

For a long time, I thought Atticus was a good guy. Maybe, he was all along; it's hard to tell where to draw the line between good and evil and, for that matter, who holds the chalk. It's fuzzy, indistinct, and perhaps relative to the circumstance. The court convicted him of gross sexual misconduct and statutory rape. According to Atticus, his wife had turned off the proverbial faucet, leaving him confused, hurt, frustrated, and possessing testicles that were quickly turning a shade of color resembling blue jeans.

Finally, self-maintenance wasn't cutting it, and Atticus started paying for his pleasure. He wasn't seeking underage girls; he didn't think a minor should be in the sex trade. Well, since participants in that line of business rarely check photo I.D's, Atticus assumed he was enjoying an evening with a female who looked every bit in her mid-twenties. It turns out she was sixteen. The young woman tried to blackmail him for her silence. Atticus thought it was a bluff; it wasn't. As a side note, it turned out his wife was having an affair.

So, Atticus, whose previous and devious criminal record consisted of three speeding tickets, found himself among the caged. Five to ten years incarceration and a registered sex offender for at least ten years after release. The convictions ruined the next twenty years of Atticus Crabtree's life. Given that he was in his late thirties, or so I thought, prison would eat some of his prime years of life.

Having done this before, it looked as if the young prostitute's luck finally ran out. She eventually threatened to blackmail the wrong guy. She was found dead, her tongue cut out and laid over her lips. The police never found her smartphone.

Atticus and I shared a cell. At first, he seemed nervous; his eyes were darting around inside their sockets. Still, he was better than most first-timers. Once, I saw a teenager piss himself when shown his cell.

A couple of inmates tested Atticus; they both lost. In an argument, Atticus twisted the other man's own words around the guy like a blanket. However, Atticus relented. He seemed to want to make a point, not an enemy. The man walked away with hurt pride, but his reputation was mostly intact.

The second wasn't so lucky. Atticus walked by the common area, towel over his shoulder, and into the shower room. A dumb, arrogant brute named Bucky Brandenshaw looked at Atticus, informed his buddies that he had found his new girlfriend, and then followed my cellmate into the shower.

Atticus came out fifteen minutes later. He had a small, red mark on one of his cheeks, and a couple of knuckles looked cut. His hair was still damp. It was apparent, after the altercation, he finished his shower. His level of nonchalance was stunning. The guards found Bucky viciously beaten. He spent eleven days in a local hospital. No one knew how Atticus was able to brutalize Bucky. The latter towered over the former and was an experienced prison fighter.

The guards and the highway patrol, who are responsible for investigating crimes inside Ohio prisons, inquired, but that was a formality. The investigation, as many in prison do, hit a stonewall. Everybody interviewed denied any knowledge of the incident. The lack of witnesses willing to testify was all the authorities needed to fulfill their paperwork and close the case. They knew the prisoner's code; *snitches get stitches*. After that, no one messed with Atticus.

For his part, my cellmate seemed unperturbed by the confrontations. I wanted to know how he had beat the hell out of Bucky but didn't want to ask. I was working on my twelfth year for stealing a car, and that wasn't my first time in the pokey. In that entire time, I had only met two, maybe three men who I thought could hold their own against that thug, and I figured even they would take a beating in the process. He said nothing about either of his confrontations. By the end of my time with him, the answer was obvious.

One day, out of the blue, Atticus said, "Jackson, I'm glad you're my cellmate. You are a good friend."

I choked up and turned away. Crying isn't something you show in prison. Any emotion other than anger is regarded as a weakness, and the last thing you want in prison is to be considered soft. When I recovered, I responded, "Me too, Atticus. Me too." It was all I could get out without breaking down. I hadn't, until that moment, realized how long it had been since someone told me they were happy for my company and that I was their friend.

***

After our Kumbaya session, we became even closer. Atticus was a voracious reader. He memorized dozens of poems, including Coleridge's *Rhyme of the Ancient Mariner*. He often recommended books, and we spent many an evening discussing what they meant. After I read *To Kill a Mockingbird*, I figured out the origin of Atticus' name. If you could call any time of your life spent in incarceration as happy, those were the months.

It made the horror to come all the more heartbreaking.

The first to die was a man named Brent. He worked the night shift in the basement boiler room. He was a lifer and had long since given up seeing the outside world, except inside a coffin. Some men in his situation become mean, and some go into a permanent state of despair. Both responses are from an unwillingness to accept their fate, and worse, their hand in their downfall.

Brent was different. He had long ago forgiven himself of the murders he committed yet recognized he deserved his punishment. So, if anyone was ready to die, it was the man who was the most alive. A guard supervised him, yet it was a light oversight. No one was going to mess with him, and he wasn't going to try to escape.

The man guarding Brent, a fifty-something man named Mason, informed the inmate he was going for a cup of coffee and asked him if he wanted some. "Yes," Brent responded, "Cream and…."

"I know," Mason interrupted, smiling as he did so, "two sugars." The two had worked the night shift together for over five years and were dangerously close to being friends. That was something neither convicts nor guards encouraged. "I'll be back in ten."

Brent just nodded and strolled deeper into the room, checking gauges as he went. Mason returned ten minutes later and leisurely drank his coffee. The guard finished his drink but had yet to see Brent. *Where is that knucklehead?* thought Mason.

He yelled down the dimly lit aisle he last saw Brent travel, “Hey, Brent, your coffee is getting cold.”

He knew from long experience Brent may not hear him over the sound of the boilers. Sighing, Mason placed his empty cup on a bench and walked down the narrow path between the wall and the boilers. He turned a corner and gasped, dropping the still cooling cup of coffee, complete with cream and two sugars, onto Brent’s corpse.

***

The prison administration, Ohio Highway Patrol, and the union tried to keep news about the death hush-hush. The warden placed the prison on lockdown, and the investigative team questioned several inmates. The Highway Patrol picked over Brent’s cell with a fine-tooth comb. A couple of the men who did outside lawncare said they saw a forensics van pull around back, near the only door leading from the boiler room to the outside. They said the guards didn’t even wand them with a metal detector, let alone the usual security measures anyone must submit to before entering a high-security prison.

As for us, the convicts, there was little to do other than

speculate about all the commotion. We couldn't figure out who would have murdered Brent, universally respected and the only convict who could keep the old boilers working. In Ohio, especially in the winter, that meant a lot. No one was going to mess with him.

Knowledge is a valuable commodity in prison. I overheard white supremacists talking to Nation of Islam members. I listened, fascinated. For these two groups, hardly friends, to openly share what they knew meant they were desperate for answers. They didn't buy the story of an accident. There was fear that there was a new player inside the prison. No one seemed willing to risk being blindsided, so each group was willing to share information.

One thing worked against a convict murdering Brent; everyone, except for ten convicts, was locked in their cells for the night. Prisoners tend to show bad judgment; that's how they usually become prisoners. However, several become excellent judges of character.

No one believed the guard, Mason, killed Brent. He was devastated by his death. He carried a hollow look on his face, and his eyes were two pieces of black coal. As we sat in the common room, whispering conspiratorially, we whittled down the field of killers to the nine other prisoners or the twenty-something prison staff working that night.

During all this, Atticus listened yet didn't utter a word. He leaned against the wall, reading. We eventually turned to him, silently staring at my cellmate. I asked, "Atticus, you're one smart son-of-a-whore; what do you think about the murder?"

Atticus marked his place in the book he was reading, *The Man in the High Castle*, and asked, "Are you sure it was a murder; couldn't Brent have died in a boiler accident? Lord knows he wouldn't be the first to meet his maker from those things."

We quietly contemplated Atticus' comment when George Ecken, who cleaned the administrative offices, sat down next to me. He leaned in over the table, trying to look casual; he appeared anything but relaxed. It was apparent he wanted to tell us something, and our ears perked up, all except Atticus, who had returned to his book. George leveled his eyes with the man on the other side of the table but whispered his gossip just loud enough we could all hear. "I was cleaning the Warden's office when I saw papers lying on his desk. Now, I'm not one to snoop, but…."

"You are a lying sack of shit," interrupted Jessie Garcia, in his thick Dominican accent. "Fucking say what you have to share or shut the hell up."

George looked cross at Jessie for a second but then continued. "Brent's family got themselves a court order to have an independent autopsy. It disagreed with the county coroner's findings. Get this; they did bite casts on some of the wounds."

At that, out of the corner of my eye, I saw Atticus frown ever so slightly. If I hadn't spent months talking face to face with him, I would have missed it.

We all became quiet, absorbing what George had just said. Then, in a tone of disbelief, Jessie asked, "Are you saying someone bit Brent to death?"

"No," George choked out, "the incisors were way too long and large. Whatever killed Brent was a large animal, bigger than a dog. He was ripped open from his cock to his chin. Part of his liver was missing. They think the animal probably ate it."

Jessie gasped, "Mother of God, protect us." He mumbled something in Spanish so low we couldn't hear and crossed himself several times.

Suddenly the thought of heavy, iron bars, which I always saw as demeaning, now felt reassuring.

***

For two months, nothing further happened, and we all slowly exhaled a collective sigh of relief. We let Brent slip from our minds; maybe it was more comfortable that way. It caused us less stress to believe he died from a boiler accident. Or perhaps, the outside door wasn't shut tight, and a black bear came through, saw Brent as a quick meal, and the animal left the way he came. After all, a predator would probably go after the most calorie-dense organ, which is the liver. That was the part of Brent's body with a bite out of it. Poor bastard, he was stone-cold dead, and we were going to have icicles hanging off our sacks unless someone else could keep the old boilers working.

By September, things were looking up. A man who knew boilers, and drugs, transferred into the prison, meaning we were going to have warm water and heat for the winter. Brent's death seemed to be an aberration, a foggy mishap in a system that regularly produced grief. Atticus introduced me to *Beowulf* and informed me that we would read *God's of the Nowhere* in October in honor of Halloween.

Then came the next death.

The man's name was Donovan. He earned his way into a high-security prison due to his seemingly endless reservoir of stupid, violent behavior. He appeared determined to fight his way throughout his five-year sentence. After yet another fight, he was placed into solitary confinement and left to rot.

Donovan received the opportunity to leave solitary. There was a caveat in exchange for limited freedom; he would work nights on a crew, cleaning the top floor of a large outbuilding. Their main job was disposing of bird and bat shit, as well as minor repairs.

Donovan's answer would never make the print in a Christian magazine. "Go fuck yourself," he said, with the smile of a man who had yet to realize he was the bottom totem on the pole.

"Fine," said Sergeant Gilliard, the head guard of the third shift. "With your record, you can kiss early release goodbye. Stay in your hole. Speaking of holes," Gilliard sadistically added, "how long do you think your wife waits until she finds someone to fill hers?"

Donovan went nuts, trying to reach the sergeant but came nowhere close to inflicting any pain. Gilliard had spent two decades dealing with the Donovans of the prison. A boot to the convict's crotch dropped him in his tracks. Leaning over the withering prisoner, he taunted, "see you at ten."

Donovan arrived at the outbuilding in a sullen mood. His crotch ached, and he was terrified his wife was banging the neighbor. Looking back, the other crew members concluded he planned to murder Gilliard. Several overheard him talking under his breath, confiding to himself how he would fix Gilliard for good. The prisoners universally despised the sadistic guard, so no one informed him of Donovan's threats.

Donovan went around a corner to a short space that

dead-ended into walls of cinderblock. A few crew members later said they saw a poorly hidden shank in his right shirt sleeve as he passed them. Donovan called out from around the corner, "hey Gilliard, water is leaking from the ceiling."

"How much?"

"A…" followed by a sudden silence.

"Donovan." No answer. "Donovan, answer me!"

Kareem, a member of our small clique, was temporarily assigned to the crew. He pretended he was unconcerned about the exchange. He later said he thought Donovan was luring the head guard to his death.

"Damn it!" Gilliard bellowed and rounded the corner.

The crew said they heard Gilliard scream. Kareem stopped scraping bat shit off the wall; he, along with everyone else, assumed Donovan had carried out his threat. He was facing the bend when the guard stumbled backward, his hands held in front of him as if warding off an attack. Kareem said the guard's eyes were bulging with fear and not a drop of blood on him. Gilliard looked at the stunned crew and recovered enough of his senses to press the emergency indicator fastened onto his belt.

The emergency response team charged into the room in less than a minute. In that short space of time, Kareem looked around that bend in the room. He said Donovan lay spread-eagle, eviscerated with half of his liver lying on the floor, the other half gone.

Frozen in terror, Kareem started a Dua to Allah for protection. He heard the door on the first level crumple from a hard blow, followed by many footfalls charging up the staircase. Kareem quickly returned to the rest of the crew, and like them, sat on the floor, entwining his fingers and placing them on his head. As guards poured into the room, he kept his eyes down and mouth shut. There was a cacophony of sounds made by the many guards running and yelling, almost drowning out Gilliard, who was still screaming.

***

Warden Kelvin Davis studied the video; Captain Erik Zeitler of the Ohio Highway Patrol sat next to him. Each was becoming more agitated by the minute. They replayed the recording of the outbuilding the night of Donovan's death. They had viewed it together and separately several times without finding anything unusual or suspicious.

"Warden," Zeitler asked, "what are Ohio Department of Rehabilitation guidelines for guard interaction with groups of prisoners above a census of five?"

Davis sighed. "Look, Zeitler," he replied reluctantly, "we screwed up. What do you want me to say?"

"What I want you to do is give me an answer! The Ohio

Attorney General is breathing down my neck, demanding an explanation of how and why two prisoners, both under your care, were gutted and partially eaten. By the way, Warden, we can't cover up Donovan's death. His widow has informed the press. She appeared in front of the cameras, crying for all she was worth.

Zeitler droned on. "In addition to this happy news, now Brent's family have come forward, handing out copies of their independent autopsy. Trust me, many people, including the press, are now in possession of that report. The state capital is in an uproar. These deaths are bigger news than the Ohio State vs. Penn State game. Do you know how big a story has to be, in *Columbus*, to supersede OSU football!?"

Davis decided he wasn't going to enter into a pissing contest with the captain. Stuffing his anger, he asked, "Officer Zeitler, do you have any idea who or what killed these prisoners?"

Zeitler's face said it all. His bottom lip shot forward in a prominent pout. He simultaneously stumbled over his words, mumbling something about unknown variables. Davis smiled, tempted to gloat, but the circumstances were too gruesome, and Brent's death still weighed heavily on his mind.

"You don't have any idea who or what killed those two men, do you?" Davis asked.

"No, none at all," Zeitler conceded, tucking in his lip.

Rubbing a little salt in the wound, Davis asked, "Since we are discussing policies and procedures, let me ask, who is responsible for the investigations of Brent's and Donovan's deaths?"

"Alright, I get it," Zeitler growled, shooting daggers with his eyes.

Now that he had knocked Zeitler down a peg, or as his grandmother called it, *seasoned the meat*, Davis thought Zeitler was ready to get down to business. He was about to speak when the patrolman beat him to the punch.

"Kelvin, we need to get to the bottom of these deaths and eliminate the threat to this prison. I don't know what to do because I don't know what's causing these deaths, nor the rationale behind them."

Davis nodded but otherwise remained silent; the warden was deep in thought. An idea was churning through his brain, yet he didn't think Zeitler would go for it.

The Captain, seeing Kelvin's eyes, knew he was thinking. He waited patiently for several minutes while the warden silently chewed over the idea. Finally, the highway patrolman could take it no longer and barked out, "Damn it, Davis, spit it out!"

"Erik," he said calmly, "we need a hunter."

***

I knew something was up when the man walked down our hall. His muscles rippled as he moved, each one seemingly in concert with the others. It was his eyes, however, that told his story. Everyone owns a tale, the chapters written on their face. Some convicts, hell, most of us, try to hide our true selves. But if you are literate in optics, you will always read an autobiography.

I was mopping the hallway, lost in thought, when I was startled by officer Lee's bark, "Jackson, move your ass!" I complied without thinking. Years in prison will do that to a person. I kept my eyes down, but my line of sight was just high enough to see the group, yet not noticed.

The Warden, a highway patrolman, several suits, and this guy was in the group. As they walked, the warden was describing the prison's layout. No one seemed to notice I was still there. When he walked by me, the man said under his breath, "Good eye level, nicely done."

"He looked confident, yet not smug," I said. I was talking to the other members of our group. "I'm telling you, he isn't the typical visitor to prison. They're either arrogant or scared. This man didn't act like he owned the place, but he didn't seem afraid, either. He was asking questions about the distance between deaths and wanting to find common corridors between the murders. He appeared relaxed, but he was storing everything, sights, sounds, hell, maybe even smells, in his brain; you could see it on his face."

"No shit," responded George, the words more of an exclamation than a question. "That explains a lot."

"A lot about what?" I asked.

"Yesterday, I was cleaning the warden's office, and there were papers on top of his desk. Now, I'm not one to snoop, but…."

I rolled my eyes while a chorus of "You liar" erupted from the table, cutting him off.

"Do you want to hear what I know, or are you going to punk me?" George replied with a scowl.

Jessie shook his head but said, "Empty your mouth, George."

Appearing satisfied by our acquiescence, even if it was blatantly apparent we lacked contrition, George began to share. "Jackson, the guy you saw is most likely Everett Thompson. The man is ex-Special Forces and now a professional tracker-hunter."

"¿Que?" Jessie sputtered. Seeing our confusion, he stated the question in English, "What?"

"That can only mean one thing," said George. Knowledge, and with it fear, slowly dawned in his brown eyes.

"What's that?" I asked.

But Jessie answered for him. "They brought in a hunter because they are looking for a predator."

***

A week later, we sat in the cafeteria, eating breakfast and taunting Jessie about his favorite sport. "Jessie," asked George, "how in the hell did a Dominican become a college hockey fan?"

"I attended Bowling Green State University, and they have a hockey team. They are quite good, muy bueno. I thought all you creamsicle-skinned dudes love hockey."

"How long did you attend BGSU?" I asked.

"That's not important," he responded.

We all burst out laughing, and then we saw Kareem walk into the room. I hadn't seen a black man look that white since Michael Jackson.

We stopped laughing and stared from him to each other. He walked through the food line with all the concentration of a concussed man. The lights were on, but it was sure as hell apparent no one was home. He sat across from George, never saying a word. Kareem thoughtlessly stuck his fork in a piece of food and was about to put it in his mouth when George grabbed his wrist and pulled the food away.

George quietly, yet forcefully, said, "Damn it, Kareem, that's pork!"

Kareem dropped the fork onto the plate, still impaling the sausage patty. With a monotone voice, he said, "it got Crusoe," and with that, a single tear ran down his face. Crusoe's real name was Castway, which we turned into Castaway, and then Crusoe was only another step away. He and Kareem lived in different blocks, but they worked the woodshop and were close friends.

I involuntarily placed my hand to my mouth, but not before I gasped, "oh God."

Kareem's face twisted into a snarl. "God has nothing to do with it," he spat. "Crusoe was a devout Christian; I'm devout Muslim, God neither spared his life nor my grief. The only god who is willing or able is that thing's. It protects the beast night and day." With that, he stood, all arms and legs, nearly flipping over his tray. Kareem stormed out of the cafeteria, a faithless man.

Atticus was lying on his bunk, his eyes shut, when I walked into our cell. He had skipped breakfast, which was unusual. "Atticus, are you all right?"

Without opening his eyes, he responded, "Of course, I am Jackson. Why do you ask?"

"You never miss breakfast, and when you are awake, you are always doing something."

"Just relaxing, Jackson, just relaxing."

"Atticus, there has been another murder."

"Poor Crusoe," he responded. I wondered how he knew.

"Yes," I responded judiciously, "poor Crusoe. Kareem's pretty busted up about it. They were friends."

"What?!" Atticus spat, his eyelids flying open.

"Didn't you know Crusoe and Kareem were tight?"

"No," Atticus said slowly, "I didn't."

It was at that moment I saw something different in my bunkmate. There was no sorrow, yet, I saw a definite look of regret. While serving time, I've seen that look untold times on countless faces.

The day passed with no further comment on the subject. That afternoon, Atticus quietly continued my chess lessons. He explained the use of rooks and bishops, in conjunction, to neutralize an opponent's queen.

The same evening, Atticus made a point of talking to Kareem. He liked the young man, and it was obvious Kareem's pain bothered him. The two men conversed privately, but I overheard Atticus encourage the young man to wait until his grief ebbed before deciding whether to abandon his faith.

***

Everett stared at the large copy of the prison's blueprints pinned to the wall next to the window. The Warden,

Zeitler, the top-ranking guard - Taylor Gonzalez, and Rachel Gomez - a representative of the Ohio Attorney General's office, were also present. On the design print, circled with a red grease pencil, was the sight of each death. In blue pencil, leading from each kill, a line was drawn and extended until it intersected the other lines.

Gomez stepped forward and, with an index finger, followed a single line from the main facility to the outbuilding, the site of Donovan's death. It indicated the presence of an underground tunnel. With her finger still on the line, Gomez turned her head to face Everett.

"Mr. Thompson," she said, "I'll bet you a nickel this is the path our killer traversed the night it killed Donovan."

"No bet, I was thinking the same thing," Everett responded with a slight smile. "Mr. Davis, I'd like to take a look at that tunnel."

"There is no need to," the warden answered. "That tunnel was closed years ago; the doors on both ends were welded shut. So nothing could get in or out."

"I'd like to see it all the same."

Sighing, Davis walked to his desk, unlocked a drawer, and pulled out a ring with several older keys attached. "Let's go."

***

"How?" Davis asked. It was the third time he had asked the question and was yet to receive an answer. The sealed door was open, bent, and upright only by the grace of God and a sturdy bottom hinge. The top hinge was lying in pieces, sheered from both the door and the wall.

"Anyone still think this was a bear?" Thompson asked, knowing only a fool would answer yes.

Zeitler examined the pieces of the hinge and the welds, which held the door, didn't. "This door is old, but its construction is still solid," he said. "And, by the looks of the welds, they weren't the weak link."

"Alright," Thompson said, "let's see if our friend left us anything."

"I'm not going into that tunnel," Davis cried out. He was sweating despite the coolness of the room.

"Mr. Davis," Gonzales said, "we have to find whatever is killing people."

Zeitler spoke. "The tunnel is wide enough for two abreast. I'm in charge of the investigation, so I need to walk in front, beside Everett. Davis and Gomez are next, with Gonzales in the back. Is this acceptable to everyone?"

A unison of *yesses* replied. Thompson nodded appreciatively at Zeitler, obviously pleased with the patrolmen's directions.

Turning to the warden, Gomez asked, "are there working lights in this tunnel?"

"How the hell should I know?" he barked back.

Gomez was about to inform Davis that as warden, it was his job to know. But she stopped when Gonzales looked above the door and spoke. "Ms. Gomez, if you look at the wires about three feet above the door, you can see they are wrapped in electrical tape and capped off. They most likely cut the wires when they sealed the doors. In other words, no lighting."

Everett immediately responded to the news. "Turn on your flashlights; it's about to get very dark." With that, he and Zeitler led them into the tunnel.

Thompson remained alert yet unafraid. He felt none of the uneasiness he sometimes experienced when clearing out Iraqi tunnels. The man had a knack for picking up danger as if it was broadcast through the dark spaces and into his brain. His Ranger team swore he was psychic; he knew he wasn't. Thompson accepted and was grateful for his ability. Still, he realized it was almost certainly his brain processing stimuli he didn't even realize existed. A whiff of air carrying the odor of someone's breath, a subtle shift in the degree of darkness, all undetectable with the conscious mind, yet, a signal to his brain stem of impending danger or prey.

The tunnel was straight, running sixty-two yards, always ten by ten feet in size, from the cellar of the main facility to the outbuilding.

"People," said Everett, "you can relax a little; whatever used this tunnel is gone. I still need you to stay alert. We need any clues we can get our hands on. Davis let out a sigh of relief that was almost pitiful. There was a stench emanating from somewhere in their front.

The group walked about fifty yards when Zeitler commanded, "everyone stop!" The group froze.

Zeitler pointed his flashlight to an old fruit crate. Its wood, shrunken by years of dryness, no longer met evenly with the small nails holding it together. What caught the patrolman's attention wasn't the crate but what sat on top of it - small pieces of organs, presumably Donovan's.

"Whatever this is," Gonzales said, "possesses a high level of intelligence."

"Why do you say that?" Gomez asked.

"Because it's taunting us."

"How do you know?" She responded.

"Ms. Gomez," Thompson said, pointing with his flashlight at the gory display, "the arrangement of the organs."

"What do you mean?" Davis asked. Panic was clearly in his voice.

"They are," Thompson said judiciously, "in anatomical

order. Whatever did this wants us to find this trophy."

"We have a serial killer on our hands," Gomez stated bitterly. A brew of disgust, fear, and anger were roiling in her stomach. "There's only one question left to answer."

"What's that?" Davis choked out.

Gomez, not taking her eyes off the grate, answered, "is it human?"

***

The group was back at Davis' office. Gomez had contacted the State Attorney General, Allison McDonald, advising her of the find. McDonald listened to the grim report Gomez gave to her, in disturbing detail, then handed the phone to Davis. The warden had shut his panic out, if not away, and finished his time in the tunnel in a dignified state. No one blamed him for panicking; they were all close to losing control.

"Yes, Madam Attorney General," Davis stated, expecting to receive his termination notice. He certainly felt he let down his staff and prisoners. The warden felt hopelessly outmatched by the predator inside his prison. He was surprised and deeply grateful for the words the Attorney General gave him.

"Kelvin, I spoke to the governor; he wants you to know you have his full support. You also have mine. We're not giving you lip service; we mean to back you up with whatever it takes to catch this maniac."

"Thank you, Madam Attorney General," Kelvin spewed, on the verge of tears.

"Kelvin, call me Allison or Ms. McDonald."

"Yes, Ma'am ... I mean, Allison."

McDonald, having pumped some air into Davis' psyche, turned in a different direction. "I need to speak to Thompson."

Without so much as a word, Davis handed the phone to Everett. "Thompson here."

"Well, Mr. Thompson, what do you think of all this?" McDonald authorized a contract with him, over the state auditor's howls, on the grounds the Department of Wildlife couldn't get a handle on what animal, if any, killed the first two prisoners. It was apparent it was a serial killer; she wanted the last report before utilizing the contract's opt-out clause.

"Ms. McDonald, in all my years in special forces, and as a hunter-tracker, I've never seen anything like this."

"That's because this isn't war, and animals aren't serial killers," Allison responded.

"Ms. McDonald," Everett replied, "that's not true. Predators can, and have, become maneaters. In the nineteenth century, two lions in Tsavo, Africa, hunted and killed several people before being hunted and killed themselves."

"Yeah," Allison said, sarcastically, "they made a movie, *The Ghost and the Darkness*. My parents dragged me to the theater to see it. I wouldn't camp for a year. What do Val Kilmer's and Kirk Douglas' lions have to do with our psychopath?"

"I'm not convinced," Thompson said with a distinct note of irritation, "our culprit is a man, at least not a man working alone."

The statement piqued the attorney general's interest. "You think there are two people involved in the murders?"

"I don't know how many people are involved, but there is an animal involved, and it's damn strong. You received Gomez's report less than ten minutes ago; she accurately described the damaged door. Now, I know you'll send a forensic team, but I damn well know they won't find any marks from a crowbar or jaws of life, indicating protracted work to break the lock and welds. Whatever ripped it off the hinges must possess extraordinary strength.

There was a silence that stretched out for several seconds, then Everett heard a brusque demand, "tell Davis to put me on speaker."

Everett was about to relay the command when Davis said just as tersely, "I heard her."

McDonald immediately took charge of the conversation. "Officer Zeitler, you haven't added to the conversation.

Why?"

Zeitler's face turned red, and sweat began to form on his nearly bald head almost immediately. "Why?" he repeated, taken off guard.

"Yes, Officer…why?"

"Because I agree."

"Agree with what?" McDonald asked.

Zeitler knew his career would soon end, yet he felt his duty to do what was right. "There is a serial killer, and it is eating part of the remains of its victims. It's also, in classic character, taunting us, letting us know it has the upper hand."

"Male or female, Officer?" She queried.

"I can't say with certainty, yet my gut tells me it's male."

"Just one?" asked McDonald. Despite the highway patrolman's reluctance to speak, he mentally cataloged everything he had witnessed.

"That's my hunch, Ma'am."

"Then, just one man, is that correct, Officer Zeitler?"

"No, Madam Attorney General," Erik Zeitler responded.

"Then, you subscribe to Mr. Thompson's hypothesis that the killer may use a large animal to make his killings?"

Here goes my career, Erik thought. He visualized water swirling in a white porcelain toilet bowl. "No, Ms. McDonald, I don't. The animal is the serial killer."

"Officer," McDonald quietly asked, "are you telling me the killer is an animal that is intelligent and sadistic enough to be a serial killer?"

Zeitler closed his eyes. Davis placed a hand on the officer's shoulder. "Yes, Madam Attorney General, I do."

Before McDonald could even form a thought about the highway patrolman's statement, she heard Davis say, "I concur."

That was followed immediately by Gomez's "Me too."

She did not know what to say to an impossible conclusion, yet three highly respected professionals formed it, she fell back to her fail-safe. "I'm going to ask the governor to request FBI assistance. In the interim, Mr. Zeitler, Ms. Gomez, and Mr. Thompson, you are to lend all assistance to Mr. Davis' efforts to secure the safety of prisoners and staff. Do all of you understand my order?"

A chorus of, *Yes Ma'am* rang through her phone's receiver. Upon receiving the affirmative responses, she immediately disconnected the call, no longer wanting to hear what they had to say.

***

"What are you thinking, Jackson?" Atticus asked from the upper bunk, or as he called it, his second-class berth.

"The murders," I responded. "I can't stop thinking

about those dead men."

I could hear Atticus place a mark to indicate his place in the book he was reading, Thomas Merton's *The Seven Storey Mountain*, and quietly lay it on the covers. It's funny the things a person can notice when he shares a small space with another. A year before, I wouldn't have noticed the sound of a book touching a wool blanket. Now, I can tell if the volume is thick or thin, hell, even if it's paperback or hardbound.

"Jackson, you need to let these deaths go; they are consuming you," Atticus said.

"Atticus," I responded, "what if one of us is next?"

Atticus leaned over his bunk, his waist bending where it touched the frame. He looked at me; his features, even upside-down, were confident. His cheekbones showed in sharp relief due to his facial muscles contracting, which accentuated the harsh look in his eyes. His countenance reminded me of a parent upon hearing an incredulous statement from their child.

"That," he said tersely, "will never happen."

"You can't know that! We are cattle to this thing. Any of us could be next," I countered.

Still hanging over the bed, but with a calmer countenance, Atticus asked, "Do you trust me?"

"Of course, I do," I answered truthfully, "but….."

"But nothing," my cellmate gruffly interrupted. "I told

you before; you are my friend. I need you to trust me when I say our little group will escape danger."

"All right," I quietly answered, still not understanding Atticus' confidence yet somehow feeling a sense of comfort.

"Jackson, I'm rereading *The Seven Storey Mountain*. When I finish, I intend to offer it to Kareem. I think it will help him deal with his recent issues of faith."

I held my arm up, just outside the bunkbed's frame, my knuckles softly rapping the steel that held his mattress in place. He passed the copy to me without comment. Atticus didn't ask if I wanted to look at the book. He knew I would, and placed the volume in my hand, probably without questioning if my fingers would be waiting to grasp the autobiography. As I said, you get to know a person when you share at least twenty hours a day, confined to an eight-foot by ten-foot world.

I asked, "why is the word *Storey* in the title spelled with an *e* in it?"

"It's the English spelling of the word story, but it only refers to the floors of a building. Think of the mountain as seven stories tall. Of course, that's a metaphor for…."

"All right, all right, Judas Priest, Atticus, you're cramping my noggin." It was in the times when Atticus' brain peaked out from behind a book or a chess piece; I was reminded the state of Ohio was wasting a brilliant mind by placing him in that shithole prison.

***

Everyone in the warden's office stood when the man stepped into the room. Davis announced, "this is Special Agent Bernard Kaplan of the FBI. He joins us from the Chicago Field Office. The FBI assigned Agent Kaplan to this case due to his expertise in serial killers. He was instrumental in identifying, capturing, and successfully prosecuting the Capote murders in Missouri and Kansas. This man knows as much about the subject of serial killers as anyone in the nation."

Agent Kaplan shook hands with everyone, identifying each person by their title and name. It was evident to all involved that Kaplan had studied the case. Zeitler, who attended a conference in which Kaplan was a speaker, was relieved to have the agent join the investigation.

"Well, agent Kaplan," said Gomez, "I see you already know all the players in this little game."

"Quite the contrary," Kaplan said with a smile, "I don't know who the murderer is, and he, or she, is the most important person. However, you are correct, at least from the killers' point of view."

"How's that?" Gomez asked.

"To him," responded the agent, "it's a game. He wants

to show us he is smarter, cleverer, and therefore superior to us."

"Hell of a game," Thompson interjected. "People are being ripped wide open, and their livers eaten."

"How do you know this?" Queried Kaplan.

"We've seen it with our own eyes," responded Davis.

Zeitler, however, knew the agent was more than questioning the crime; he was challenging the group's assumptions.

"You believe," Kaplan responded, "the victims were dead, and part of the livers eaten. You are assuming the victims were dead at the time of the cannibalism. I saw nothing in any of the autopsy reports, including the independent exam of Brent's body, which conclusively states removal of the victims' livers were post mortem."

"Agent Kaplan," said Thompson, "I know you are…."

The agent interrupted him. "Bernie, please call me Bernie. My parents named me after Browns quarterback, Bernie Kosar."

"Okay, Bernie," Thompson responded, "what point are you driving at?"

"What I'm stating," Kaplan judiciously answered, "is that this group has made assumptions, not unreasonable ones, yet assumptions, nonetheless. We need to wipe the slate clean and focus only on the facts, and in case we are not certain, use professional estimates and conclusions.

We must always leave the door open to change based on the evidence, as it becomes clearer."

"Where do you suggest we start?" Asked a flustered Gomez.

"At the beginning, of course."

***

The small group assembled once again in Davis' office. At Kaplan's request, Chief Officer Taylor Gonzales was also in attendance, as he supervised all guards and saw the tunnel's evidence. They were, once again, staring at the map. With his finger, the agent traced the site of the first murder to that of the second. Then, he ran it to the location of the third murder - Castway, aka-Crusoe.

"Mr. Thompson," Bernie asked, "am I correct the third murder occurred after you inspected the prison?"

"Yes."

"What do you think of the crime locations?"

"The assailant is following an orderly path, yet…." Thompson paused.

"Yet, what, Everett?"

The hunter sighed, staring hard at the prison's design prints. "Mr. Castway's murder seems risky, out in the open. It doesn't make sense."

"Mr. Thompson, you have a good eye," Kaplan

remarked. “If you follow the progression, where does our killer strike next?”

Everett leaned in and placed his finger on the map, showing an isolated section of a lower level. “Here,” he said. “It’s isolated, one way in and out. The assailant would corner and eliminate his prey without prying eyes.”

“I don’t know,” Gonzales stated. “Who would be there? Neither staff nor inmates go to that location.”

“Officer Gonzalez,” replied Kaplan, “you hit the nail on the head.”

“What?” asked the chief officer.

Thompson’s eyes grew wide, yet it was Zeitler who suddenly understood, with horrifying clarity, what the agent and the hunter already recognized. Zeitler said meekly, “Mr. Thompson, the trap is for you.”

***

The lockdown entered its second week, and the strain on the prisoners was taking a toll. I was battling insomnia. I struggled through Shakespeare’s *The Merchant of Venice* while Atticus worked his way through volume two of Shelby Foote’s narrative of the American Civil War. In frustration, I jumped out of my bunk and whipped the volume against the wall. Atticus had loaned it to me, and I immediately regretted my action.

Atticus climbed off his bed and retrieved poor, abused Shakespeare. He examined the book, and without turning to me, said, "it appears she weathered the tempest."

"Atticus," I said in near tears, terrified I hurt my best friend. "I'm so sorry I threw your book. I felt the walls closing in on me, and I just lost it."

Genuine kindness isn't an abundant commodity in prison. So, to disrespect its offer is considered by both convicts or staff as ludicrous. Atticus had every right to turn his back on me, yet he gently placed his hand on my shoulder and quietly said, "please don't do that again."

I nodded yet said nothing for fear of breaking down.

"Jackson," he said, with a smile, "we need something to break the monotony. How about a game of charades?" He must have seen the shine in my eyes because he added, "let's have some fun."

We began the game, me shouting guesses. Soon, other inmates, hearing the clamor, asked to join. Atticus or I would hold drawings of what the person was doing through the bars. The other inmates extended handheld mirrors through the bars to see the pictures. They would yell their guesses. Eventually, even some of the guards joined in, and a great deal of stress was released. That night I slept like a baby.

***

"Thompson, are you nuts?" Davis asked angrily, almost hissing his question.

"Warden," he responded angrily, "do you want to catch this prick or not?"

Davis sighed, nodding his head with an air of reluctance. "Yes, Mr. Thompson, I want to apprehend this killer; however, I'm worried for your safety. Why has he, pardon the phrase, targeted you?"

"Because," Gonzales stated, "this person or whatever it is, wants more interesting prey. Thompson has Special Forces training, and the prisoners know he is a hunter-tracker."

"Why didn't the killer go after someone like Bucky Brandenshaw," Davis countered. "He's massive, and if his reputation is right, a hell of a fighter. It must have taken a tough group to beat him the way they did, putting him in the hospital."

"There was no group," Gonzales stated. "One man beat him."

"The investigation was inconclusive," Zeitler chimed in.

Gonzales looked at both men harshly. "You both know damn well inmates won't talk, at least not to us. Trust me;

it was one man."

Kaplan sat quietly, taking in every piece of the exchange.

"Who?" Davis growled.

"Are you going to punish him?" Gonzales asked.

"No, but I want to know who crushed Brandenshaw."

Gonzales checked Davis' eyes but knew the man didn't lie. "It was Atticus Crabtree."

"The bookworm and chess player?" Davis asked incredulously. "How?"

"No weapons," Gonzales replied. "Just him and Bucky in the shower. Bucky bragged he was going to make Atticus his bitch."

"Warden," Gomez responded, "why are you so surprised? Fights don't always end the way we thought."

"Because," Davis answered, "Atticus has no business winning a brawl against Bucky, let alone the severity of the beating. That ass-kicking hospitalized Brandenshaw. Bucky is massive and an experienced prison brawler. It would take a miracle for Atticus to hold his own, let alone inflict that much damage on that thug."

Gonzales nodded and added, "Crabtree had no business coming out on top, let alone how well he looked."

Thompson and Kaplan showed noticeable interest while Zeitler sat in the background, his eyes alert.

"What do you mean by how well he looked?" Bernie asked.

"I remember looking for marks of a fight, trying to identify who fought Bucky. I remember seeing a slight red mark on Atticus' left cheek, and the knuckles on his left hand were slightly scratched. Other than that, he looked unscathed."

Davis glared at the guard, shook his head, but said nothing.

"Officer Gonzales," Gomez harshly asked, "why didn't you volunteer this information during the subsequent investigation?"

"Because," Gonzales stuttered, "it was Atticus Crabtree. I didn't see him as a possible participant in the altercation. I couldn't fathom him winning a shower-room fight against Brandenshaw, let alone walking away with only superficial injuries. By the time I overheard two prisoners talking, the investigation was over, the case closed. The inmates would never testify, and Brandenshaw refused to identify his assailant."

"I agree," Zeitler interjected. "I would have also eliminated Crabtree from the list of possible suspects. The man doesn't come close to fitting the profile of a fighter. One look at him by the prosecutors, and they would laugh us out of their office."

Kaplan examined the group, checking each person's face for their reaction to the news. Seeming satisfied, he said, "bring him in. Let's talk with our enigmatic, Mr.

Crabtree."

***

The investigative group sat in a semi-circle with Atticus facing them. The room was silent, each person sizing up the medium-sized man wearing prison blues. Zeitler noted Crabtree was silently returning the favor. His eyes gleamed with a quiet intelligence and thoughtfulness that impressed the highway patrolman.

Kaplan started the conversation. "Mr. Crabtree, I'm Special Agent Kaplan, FBI. Do you know why you are here?"

"I originally thought for organizing the game of charades. Yet, unless parlor games are an F1 felony, this seems to be overkill."

"No, Mr. Crabtree, you wouldn't be here for a simple game. We want to talk to you about Bucky Brandenshaw."

"I don't associate with the man," Atticus responded.

"But you did about six months ago, in the shower." The agent quipped.

"Am I being charged with his beating?"

"No," the agent replied, "I have no interest in prosecution, and the prison has assured me that you will not face the consequences for anything related to your alleged involvement in the incident."

Atticus turned his attention to Gonzales, quietly studying the man.

"Atticus," the guard said, "it's the truth; you don't have to worry."

Atticus sighed and turned his attention back to the agent. "Am I to talk to you directly, or is my confession to the group?"

"The entire group," was Davis' quick reply, not waiting for Kaplan's answer.

"If that's the case, I ask that you wait until I finish before asking me any questions; they play hell with my train of thought."

There was no answer; still, everyone grabbed a pen and paper. Atticus nodded; his face, however, remained neutral. When everyone returned their attention to the prisoner, he began his story. "Before this charge, I had not spent a second of my life incarcerated. My attorney told me, given my lack of priors, I would receive a low-security assignment. Instead, the assessors at the Orient Facility placed me in a high-security prison." Atticus stopped long enough to allow the investigators time to write his opening statement. There was no sound except pens being drug across paper.

"Being new to the prison system, I was ignorant of its culture. I believe the term is *fish*. I'm not a big man, nor particularly imposing. I suppose I looked the part of an easy target. It will come as no surprise to Officer Gonzales that Bucky Brandenshaw is a bully and an extortionist. In the outside world, if threatened, one could call the police. Prison, however, is, to a large degree, a closed system. There is nowhere to run, no one that can guarantee a just resolution."

Zeitler and Gonzales were nodding their heads in acknowledgment of Crabtree's observation. Atticus appeared deep in thought. A slight frown and sad eyes accentuated his face. Kaplan was about to ask Atticus to continue, but the prisoner beat him to the punch.

"I walked into the shower with no plans other than to bathe, brush my teeth, and apply some of the commissary's deodorant." Atticus chuckled in remembrance. "My cellmate, Jackson, told me the first giveaway that I was new to prison life was that, at the commissary, I bought candy instead of hygiene products. I already possessed toiletries, but my gaff was a big no-no. He also told me *never* to call a prisoner by the term inmate. They identify themselves as inmates. I'm sure I gave off a hundred different signals I was new to prison life. Apparently, that made me a target for violence."

Gonzales nodded involuntarily; the muscular officer had witnessed the same scene countless times.

"I apologize for my digression, time to move onward with this tale. Mr. Brandenshaw followed me into the shower. He informed me that I was to be his new bitch. Pure providence provided that I had already completed using soap on my face and shoulders, allowing for unabated eyesight. I said a succinct *no thank you.* He responded that he wasn't asking. He walked forward, fists clenched, no doubt intending to rape me. That's when he slipped on the soapy floor. I didn't waste the opportunity; I immediately kicked him rather viciously in the groin, several times in the ribs, and proceeded to beat his face for all I was worth. Even battered, he connected a glancing blow on my left cheek."

"What happened next," Kaplan inquired.

I knew I could make a statement that I wasn't easy prey. I forced myself to calm down, then finished my shower, afterward even using the ubiquitous prison deodorant. I then walked casually out of the shower room as if nothing happened. I've had no contact with Brandenshaw since the incident."

Other than the sound of scribbling, the room was quiet, and then even that gave way to silence. Kaplan observed the man Davis described as a bookworm and chess player. In his experience, most people are uncomfortable with long periods of silence, yet, Atticus appeared at ease with the lack of conversation. The agent didn't see the usual passive-aggressive signs prisoners often exhibit in the presence of the law: yawns, crossed arms, looking away

- desperate attempts to grasp some sense of power in situations where they lacked any sense of self-direction. Atticus, on the contrary, appeared relaxed and confident, but not in the least smug or defiant. Although not knowing Jackson's opinion, the FBI agent had arrived at the same conclusion. It was a waste to incarcerate this prisoner.

"You don't talk like most prisoners," Davis stated.

Kaplan and Zeitler cringed, knowing they just lost the opportunity to open and direct the questioning with focused inquiries.

"Was that meant as an insult or a compliment?" Atticus responded.

Davis' face turned a deep shade of red, but he didn't respond. Gomez openly glared at the warden.

The agent waited for the prisoner to push his advantage, yet he didn't. It became evident to everyone that Crabtree didn't feel the need to manipulate the conversation; he didn't see the interrogation as a contest.

"Mr. Crabtree," Kaplan asked, "you want us to believe you single-handedly beat a man at least one hundred pounds, mostly muscle, larger than you?"

"It does seem fortuitous, doesn't it, Agent Kaplan?"

"Yes, it does," Bernie judiciously replied.

Atticus nodded and softly chuckled, "I'm in prison, yet I'm saved from a rapist by a few drops of shampoo that I unknowingly spilled on the floor. If I possessed a higher opinion of my station in the cosmos, I might consider it a left-handed gift from the gods."

"Left-handed gift from the gods," Davis spat out with disdain. "Where did you learn that phrase, Bookworm; Dickens, Aristotle, Nietzsche?"

Atticus responded, glaring at the man, "Nietzsche and Aristotle were atheists, and as for the phrase, I've not come across it in any of Dickens' works. I first discovered the term in a piece of work by King, Stephen, to be exact."

Minus the warden, the investigators wore looks of embarrassment on their faces. Bernie couldn't believe Davis had shot off his mouth during an interrogation. The agent forced his body to relax, allowing his hands to stop shaking from anger. "Thank you, Mr. Crabtree," Kaplan stated, "that will be all. Please close the door behind you." Kaplan controlled his voice only with great effort.

When they knew Atticus was beyond earshot, Kaplan exploded. "You stupid shit, he was talking with us! Now, we can forget getting any more information from the man."

"Oh, good God," Davis sarcastically responded, "the man is a wussy. He lucked out and made a reputation for being tough. Good for him, but it's not real. He's not our killer, and since arriving, his most dangerous behavior is instigating a game of charades."

"Kelvin Davis," Zeitler sadly stated, "you did worse

than ruin an interview; you insulted a good man. We all know he didn't deserve a high-security assignment."

Gomez studied the highway patrolman, frankly stunned by his statement. "Erik, when did you become soft on criminals?"

"Rachel, I'm not, and you know it," Zeitler snapped. "But, there is something about this man; he's not a normal prisoner. Gonzalez, what are your guards' opinion of Atticus?"

Gonzales looked around the room before answering. "The guards report he is compliant, respectful, and they've had no trouble with him."

"That's great for the parole board," Bernie responded. "But what do your guards *think* about him?"

Gonzalez exhaled, looked at the agent, and said, "I prefer not to repeat what is confided to me by those I supervise, especially when it doesn't affect their work."

Davis sighed, regret clearly written on his face. He had already decided when they closed the case he was taking two weeks of vacation to the Bahamas. "Officer," Davis said, "we are beyond niceties and protocols. We need to know if we can close him off as a suspect or dig further. Nothing your officers said could be worse than what just spilled out of my mouth. Please, Gonzales, we need to solve this case quickly."

The supervising officer nodded reflectively, consenting

to the warden's logic. "The guards don't understand Atticus. They can't figure out what he did to deserve a high-security prison. They worry they're missing something about him. That he may be dangerous, and that makes them nervous."

"Then there is Atticus' behavior; he isn't a phony intellectual trying to impress others. He's far smarter and infinitely more educated than the average prisoner, yet he shows no signs of trying to manipulate others. The game of charades he started diffused considerable stress in that ward. A man of Atticus' intelligence could easily parlay the goodwill he built into some sort of advantage, yet there is no indication he did it for any reason than to help the prisoners and staff."

"He belongs to a small, unremarkable clique. That tough Dominican, Jessie Vazquez, is a member, and that tends to dissuade other prisoners from bothering them. Even among that group, Mr. Crabtree appears to occupy the fringe, though he seems genuinely fond of them, and they of him. After his incident with Brandenshaw, he now has a formidable reputation, though I haven't heard of him extorting other prisoners. Neither my officers nor the prisoners know what to make of him, and they tend to leave him alone."

"What about his cellmate, Jackson Mack?" Davis asked.

"Anyone who reads his file knows he is a chronic thief. Like Crabtree," Gonzales continued, "he probably shouldn't be in high security, but while he was in the Lima Penitentiary, he was involved in a messy fight with a guy who tried to steal his food. The state didn't file charges against him, but it was thought he inflicted more damage than was needed. The guards don't share that opinion. If left alone, he is harmless."

"What about Brandenshaw," Bernie asked, "Do any of you think he could be our killer?"

"No," Gonzalez immediately answered. "That man is a thug, a stupid, hot-tempered bully, nothing more. He isn't smart, patient, or creative enough to plan and carry out these murders. In addition to the inmates, I checked the staff records. None were at the prison for all three deaths. I don't know who is capable of carrying out these crimes. It could be anyone. Not knowing that's the thing that scares me the most."

"Trust me, Officer Gonzales," Kaplan quietly replied, "it takes more than just anyone to be *our* killer."

***

"Busted for stealing milk money?"

"Excuse me, Jackson?" Atticus asked.

Without looking up from my book, *The Shadow Land*, I

continued my inquiries. "The investigating team brought you into the Wardens' office. I figured it couldn't be for the murders, so I paired down the charges to the worst thing I could imagine you doing, and even that seemed to be stretching reality."

"You would be wrong, my dear friend. The interrogation concerned the assault committed against Bucky Brandenshaw."

"What?" I exclaimed, laying aside the dictionary I continually used when reading Kostova's books. "They aren't going to charge you, are they?"

"The people in the task group say no. They only want to know what happened."

"But, George said he saw the paperwork on the wardens' desk; the case is closed," I replied, fear seeping into my voice. Worry etched on my face.

Atticus sat on the single chair we were allowed and rested his elbows on his knees, his hands between his legs, interweaving his fingers, his head bowed in thought. "I don't think they care about my fight with Brandenshaw. I believe they wanted to find out if I was somehow connected to the killings, though they never said."

I felt an instant surge of relief; I thought there was no way in hell Atticus could be involved in something so twisted. "That's a relief," I cheerfully replied.

Atticus raised his head, then his eyebrows. "Why do

you say that?"

"Because you're Atticus," I replied, flustered over his lack of insight. "You were just someone they needed to cross off their list. They'll probably question all of us."

"The FBI agent didn't believe my story about the fight. The warden believes me but doesn't like me. He calls me *Bookworm*."

His response startled me. He was the best friend I ever had, and the thought of him being charged, or moved, caused me a sensation, not unlike the squeezing of my bowels. The warden's dislike was also not good. I don't think anyone who hasn't experienced prison can genuinely understand the power a warden possesses. In prison, the warden is God, with an extra-large *G*.

I also knew enough of American justice that if the law, and those who wielded it, decided you committed a crime, whether they possessed good reason or not, were going to work until they had a conviction. Still, there were limits, and I thought Atticus was probably beyond them. I knew if charged with the murders, he wouldn't be convicted. And, no one, including the system, really cared about Brandenshaw's beating.

"Jackson, will you play a game or two of chess with me?"

"Another lesson?" I asked.

"In a way, just games and try to set traps."

"Why?"

"So, I can practice turning them to my advantage."

***

"They're working," Gonzales said into the walkie-talkie."

The I.T. department had spent the better part of two days installing cameras in the area Thompson would occupy. The extra cameras fed live streams directly into screens placed in Davis' office. After a heated debate, the hunter had received permission to wait in the next probable kill zone. He knew he was simultaneously the hunter and the bait.

Kaplan and Gonzales would occupy the adjoining halls. Once the killer entered the room, they would close the escape route. Zeitler wanted to join Everett, but he told him he wanted the patrolman to watch the screens. What he didn't say was that he lacked faith in Davis to remain emotionally calm enough to relay information. Zeitler was also familiar with the prison and likely to locate the killer's position. Gomez, as a representative of the state, would observe but no more.

"I want those areas mopped with a strong disinfectant," Thompson stated.

"Why?" asked Zeitler.

"I want to mask our odors."

"Do you think that's necessary?"

"I want every advantage. Remember what Bernie said about assumptions; we can't assume the killer doesn't possess a keen sense of smell. Plus, it will reduce the risk of infection if we are injured."

"I'll get multiple guards to accompany the janitorial crew when they enter the area," Gonzales interjected.

"That's good," stated Thompson, "but unnecessary. He wants me."

***

I remember doing pushups in our cell. Physical fitness is a requirement in prison, given the heightened threat of violence, as well as the lack of quality healthcare. Atticus laid on his bunk, silent, his eyes closed. As I switched to sit-ups, I could see him. His body appeared relaxed, yet something told me his mind was in motion. He looked as if he was deep in concentration. He seemed oblivious to my grunting as I pushed my body. Not wanting to disturb him, I quietly grabbed my clothes and headed for the shower.

When I returned, Atticus was reading a paperback novel. Other than Ray Bradberry's *The Martian Chronicles*, I rarely saw him read science fiction. But what caught my attention was that, by the cheesy cover, it was a B-quality tale. I had never seen him read anything other than high-quality work. "Atticus, why are you reading that piece of crap? The cover alone is shit."

"You know the adage: *never judge a book by its cover*."

"Is it good?"

"No, in fact, it's horrible."

"Then why are you reading it?" I asked.

"Change of pace. Reading relaxes me, but I didn't want anything that would require intense concentration."

I was about to ask why but stopped. Atticus' eyes grew large; he looked the same way when he had pieced together the strategy of a chess opponent.

"Jackson, you're wearing deodorant!"

"I always do," I said a little defensively. "I don't want people smelling me."

"Exactly," he stated.

Atticus' face took on a gleam as if he discovered something no one else knew. The way he looked was unnerving. Despite the slight smile, there was something sinister about my cellmate's countenance. For the first time since we met, I feared him. He must have read my face because his features relaxed, and he tossed the novel on his bunk.

"Jackson, you're right; I should elevate my sights. I think I'll start volume two of Ulysses S. Grant's autobiography. Did you know he finished the work a mere ten days before his death, and Mark Twain was his editor?"

"No, but I'm not surprised you do. So where do you find these tidbits of information?" I asked, relieved to have my old friend acting his usual self.

"They hide that information in books," he laughed.

I rolled my eyes, fell back on my bed, letting out a deep sigh. I knew Atticus was smart. Hell, everybody knew that. They also knew he was kind. However, for the first time, I suspected my friend was more than he appeared. While I lay on that bunk, I received an epiphany. I knew with sudden clarity, Atticus Crabtree was also dangerous.

***

"We've waited three nights and nothing!" Davis bellowed. "Has the killer skulked away or just plain stopped?"

"Neither," Thompson responded. "He was there, just not engaging us."

"Why?" Zeitler blurted out. The frustration of the case was revealing itself on his forehead in the form of contracted muscles, causing ridges to build above his eyebrows.

"It's called reconnaissance," replied Thompson. "He wants to understand our trap before he enters it. And the killer was there, though I'm embarrassed to say how I know."

"You could feel him, couldn't you?" Gonzales asked. "I know I did, sitting, waiting in that lonely hall."

Kaplan and Everett nodded in agreement.

"Do you have any clue as to when he will make his move against you?"

"Tonight," Thompson replied. "He wants to bag his trophy and move on. If the killer is, as I suspect, a prisoner, he will be gone by morning headcount. If I don't survive this night, you can follow the trail of the missing prisoner."

"And what if two or more prisoners are missing?" Gomez responded. "Maybe the killer is killers…plural."

"No," replied Kaplan, "this is a single murderer. If more than one prisoner is missing, then it's meant as a distraction. I agree with the FBI profile; this is a lone wolf. The circumstances are extraordinary, but the insight is valid. This person is cunning, intelligent, and worst of all, experienced. He's done this kind of business before. We either get this guy tonight or not at all. There's no in-between."

Thompson looked around the room and asked, "Can any of you buy flowers for tonight?"

"Why?" Kaplan queried.

"I want to change up the fragrance a little, give him something new to consider. Also, leave only the emergency lights on. I want his eyes large and wide when we turn on the high illumination. I want him blinded for a couple of seconds. I will need that time to put my Bowie knife and a few rounds into him."

"And if that doesn't bring him down?" asked Davis.

"Then look for my liver; he will leave it somewhere obvious."

"To mock us, no doubt," Gomez complained bitterly.

"No, as a concession," Zeitler interjected. "He's brutal and efficient, but there's still a sense of fair play. Our killer doesn't boast. He may be merciless, but he isn't impolite. I thought the arrangement of Donovan's organs was a taunt; now, I see it as a warning. It was telling us of what we were up against. I don't think he murders to show anyone he is superior; he kills to improve his hunting abilities. He probably tries to better himself in every area of his life. His arrangement of Donovan's remains, which at the time appeared to be the hallmark of grandiose, sociopathic behavior, was meant to draw in an FBI agent. He needed better competition to sharpen his skills. Mentally, he is trying to outwit us, and tonight will attempt to use his skills to their best ability."

"So, you're not convinced he enjoys killing?" Gonzales asked.

"No, I'm not. But whether the killer finds pleasure or not, he is slaughtering people and must be killed."

"Whoa, hold on there," Gomez emphatically stated. Her

hands went into the air, fingers spread apart. It reminded Kaplan of someone trying to quiet a room. "If this man surrenders, you must not harm him. He is to be restrained according to Ohio Statutory Law, and isolated from the rest of the prison population, pending legal disposition."

"And then what, Rachel?" Davis asked. "Is he to stand trial? Even if convicted, and with this set of circumstances, it's a big if, will he remain in prison? He has already shown doors are no hindrance. So how do we keep people safe?"

"Rachel, I get what you mean," Kelvin continued, not unkindly. "You know me, I have always stood up for prisoner rights, even when it made me unpopular. But this man is more than human, and we can't let our incredulity guide us into self-deception. This thing cannot be allowed to see another sunrise."

Gomez nodded, her head slightly bowed. She knew the warden was right yet hated the part of herself that agreed with his assessment. Rachel had spent her career in pursuit of justice. She believed whole-heartedly in the concept of America as a nation of laws, not given to petty tyrants, ruling elites, or mob justice. Now, she accepted putting a man to death, even if he attempted to surrender.

She felt a steady hand on her shoulder; it was Erik Zeitler's. "Rachel," he said, "I think I know what you are feeling. I, too, have sworn to uphold the law; but innocent people will die if we don't eliminate him. They may be prisoners, but they are still humans and deserve our best effort to protect them." Without looking up, she placed one of her mocha hands on top of his and squeezed it slightly.

"These are all philosophical questions," Gonzales interjected, "and good ones, but they will have to wait until we're finished. We don't have the luxury of time. We can congratulate or self-recriminate ourselves later."

And with that statement, the group tucked away their doubts and went about preparations for the night.

***

"Atticus," Jackson asked, "how far are you into the Grant autobiography?"

"The part where Lincoln gave Grant control over all Union forces. It seems the general had a high opinion of General Meade. That despite the fact the latter could've annihilated the Confederate Army of Northern Virginia after its defeat at the Battle of Gettysburg. He instead hesitated to pursue it. That time allowed it to slip to safety south of the Potomac River."

"Goodnight, Atticus," I said and rolled onto my side, facing the cinderblock wall, painted a dark brown to cover any stains…or hope. Pulling the sturdy sheet and wool blanket up to my chin, I was asleep in under five minutes.

***

Thompson had just finished a walkie-talkie check. The use of a newer model and a headset eliminated the necessity of pressing and depressing any buttons. Everyone was communicating without difficulty. The three were also able to speak with the makeshift control room in Davis' office.

Come quick and clean, with no malice between us, Thompson thought, as he lowered himself into an ergonomic, swivel chair.

He had killed many combatants in his tours of duty, including a member of the Russian Special Forces, who was using a laser to help a fighter jet lock its missiles onto a Marine base in Syria. There was so much fear and mistrust between the belligerents that he often wondered if they just sat down and talked, would they find a tangible reason to fight. He didn't want such impurity in this conflict. He accepted the real possibility of death and only wanted to match skills with the best predator he'd ever come across.

"No ideology, my friend," he muttered. "Let's do this right."

Gonzales heard a faint noise about thirty yards down the hall. Before the killings, he would have passed it off as a noisy water pipe. Now, however, his sharp mind processed every sound. Every shadow in the corner of his eye was a potential threat. He forced himself to breathe deep and slow, holding each breath for three seconds, counting before exhaling.

Only when he felt his muscles and mind release the stress did he press the button on his walkie-talkie. "I have company."

Kaplan heard Gonzales' calm announcement, signaling the killer's arrival. The smell of flowers filled the hallway, engulfing it with a sickish scent. The aroma seemed to pull the air from his lungs, replacing it with gas as alien as that of another world. His increasing stress only compounded the difficulty he was enduring in breathing. That, combined with the claustrophobic feeling of sitting in a narrow hallway, was playing havoc with his mind.

The sensation caused a level of panic he hadn't felt since his first raid. The atmosphere reminded the FBI agent of a funeral parlor. He fleetingly wondered if he was experiencing what the dead feels when the living closes the coffin lid, leaving them with only darkness, cramped space, and the disgustingly sweet smell of floral arrangements. He made a mental note that if they survived the night, he would kick Thompson's ass for requesting flowers.

Everett spoke into the walkie-talkie, “Gonzales, give me some intel.”

“The light is too dim to see that far down the hall, but it’s moving slowly toward me. The sound is getting closer. Hold it; I hear panting like a large animal. Maybe we have a bear, after all.”

Thompson considered the possibility of a simple case of a rogue bear, but he knew it was wishful thinking.

“Gonzales,” he said, “get ready to bail out of that hallway. I’m coming to the adjoining door.”

“I hear a click like a dog makes on a linoleum floor, but there is something else.” Everyone heard Gonzalez gulp, most likely from fear. “The nails are also being raked against the bricks.”

Davis interjected, “Officer Gonzales, are you sure? The brick portion of the walls starts at four feet off the floor.”

“Do you want me to switch on the main lights?” Zeitler asked, with tenseness in his voice.

“No,” Gonzales’ replied quickly. “This is our chance to bag this bastard. We’ll keep with the plan.”

“Erik, what do you see on the cameras?”

“I see something dark, but it’s hugging the wall tightly. I can’t tell you anything other than it looks big and stopped moving, about twenty yards from you.”

Thompson was listening to the conversation; something

didn't seem right about the thing's behavior. "Is it still running its nails across the wall?"

"Yes, and it's growling." Gonzales sounded nervous; Everett couldn't blame him.

"Don't raise your gun," Everett said emphatically.

"It's already drawn," was the curt reply.

Thompson could tell if the issue didn't quickly end, Gonzales would crack from the stress. Like everyone else's, the guard's brain was wired by countless centuries of evolution to choose fight or flight. He had to cut through the fog of fear the man was experiencing. "Officer Gonzales!" he said in a rough, mean tone. "Holster your weapon."

After a couple of seconds of silence, Gonzales answered, "Done, but I don't like it."

"There's a reason I instructed you to put away your piece."

"What's that, Mr. Hunter-Tracker?" Gonzales asked sarcastically.

Good, thought Thompson. *If he's pissed at me, at least he won't be frozen with fear.*

"For your safety. The killer picked you as bait, hoping we would rush to your aid. He is hoping I will come to you."

"I'm a good shot; why not let me throw some lead at him?"

I don't doubt your accuracy, but you said it yourself; you couldn't see him well. If you shoot him, you may kill him, or more likely, piss him off. Then, he would probably murder you. You are carrying a .32 caliber handgun; do you think that will stop the thing that tore off that bulkhead door? You aren't on his menu; don't put yourself there."

There was a sudden roar that eliminated any remaining hope the killer was human. Gonzales felt paralyzed, but not by fear. Instead, he could feel the sound pulverizing his insides.

Thompson, in the adjoining hallway, could feel it to a lesser degree. The last time he had that physical sensation was when he hunted a tiger that was a habitual maneater. At one point during the hunt, the big cat had roared, causing him temporary paralysis. Now, he felt his guts churn, and it was hard for him to move. Fleetingly, he thought, *our boy has low hertz infrasound, nice addition…for him.*

"Gonzales?" No answer. "Taylor Gonzales!" yelled Zeitler into his microphone.

He finally responded. "It's gone, but I'm here, just taking a leak. That thing shook the piss out of me."

"Where are you?" asked Davis.

"In the hall."

"You're not allowed to urinate except in designated areas," said Davis. "Peeing on the floor sets a horrible example to those under your command."

Gomez and Zeitler looked at the warden incredulously.

"Warden Davis?"

"Yes, Officer Gonzales?"

"Fuck you."

***

Jackson woke with a start, sweat running down his face, a feeling of dread gripping his chest, stomach, and, most noticeably, his testicles. He placed an arm over his eyes, which was unnecessary, given his eyes were closed, and the light in the cell was the equivalent of twilight. It was more a sign of mental reflection than to relieve physical annoyance.

Something wasn't right; Jackson could feel it in his bones. Still, the issue alluded his attempts to identify. He also remembered Atticus' proverb*: you must define the problem before you can articulate it, and you must articulate the problem before you can hope to solve it.*

Sighing, Jackson quietly climbed out of his bed, not wanting to disturb his cellmate. He walked to their small, stainless steel basin and splashed his face with cold water. Jackson didn't bother drying himself; the man enjoyed the crisp, fresh feeling. He felt his skin tingle, reminding him of the summers he and his brother, Jimmy, would dive into Lake Erie every morning, just after sunrise.

He smiled in remembrance, the two of them roaring out of the cabin, running headlong toward a beach occupied only by seagulls. The water was cold after a night with only the moon for company. Plunging into the water, he always felt like there were a thousand needle pricks on his body. He and his brother would rise to the surface, treading water, smiling at each other with the ease of hearts only the young possess. By then, his skin had morphed into goosebumps. They would splash each other and laugh.

"That world is still out there, waiting for you," Jackson said to himself. At that moment, he swore he would never return to jail. He thought, *I'll take the psychiatric examination the prison has wanted from me for years. I'll follow the recommendations and learn to live like people who don't steal or break the law. I will ask for my brother's forgiveness for taking money out of his dresser while he was with his family at the movies.*

Jackson straightened himself, pushing his chest out with a sense of resolve he hadn't possessed in years. *Jimmy and I,* he thought, *will dive into a frigid lake, splashing, laughing, and watching the sun rising toward its zenith, bringing blue skies and wispy, white summer clouds along for the ride.*

Jackson experienced a sense of peace he hadn't felt in

years. He resolved to write his brother in the morning. Jackson felt so at ease he had forgotten why he awoke; until he turned and saw with surprise and despair, Atticus' bunk was empty.

***

Thompson's back was against the wall where the hallway ended. He was staring straight ahead at the steel-reinforced door, fifteen yards to his front. Three metal bars ran along the width of the door, each resting in slots fabricated and welded to the strong entryway. Everett knew they would not stop an animal capable of ripping away a hatch door that was welded shut. But that wasn't their reason. He wanted the thing to work, expending energy to get to him. The time the murderer spent tearing apart the door might give him a chance to line up his shot.

Everett was grateful Kaplan and Gonzales protected his flanks. He pondered if the thing, unable to lure the chief officer away from the adjoining door, would try something with the FBI agent. Bernie would be more challenging than Taylor, yet he gave only momentary speculation to the idea; the thing wanted to hunt the best the investigatory group offered, and that was him.

A rush of adrenaline hit him. Everett realized, without questioning why, the thing was on the other side of the door. He asked himself what he would do if he were in its position. His answer was to kill Gonzales and enter through the weaker door. He knew the thing wasn't going to take that route, or it would have eliminated the chief officer by now.

Davis confirmed Thompson's thoughts. "Everett, you have company right outside your door."

Zeitler added, "it isn't doing anything, in particular, just touching the door. That seems odd."

"Trust me, Erik," Kaplan responded, "it isn't strange. Everett, it's inspecting the barrier between you and it. Get ready."

"I am," was the short reply, followed by the sound of a round chambering into a rifle.

"What the hell, Everett," Gomez said. "How did you get a rifle into the prison?"

Kaplan answered for him. "I put it in his Christmas stocking. Now, everyone stop with the bullshit regulations. He's using himself as live bai…" The FBI agent didn't get to finish his sentence as a loud sound reverberated through Everett's microphone.

The door in front of Everett shook from a strike of tremendous energy. Cracks formed along the adjoining cinderblocks like varicose veins.

"We saw it, we saw it!" yelled Zeitler. "Dear God, Everett, get out! The thing, oh, dear God."

"Erik's right," Davis said. "I don't know what this thing is, but…"

There was another tremendous blow against the door, and the reinforcement bars started to bow. Pieces of the wall were splitting and falling. Before Thompson had time to process the damage fully, another strike caused a crack in the door, and the welds that held one of the reinforcement bars gave way. He knew, at that point, the door wouldn't stand the onslaught.

The pounding on the door was now constant. Part of him had hoped it wouldn't break; he wanted to see the sunrise, to go home to his dog. The shrill sound of metal tearing told him that it probably wasn't going to happen. He flipped the rifle's safety to the off position.

The noise made it hard to hear, but he gave a final set of instructions. "Erik, when I say *now*, flip on the lights. Bernie, Taylor, you both did well; now get the hell out of here. If I can't stop him with a 30-06, nothing you have on you is going to do the trick." Then he said quietly, yet with a tone that emitted pride, "it has been an honor."

Now, the only sound was the cracking of cinderblocks and twisting metal. Thompson placed a pair of sunglasses over his eyes and said, "Erik, get ready with the lights."

"I've got my finger by the button."

The top corner of the door, on the lock side, crumpled inward. Thompson couldn't believe the hands that reached through the opening. His brain overloaded from the terrific sounds of the door tearing apart, and now, those hands. They appeared so unlike a human's, yet the end of each muscular palm possessed four fingers and a thumb.

There was a moment of silence followed by Thompson's deeply inhaled breath. He saw an eye staring through the new opening. He had seen enough combat to know the look of a killer. His brain dimly remembered Dr. Richard Dawkins stating the eye may have evolved independently, up to forty times. *Make that forty-one, Dr. Dawkins*, he thought.

Thompson quickly began to calculate the proportions of his adversary based on eye height. He looked through the rifle's sights, using a knee to support the weapon. He wanted accurate shots.

Another slam, and the door bent sharply, the metal splitting with a loud cracking sound, announcing its back had broken. There was a moment of silence. Thompson knew the thing's examination of his side of the door was reconnaissance. It was thinking through what it saw inside the barricaded room, adjusting its plan of attack to give it the best chance of success.

"Erik," Everett said, "place your hand on the button."

"It's on it," he assured.

The supports gave way as the barricade failed to

withstand a steady pressure. A hinge cracked and bounced off the walls a few times, like a rubber ball. There was no explosion, the walls supporting the barricade crumpled, and the door fell inward, sending dust in a lazy wave. The thing stood, panting from the exertion necessary to gain entrance. It took two steps into the hallway, and Thompson yelled into his microphone, "Erik, now!"

Nothing happened.

Zeitler's voice screamed in Thompson's ears, "It's not working! It must have severed the electrical connection!"

Everett cursed and threw the sunglasses aside, but the thing had closed the gulf between them and was reaching for the rifle by that time. Everett pulled the trigger. There was a yelp of pain as the kinetic energy of the bullet propelled the thing backward. Then, before the animal had a chance to recover, another high-powered round hit it squarely in the chest. This time the sound wasn't from slight discomfort; it was full-throated pain.

Gonzales and Kaplan had returned to the control room and watched the ensuing battle. "That conniving fucker," Zeitler hissed. "It tore out the electrical circuits, cutting all but emergency power to the area."

Two more shots hit the animal, making four in total. Kaplan, his arms folded, stated, "any one of those shots would have killed a man,"

Davis walked with purpose, his back straight, to his

safe. Punching in the code, he opened the heavy door and removed a Smith and Wesson .460 magnum. He opened the cylinder. The chamber aligned with the hammer was always left empty for safety. He loaded the weapon and handed it to the FBI agent.

"And just where did you get that?" asked an incredulous Gomez.

"Thompson isn't the only one with a Christmas stocking," Davis said as he winked at Kaplan.

"Bernie," said Davis, "I gave you the magnum because you are no doubt a better shot, but I'm going with you." He withdrew a .460 Casull from its place in the safe.

The highway patrolman volunteered, "Kelvin, would you rather me go?"

"Erik, I absolutely want you to go instead of me, but it's my prison. I've spent this entire ordeal acting like a chicken shit or an asshole. No more, my friend; I'm taking back my facility."

Zeitler nodded, and the men rushed out the door.

Thompson placed the fifth round in the things right eye. Blood exploded out of the empty socket. With only one round left, Everett unsnapped the strap securing his bowie knife in place. He shot the last round directly into the center of the thing's chest. The bullet thing knocked it off its feet, writhing on the floor, smearing its blood into a pattern akin to some perverse snow angel.

Everett pulled his bowie knife, not allowing himself to think about the thing before him, jumped onto the beast, straddling its stomach. He squeezed his thighs against the animal for stability while going onto the balls of his feet for traction. He did all this inside of two seconds as he raised his hands, holding the knife way above his head to build enough force to drive the sharp, hardened steel blade into and through the animal's heart. It was a mistake.

The thing on the floor knew death was imminent if it didn't turn the tide of the battle. He had cut the lights but had underestimated the rapidity and accuracy with which his adversary discharged his rifle. The thing also miscalculated the power of the firearm. He had been shot many times over the years, but the bullets were always from a small-caliber handgun.

Even while losing, when Thompson jumped on him, he saw the opportunity for a victory. The thing reached up and viciously squeezed Everett's right wrist. Everett screamed in pain, and the animal watched as the large knife fell to the floor. Though severely injured, it now held the advantage over the weaker human. With a sudden surety, it knew it was going to kill the hunter.

Everett saw a flash of movement, but his eyes couldn't keep up with its speed. The blur was followed, almost instantly, by the sound and accompanying pain of his wrist shattering. *Too long*, he thought. *You took too damn long to stab him, and now you're going to die.*

He felt his body thrown off the animal; only the chance landing of his head on his pack, instead of the concrete, saved his skull from caving in. As it was, he still received a large gash down the side of his face, from where it connected with his metal flashlight.

The animal slowly rose to a sitting position. It coughed, spraying blood and fluids out of its punctured lungs and onto the walls. It leaned over and started crawling on all fours toward its quarry.

Thompson felt woozy and disoriented. He tried shaking his head to clear it and received fierce pain as payment for his attempt. Everett started to take stock of his situation. His quick calculation didn't give him the answer he had hoped. Blood was pouring into his eye from a deep gash on his head. He knew, without doubt, his right wrist was useless, with bones not only fractured but most likely turned to pulp. Worst of all, the thing was moving toward him. At that moment, he prayed, not to live or for his soul, but that his dog would go to a loving family, maybe one with kids.

Zeitler watched the fight between Thompson and the thing unfold on the screens from the warden's office. He turned to run to his fallen comrade, but Gomez stood in his way. "Erik," she said, "I know you want to help Everett, I do too, but there has to be someone left to protect the prisoners, to give them eyes. We can do that from here."

Zeitler nodded. "You're right," he said as tears welled up in his eyes.

They turned to the screens, and Gomez, her nerves as frayed as Zeitler, said as stoically as possible, "guys, if you don't get to Thompson in the next fifteen seconds, there will be no rush to get to him at all."

Still, on its hands and knees, the thing hovered over Everett, who lay on the floor, unable to will his body to sit, let alone stand. Then, in a strangely human voice, it said, "This may be little solace, but I want you to know, you are the best prey I have ever hunted. The next closest was a Pawnee Indian I fought in 1856. Jeez, he was a tough bastard."

"Mr. Thompson," it continued, "you gave me a good fight, but the contest is over. Your wrist is useless, your eyes tell me your head is spinning, but it doesn't much matter because your body isn't listening to it anyway, or you wouldn't be lying here."

"I never met anything like you in the tunnels of Iraq," Thompson replied. He was too worn to muse at the fact he was holding a conversation with a monster.

"No, too many high explosives. I was, however, in Afghanistan, but that was long ago."

"Soviet occupation?"

"No," the thing responded, "I was part of the British

Expeditionary Force. What they say is true; that land is the graveyard of empires."

"What now?" Everett asked.

"I kill you," it responded. "But I respect you. Other than eating part of your liver, I won't mutilate your body. I'll do you a mercy and break your neck before I open your belly."

The thing reached over the hunter to place its hand behind Thompson's neck. "Goodbye, Mr. Thompson."

"You missed something," Everett responded. "I didn't think you would, but you did."

"And what is that?" The thing above him asked, genuinely curious.

"When I was shooting, the rifle was on my left shoulder. I'm a southpaw," replied Everett. "My dominant hand can still handle a knife just fine."

The thing's eyes suddenly widened in realization, just as a dagger plunged into its chest to the hilt. Thompson's broken right wrist prohibited him from placing it in the thing's heart. The animal sat up, straddling the hunter. Simultaneously, blood and bullets splattered on the wall above Thompson's head, spraying his face and torso red.

The thing turned its head in time to receive a glancing blow across the temple from a round of the Casull. The combination of lead and energy dug a groove in the thing's flesh that looked not unlike the plowed row of a field. It swayed to the side, almost falling off Thompson. From underneath the monstrosity, he could see the creature was dazed; the last headshot nearly knocked it unconscious.

He was about to push it off when it obliged its captive by lifting itself to face its new attackers. Then, shaking its head as if to clear the cobwebs, it stood, facing its tormentors, attempting to roar at them in disbelief, as much as pain or anger.

The sound that came from the animal's throat was unlike the one it had produced earlier. Instead, what emanated was a gurgle, a gasp for breath. Blood poured from the thing's mouth in a tide, telling the men their attack had inflicted massive injuries.

While Kaplan and Davis were reloading, the animal charged past them. Davis caught a glancing blow from the beast, the impact dislocating his right shoulder. His gun went flying as he crumpled to the floor. Thompson staggered to his feet, holding his wrist, grimacing as he stumbled his way to Davis. Kaplan was leaning over the warden, concern written across his face. Kelvin had his right arm protectively pressed against his side; the pain etched on his face in deep lines.

"Everett," Kaplan asked, "how are you?"

"I've been better, but other than a broken wrist and a hellacious headache, I'm okay. How are you two?"

Davis looked up at Everett as if he had lost his mind.

"Warden," said Thompson, "I'm going to pop your shoulder back in place, but with my bum wrist, our special agent is going to have to hold you steady while I do the honors."

Kelvin was sweating from pain but nodded his head. He screamed in agony when Thompson pulled his arm but received such a relief of misery that he grinned.

"Did you learn to reset a shoulder in Special Forces?" Asked Kaplan.

"No, I think I saw it on an episode of *House*."

"Thank God for overpaid British actors," Davis chuckled.

Kaplan stated, "I hate to break up the TV review, but that thing is still alive, and we must assume inside the prison. So let's finish it off before it has time to escape and kill again."

Davis picked up the pistol and handed it to Thompson. "You're going to have to fish out the remaining cartridges from my right jacket pocket; I can't move my shoulder or hand very well."

"It broke my right wrist; how do you know I can use the weapon?" Thompson asked.

"Because you are a lefty."

"You noticed," Thompson said with surprise. "The thing didn't, and I was able to get a dagger in his chest."

"That thing," replied Davis, "was never a warden. It's

my job to see everything."

"Come on," interjected Kaplan. "Tracking him won't be hard; there's a blood trail a mile wide."

***

I lay in my bunk, silently waiting for Atticus' return if he returned at all. Sometime during my vigil, I succumbed to sleep. I awoke to drops of liquid soaking through the top bunk and landing on my forehead. The coppery smell told me immediately it was blood. I could hear labored breathing. "How was your late-night excursion?" I quietly asked.

Atticus responded with a laugh that quickly digressed into a choking fit. After he brought his breathing under control, he answered, "Jackson, to tell you the truth, I've had better."

"Did you kill anyone?"

"No, but not for lack of trying."

"Are you going to kill me?"

"What did I say?" Atticus coughed out. "I will never hurt you."

"That prostitute, the one that testified against you, did you kill her?"

"Yes, Jackson, I killed her. The missing phone was because she snapped a picture of what I truly look like, not the form I showed you. At first, I don't think she even knew what she had on her phone. She called me in jail and told me she was going to the news. My identity couldn't be allowed to reach the light of day. I laid her tongue across her mouth to make it look as if she was about to squeal on someone, and they murdered her. At the time, I was firmly ensconced in the county jail, thus removing myself as a suspect," Atticus confessed.

"It's obvious cells and fences don't stop you. So why are you in prison?"

After another coughing bout, complete with blood spraying the cell walls, he asked, "why would a fox chase after chickens when he can get them so much easier inside the henhouse?"

"You wanted in!" I exclaimed in awe.

"Yes, I tried to resist killing but knew I was fighting a losing battle. When I found out my wife was having an affair, I knew it was easy to develop a cover story. I chose the tattling prostitute long before I acted upon my plan."

"Atticus," I said in a mixture of hurt and anger. "I thought we were friends."

Wheezing, he replied, "we are friends. I love you like a brother. Haven't I taught you about the joy of thoughtful reading? Didn't I teach you chess, have long conversations, and even played a game of charades?"

"That's what this whole thing is, a charade. You hid the

real you from me."

"Jackson, we all hide our real selves; it's one of the consequences of living a sentient life."

"Are you going to die?"

"I don't know," was his curt reply. "I was attacked by a saber-tooth cat, which by the way, were not tigers, about eleven thousand years ago, while hunting a tribe of Clovis People in modern-day Nebraska. I was gutted and mauled. I broke her neck before she started to eat me. In time, I fully recovered, but I have no idea about this situation; I took a real ass beating tonight."

"You need medical help."

"No, I need to leave. I can hear the footfalls of my pursuers even now; if they find me, they will finish me."

"What's your real name?"

"To you, my friend, let it always remain, Atticus."

"Will I ever see you again?"

"No. Close your eyes. I don't want you to see me in my natural form. I want you to remember me as I presented myself to you. Oh, and that old book on the shelf, it's a first edition print of *Moby Dick*. I'm giving it to you. Did you know its author, Herman Melville, is widely considered one of the first great American writers of the post-revolutionary period?"

I closed my eyes as I heard the top bunk lighten. I listened to the cell door creak, and then there was silence.

Minutes later, my eyes were still shut when the door was unlocked, and a flashlight was shone in my face.

I heard someone say, "good God, there's blood everywhere."

I opened my eyes and propped myself against my pillow, using my elbows for support.

Then Everett came forward, crouching, examining me. He turned his head toward the warden and the FBI agent and said, "it's not his blood. The thing was here, but he's probably out of the prison and our reach."

Warden Davis asked me, "Jackson, are you okay?"

I pondered his question and responded, "no, Sir, I'm not."

"What's the matter, Son?"

I had never heard a warden talk to an inmate with such kindness. He and Thompson looked wounded. They must have given Atticus a hell of a fight.

My lip quivered, and tears washed away some of the blood on my face, leaving small rivers of cleanliness on an otherwise crimson mask. "Sir, I've lost the best friend I ever had."

About the Author

Kevin Baker is a published author who has written across a broad spectrum of genres. He may be found writing anything from poetry and love stories to horror and speculative fiction pieces.

He earned a B.S. in Education from Bowling Green State University and an MBA from Heidelberg University.

He lives in Ohio with his wife and their dog.

Follow Author Kevin Baker

Instagram: @authorkevinbaker
Facebook: @authorkevinbaker

By the Same Author

Moondance

Printed in Great Britain
by Amazon

86977987R00201